Pattern for Romance

Other Books in the Quilts of Love Series

PATTERN FOR ROMANCE

Quilts of Love Series

Carla Olson Gade

Abingdon fiction™

a novel approach to faith

Pattern for Romance

Copyright © 2013 by Carla Olson Gade

ISBN-13: 978-1-4267-5271-1

Published by Abingdon Press, P.O. Box 801, Nashville, TN 37202
www.abingdonpress.com

Published in association with MacGregor Literary Agency.

All rights reserved.

The persons and events portrayed in this work of fiction
are the creations of the author, and any resemblance
to persons living or dead is purely coincidental.

Library of Congress Cataloging-in-Publication Data has been
requested.

Scripture quotations are taken from The Authorized (King James)
Version. Rights in the Authorized Version in the United Kingdom
are vested in the Crown. Reproduced by permission of the Crown's
patentee, Cambridge University Press.

Printed in the United States of America

1 2 3 4 5 6 7 8 9 10 / 18 17 16 15 14 13

For my amazing husband, Brad—
Our Master Quilter designed a beautiful story for us,
His-story.
With every stitch of love,
a beautiful pattern has emerged!

Delight thyself also in the LORD:
and he shall give thee the desires of thine heart.
Commit thy way unto the LORD; trust also in him;
and he shall bring it to pass.
Psalm 37:4-5

Acknowledgments

After a vehicle accident that injured my writing wrist, I found completing this novel to be no small task. I'm so grateful to all those who helped, prayed, and encouraged me through it.

Ramona Richards, my Abingdon editor, for your patience. Joyce Buckley, my mom and copy editor, for your tenacity. Susan Page Davis, my mentor, for your skillful assistance. Chip MacGregor, my literary agent, for your guidance. Amanda, my occupational therapist, for your perseverance. Colonial American Christian Writers, for your knowledge. Brad Gade, my husband, for your encouragement and support. Jesus, my friend, for your grace, healing, and strength.

Dear Reader and Quilt Lover,

Pattern for Romance will be unlike most of the Quilts of Love novels, in that the whole-cloth quilt featured in this book is not piecework. During my research, I was blessed to view firsthand authentic examples of this type of quilt at the New England Quilting Museum and in Colonial Williamsburg. I came to adore these beautiful quilts and often found myself poring over photographs of the beautiful extant samples for pure enjoyment!

Whole-cloth quilts originated in fourteenth-century Italy and were popularized in France. The English and other European cultures were highly influenced by French styles, and by the seventeenth and eighteenth centuries, skilled quilters in England were manufacturing the whole-cloth technique. Whole-cloth quilting was the first type of quilting found in early America in the form of bed coverings and quilted clothing such as petticoats, jackets, waistcoats, and robes. The term "quilt" was often used interchangeably for a bed quilt and women's quilted petticoat. Outer petticoats, worn as the skirt of a woman's gown, were not considered an undergarment. Open-robe gowns parted in the front and sometimes gathered at the sides into a polonaise to show the elegant needlework of the outer petticoat.

Quilted clothing and bed quilts featured exquisite motifs that were traced onto paper and transferred onto the fabric. Holes were poked through the paper and ground cinnamon sifted onto it. When the paper was removed, the design was left behind. Curves and swags of vines, ferns, ivy, and acanthus leaves, mixed with reliefs of roses, grapes, pomegranates, fleur-de-lis, geometric shapes, birds, and animals provided all manner of beautiful designs and borders. Bed quilts were not always square, but often a T-shape to fit over the side and footboards of the bedstead correctly. One husband in Colonial America has been known to have designed a bed quilt pattern, while his wife provided the stitching. Surely, many of the great works were a labor of love.

Yet the average colonial woman did not have the privilege of leisurely time for quilting. Many quilted garments and bedcoverings were stitched by professional quilters who were paid meager salaries, though wealthy ladies with the time and means to develop their fine needlework may have enjoyed the task. Regardless of who did the handiwork, the beauty of their careful stitches was often highlighted by the textile used for the quilt. Dyed in bright colors such as deep crimson and blues, worsted wool blends given a glazed treatment by pressing the fabric with hot rollers or an iron resulted in what is known as *calamanco*. Silks and satin-weaves were also chosen for garments. White fabric was rare and costly, and therefore, many bridal quilts were made of a satin-weave cotton/woolen blend with linen backing. Sometimes small bits of batting were painstakingly stuffed into the pattern to provide a raised relief for the white work, in modern terms called trapunto, a method still used today by hand-quilters.

Although quilting in Colonial America has been idealized, it was indeed rare in the founding years of our country, particularly in New England, when women worked spinning and weaving, leaving precious little time for leisurely activities. It is only in the late eighteenth century that we begin to see medallion style and chintz applique piece-worked bed quilts when textiles became more readily available, but more so in the early nineteenth century. The stitching patterns used on whole-cloth quilts were sometimes applied to the piecework quilts, lending to the dense and comfortable bedding. Yet, the beautiful and rare solid whole-cloth quilts we find from early to mid-

Colonial America birthed an appreciation of quilting, which has endured for centuries and may for centuries to come.

Come, join me in Colonial Boston as we see a *Pattern for Romance* emerge through the story of an exquisite white-work whole-cloth quilt and its humble quilter. Please visit me online at http://carlagade.com and http://pinterest.com/quiltsoflove to see historical quilting samples and research materials that inspired me while writing *Pattern for Romance*.

Blessings,

Carla

1

Boston, Massachusetts
July 31, 1769

The crack of musket fire resounded through the clouded sky. Hailstones, the size of goose eggs, pelted the cobbled thoroughfare as people ran for shelter. Thunder clapped and an onslaught of shouts and shrieks echoed nature's vehement warning. Honour Metcalf sank to her knees in a puddle of quilted petticoats and toile—her mitted hands encased her head, vying for protection against the artillery of hail and confusion.

"Miss Metcalf, Miss Metcalf . . ."

A muffled voice reached her ears and she dared peek at the one towering over her. Blue eyes—those eyes—flashed concern, then vanished as a dark cloak enveloped her. Strong arms scooped her up, pressing her against the firm chest of her rescuer.

Honour could scarcely make out the blur of damaged brick and clapboard as Joshua Sutton's long strides carried her away in haste. Glazed windows popped and shards of glass flew as hail continued to wreak havoc on shops and offices. Fallen birds littered the street amidst the frozen ammunition. Lightning flashed and Honour squeezed her eyes shut, willing away the shrill neighs of horses and the cracking of the icy brimstone beneath carriage wheels.

The pair entered through a heavy wooden door into a dimly lit foyer. Mr. Sutton rested Honour upon a long bench and stooped beside her. With trembling hands, she pushed back her taffeta calash. The boned collapsible bonnet provided some measure of protection from the torrent, but what would protect her from him?

"How do you fare, Miss Metcalf?" Mr. Sutton asked.

Honour's heart pounded, much the same as Mr. Sutton's had, as she hovered against his chest. Her eyes darted around the room before her frightened gaze locked on his. Darkened and dampened by the storm, his hair spread wildly about his shoulders, and his ocean blue eyes awaited her answer.

"Miss Metcalf. I asked if you are well."

The edge in his voice lifted her out of the fog and she rubbed her temple. "Mr. Sutton? Aye, I am well enough. Where . . . why are we here?" Honour glanced at the small leaded glass window, a piece of golden glass missing from a corner and other sections cracked.

"I found you in the street getting pummeled by hailstones. We took shelter here in the meeting house." Thunder rolled again and Mr. Sutton's eyes shot toward the door.

"How long will it last?" Her young sister was safe at the dame school, or so she hoped.

"That, only the Almighty knows." He surveyed her as if assessing a length of cloth. "Are you certain you are uninjured, Miss Metcalf?"

"I am . . . I must go." She attempted to rise, but a wave of dizziness overcame her.

"Please rest for a moment. You cannot go back out there." His mouth drew into a line. "Perhaps we should pray."

"Surely I did, as you carried me here." A warm blush rose on her neck.

"I prayed, as well. Then we shall trust the good Lord for the outcome, shall we? After all, we have found refuge in His house." The corners of Mr. Sutton's eyes crinkled with reassurance.

Honour replied with a simple nod and regarded his kind face. "It is you who are injured, Mr. Sutton." She extended her hand toward his bruised cheek, and retreated.

He instinctively found the bruise on his cheekbone, and felt his temple. A trickle of blood mixed with rainwater streamed down the side of his face. He looked at the blood on his hand and shrugged. "'Tis nothing. Perhaps some feverfew tea will help."

"You might as well have been lambasted by rocks thrown by town delinquents. If your head hurts, as mine is beginning to, it will take more than tea, I fear."

"The tea would warm me more. It hurts little." The corner of his mouth curved.

"This is no time for mirth, Mr. Sutton." Honour said, searching about for her satchel. "I would offer you a handkerchief, but I've none in my pocket and cannot find my workbag. I must have dropped it in the street."

Mr. Sutton gestured toward her cloak pocket. "May I?"

Only then did Honour notice his greatcoat draped awkwardly around her shoulders, her short chintz cape beneath, which she'd hastily donned, perchance it rained. He must have covered her when he whisked her away from the harsh elements—including British officers. When they came rushing toward her, she had crumbled to the ground, and her legs turned to porridge despite her urge to flee. But the dark sky and giant balls of ice caused her to succumb to nature's assault.

Like the fire and brimstone punishment of the ancients, God had thrown water and ice to execute judgment upon her.

She attempted to remove the coat, but he stayed her hand with his. Though cold, his firm, yet gentle clasp exuded the warmth of one who cared. Or was it her mere imagination? Her heart dared not hope.

"No. You need it for warmth. One would scarcely know 'tis a summer day." He retrieved a handkerchief from his coat and wiped at his cut. He refolded the linen cloth and placed it inside a pocket of his damp-about-the-shoulders waist-coat. "Now tell me about this satchel of yours. Is it of great importance?"

She worried her lip and nodded.

"Perhaps we can yet find it. If not, you might obtain a new one from my father's store, if you'd allow me to replace it."

Honour wrinkled her brow. "Though I do appreciate your offer, Mr. Sutton, it must be found. 'Tis not only my workbag, but of special value to me. It was a gift from my late mother."

"Let us hope, then, it may be retrieved . . . once the storm has passed." He glanced upward to the vestibule's high ceiling, and her gaze followed—the hail continuing to pound the slate roof of the church in an unnerving staccato.

"Yes, I do hope. My mother taught me to quilt and the embroidered bag once belonged to her. It is dear to me, indeed, as far as material things. Though I do hope you do not think me selfish to speak of such a small matter whilst people may yet be out there in the storm, injured and dealing with the damage." She rubbed the base of her skull, the dull ache inten-sifying, yet she wished not to concern Mr. Sutton.

The man grinned, and a darling crease appeared by his mouth. "I do not think there is one thimbleful of selfishness inside you, Miss Metcalf."

"Then you do not know me well enough, Mr. Sutton." Honour smiled shyly and lowered her gaze, her heavy lids beckoning her to succumb to the drowsy feeling tugging at her.

"Perhaps we may remedy that."

"Mmm." Her eyes grew leaden as an aura of slumber descended upon her.

"Miss Metcalf!"

Honour's head bobbed up. "Yes?" She felt as though she were floating in the ocean—submerging one moment, and above a wave another.

Joshua Sutton still knelt before her, his eyes stayed on hers, as if he could hold her up by sheer will. Then he peered down at her quilted outer petticoat. Aye, she'd worn her favorite blue silk quilt today, with her blue and yellow toile polonaise gown. Did he find her attractive? She felt her damp skirt. Mercy, how could he? She must look like a shipwreck.

"Your quilt, Miss Metcalf. It is sublime. Is it your own handi-work?" he asked.

"Aye, thank you," she whispered, trying to remain alert. "I learned from my mother. There was never a finer quilter than she."

"I have heard you are an adept quilter, but I have never seen evidence of it until now. Your mother taught you well. Perhaps my father can make use of your services for men's banyan robes and waistcoats, since we are no longer able to obtain quilted cloth from England."

Honour stared through him, her vision blurring him into two.

"Dare I say, it is a pity your hem got wet . . . Miss Metcalf, are you listening?"

Honour leaned over to inspect the hemline of her petticoat. But instead of seeing the quilted cloth, she found darkness, as the sound of hail and Mr. Sutton's smooth voice faded into nothingness.

———

"Who goes there?"

Joshua recognized the deep baritone voice at once. He looked up as the parson entered through the vestry doors, only to greet him with Miss Metcalf slumped against his chest. "Reverend Cooper, we have come to seek shelter, though the lady has just now swooned."

Lantern in hand, the reverend's eyes widened as he came near. "Good heavens . . ."

"Please help me lay her on the bench. She was battered by the hailstorm and it seems to have done her in."

"Why, of course." The parson set the lantern on a small table and shuffled over to help.

After laying her down, Joshua stood and faced the minister. "Thank you, sir." Joshua had never seen this man of the cloth in such disarray—without his powdered bob wig and crisp black suit. Instead, he wore breeches and a plain linsey-woolsey waistcoat.

Reverend Cooper became aware of his disheveled state. "You must forgive my appearance. When there was a short reprieve from the storm, I went out to assess the damage, as the sexton is away, then it started up again and soaked me through. I found these old clothes to put on."

Reverend Cooper swiped an errant lock of hair into place over his balding head, and replaced his cap. "Now what happened to the young lady? Who is she, pray tell?"

"I found her collapsed in the street being accosted by the hail. A few British officers were about to give her aid, then I arrived. I told them that I recognized her as Miss Honour

16

Metcalf, an employee of Mrs. Wadsworth, the mantua maker. Before I could say more the officers fled to help others."

"Mmmph." Reverend Cooper's brow wrinkled with concern. He pursed his lips and signaled Joshua to continue.

"Most of the shopkeepers locked their doors in the chaos and we were far from either of our own. I was greatly relieved to find refuge here," Joshua said.

Reverend Cooper clamped his index finger across his jaw. "Rather fitting, I say, to find a safe haven in the the Lord's house when mysterious elements from heaven descend."

Joshua released a slow breath. "Indeed it is."

The reverend's wiry eyebrows twitched. "Though I suspect you are not entirely comfortable here."

"Not entirely, sir."

The minister nodded, "You are Joshua Sutton, the tailor's son, are you not?"

"Yes, I am."

"How well do you know this young lady?"

"I am briefly acquainted with her, as Sutton's Clothiers and Mrs. Wadsworth's Mantua Shop have occasion to do business with one another. But we are not attached, if that is what you are asking." An embarrassed grin formed on Joshua's lips and he shook his head in denial. He had no interest in forming an attachment even to one as lovely as Miss Metcalf.

The man cocked his head and arched an eyebrow. "You might consider it."

Was the reverend jesting or accusing? Joshua swallowed. "Pardon me, sir, but I am uncertain of your implication. I assure you it is as I said. My intent was for her well-being. Would you have me marry her simply because you found me here alone with her? I assure you it is entirely innocent."

The man issued a sardonic grin. "It is why some couples seek me out mid-week. In fact, I wed a young couple this morning at Widow Lankton's home. Her niece, you know. I understand you are acquainted."

Joshua grimaced.

"Pardon me, son. I should have refrained from mentioning it. But I thought it would be of particular interest to you. You must be relieved to see her settled."

Joshua clenched his jaw and stared at the stone floor. It should have been he who wed Emily Guilfold. But now, his name was marred, and her reputation sullied, despite her attempt to "settle." Though she did not confess any sin, some assumed. Why else would she marry so soon after she'd broken off their own attachment? Because of it, some said Joshua had been inappropriately engaged with her. He hoped the gossip would abate until matters could be set straight. He'd refrain from going to taverns for a while—and mayhap Sunday meeting. Though Mother would tan his hide if he was absent from their family pew.

"Yes, Miss Guilfold informed me she was to marry by special license. Though I did not know the marriage was to occur this day."

"Mistress Leach, now," the minister said. "By all appearances the couple wed in haste, but you may put yourself at ease. Widow Lankton assured me it was for the best, though I am not at liberty to discuss it in detail."

Why must the old man ramble on so? Joshua's character was blemished; he did not need to dwell on it. Nor did he wish to hear about "Mrs. Leach."

A soft groan came from Miss Metcalf and the two pivoted in her direction. Joshua would deal with his irreverent thoughts later.

"Does she need an apothecary? A physician perhaps?" Reverend Cooper asked.

"I suppose that she does." Joshua went to the door and pushed it ajar against the pressure of the wind. Ice pellets continued to descend, now mixed with rain. He hoped it would subside soon. "I should go for Dr. Westcott."

"I have seen storms as this in my lifetime. You should not go out again until the torrent ceases. I fear it may continue for some time," the clergyman said.

Joshua shut the door. "But what of Miss Metcalf? I tried to keep her awake by talking, as I feared she might've obtained a concussion." Joshua glanced at her still form. "Perhaps we should wake her."

"Sleep might be best for now, son. At least, until the storm has passed."

Miss Metcalf murmured unintelligible words. The men shifted their attention toward her, and then the reverend bowed his head. While Reverend Cooper entreated the Lord in silence, Joshua knelt by her side. He cast aside his own misery, as a strong desire to stroke her deep auburn locks and calm away her fears emerged from some place deep within.

He brushed a loose tendril from her pallid face. "Hush now, all is well."

"Joshua?"

Reverend Cooper cleared his throat following a quiet "Amen."

Joshua withdrew his hand. He would not allow himself to succumb to such feelings.

Yet, as the beauty slipped into unconsciousness once more, it occurred to him that she'd called him by his Christian name, Joshua. Worse yet, he addressed her in kind. Honour. Sweet, talented, and lovely Honour. Everything the beguiling Miss Guil—Mrs. Leach—was not.

2

Honour stepped around a puddle in front of the manse and drew in a refreshing breath of air. Though midsummer had been remarkably cool, with the dismal weather that had settled upon Boston of late, today the sky was blue, with nary a cloud to see. A chill remained in the air, but the day was indeed sublime, and she relished the opportunity to ride in the carriage parked before her. The carriage made a grand impression with its cheerful shade of green. Temperance would love it.

How Honour hoped Tempe was all right since she had been unable to tend to her sister while absent from her. It was so kind that the Reverend and Mrs. Cooper allowed Honour to convalesce overnight in their home.

"Shall we?" Joshua Sutton extended his hand and helped her into the carriage. "Please sit here. Facing forward will be more comfortable."

Honour offered a meek smile. "I thought you would sit there. It is your conveyance."

"'Tis my father's coach. And I shall, if you do not mind."

Honour settled onto the tufted black leather seat, and Joshua sat beside her. "Thank you. It was most kind of your father to allow you to bring me home."

He grinned. "I shall thank my mother for you. She is the generous one in the family and suggested it."

"You must favor her then." Honour adjusted her calash, averting her eyes from Joshua's. When he chuckled, she found that it could not be done. She simply had to look at him. His eyes were as blue as the cloudless sky, with rays of sunshine spilling from the corners.

The well-attired driver turned back, his silver buttons gleaming in the sun. "Ready, Sir?"

"Yes, Redmond. To Mrs. Wadsworth's Mantua Shoppe on Hanover, at the sign of the needle—should it still be up."

Honour shot a glance at Joshua. There was so much damage in evidence from the storm, despite the pleasant day. How had Mrs. Wadsworth's shop fared? The carriage lurched forward at the driver's command, jarring her aching body. A tiny moan rattled in her throat.

"Miss Metcalf, are you well enough to travel? I hope I have not presumed too much."

Honour rubbed her arm. "Not at all, Mr. Sutton. I am sore yet, but well enough and anxious to go home to see my sister."

"She will be waiting for you then?"

"Oh, yes, I hope so. She is only eight years of age."

"So young. Have you other siblings?" he asked. "I, myself, have a younger brother and two older sisters. Both married and with a few youngsters of their own."

"No . . . it is only the two of us." The spoken words pierced Honour's heart and she released a ragged sigh.

"Forgive me, I meant not to intrude upon your personal matters."

Honour looked straight ahead to the cobbled street before her, holding back unshed tears, and thankful her over-sized bonnet concealed her moist eyes. An awkward silence descended upon the pair while she regained her composure.

"There is no harm done, Mr. Sutton. I have spoken little about my family since their passing, except to Mrs. Wadsworth and Reverend Cooper and his wife."

"I beg your pardon; I did not mean to intrude. But if perchance you should like to talk, I am happy to lend you my ear." Joshua tugged on his earlobe beneath his cocked hat and grinned.

Honour released a small laugh, but doing so brought a fresh wave of pain to her head. She cupped her face in her hands and rubbed her temples.

"Forgive me, I meant not to aggravate your headache."

"The city shall soon recover and so shall I." *I must.* Though the roads were mostly cleared of the hail and debris, crews of men and boys were busy shoveling the balls of ice into waiting wagons. "Whatever will they do with it all?"

"Some of it melted with the rain last night. I suspect that businessmen will harvest what they can for icehouses. The rest, I suppose they'll dispose of in the harbor. I heard the hail measured a foot high in some places."

Workers bustled about repairing the exteriors of the many buildings lining the street—chipped bricks, damaged clapboards and shingles, broken windows and signs. "This fine day certainly bears no resemblance to yesterday."

"'Tis a new day indeed," Joshua said. "Yesterday was a day of destruction, while today offers promise. If these citizens had not hope, we would not see them working so hard to restore what belongs to them . . . or paying another to do so. The colonial spirit endures, despite the burdens we find so cumbersome."

Honour hiked her chin. Surely he referred to the Townsend Acts imposed on the colonies by the king. "What if one owns nothing? What motivates a person then?"

Mr. Sutton narrowed his eyes and replied with a grin. "Faith?"

"And what if one *has* lost faith?" She regretted the question as soon as it was upon her lips. Would he guess it could be someone like her?

Mr. Sutton crossed his arms and thought a moment, then donned a smile and said most assuredly, "Love."

"I have heard it is the greatest of all three."

"Indeed it is. What is it that motivates you, Miss Metcalf?"

"All I do is for Temperance, my little sister." Honour fiddled with the ribbons of her bonnet, her thoughts drifting afar. "She is all I have left in the world, and all I have to love."

Joshua squeezed her hand, this time allowing his hand to linger. Her gaze floated from their hands toward the bruise on his cheek, shadowed beneath his brown felt brim. How different he looked today, from the man who spirited her off yesterday looking more like a pirate than a gentleman. Now he dressed in a fashionable day suit befitting the son of a merchant tailor. His ash-brown hair, pulled neatly in its queue, peeked beneath a cocked hat, his face freshly shaven. His countenance now vacant of alarm instead held calm concern.

The glow of sunlight shone in his eyes and she could see her faint reflection in them. Unspoken reassurance drifted through the soft breeze, encouraging her to continue.

The carriage rocked back and forth in rhythm with the team's gait as Honour bared her soul. "We were on our way to America when a ship of French pirates came upon us. My mother, father, and my brothers, Thomas and Wesley, were on deck when they fired upon us. We were making our way up the stairs from our cabin, Temperance and I, and the explosion knocked us down. We huddled under the steps and heard their screams. My sister tried to go up, but I pulled her back and swaddled her against me in the quilt I was carrying and covered her ears from the thunder of cannon shot and ammunition battering the deck above."

"How frightful," Joshua said.

"An American frigate arrived to rescue us, but it was too late. Too late for our parents and brothers." Honour trembled, and Joshua wrapped his arm around her shoulders. There she found the strength to share her innermost fears. "Yesterday afternoon, the sound of the hail on the cobbled streets brought me back there again. This time alone."

A torrent of long pent-up tears released, and she buried her head against Joshua's chest, wanting never to be alone again.

Joshua held her so close she could almost feel their hearts beat in one accord. In his smooth, deep voice, he spoke barely above a whisper. "You are not alone now, Honour. You are not alone."

<hr>

The carriage came to a stop in front of Mrs. Wadsworth's Mantua Shoppe. Joshua slid his arm out from behind Honour's warm back. He straightened in his seat and tipped her chin up with the back of his fingers. "We are here, Miss Metcalf. You are home."

He looked into her eyes, still dampened with tears, and offered a gentle smile. "Allow me to help you."

Honour took some shallow breaths, and stood while he supported her elbow. The driver opened the carriage door and lowered the steps. Joshua climbed and reached up to assist her.

As she began her descent, Honour wilted. Joshua captured her in his arms and carried her to the shop. Mrs. Wadsworth greeted them, holding the door as they passed through. "My dear girl. Thank you for sending us the message, Joshua. We were sore afraid."

Face-to-face, Honour said, "You may set me down, now, Mr. Sutton."

Releasing her was the last thing he wanted to do. Sometime, within the past day—nay, within the past mile, as the brick and clapboard buildings blurred by, something akin to affection stirred within, and altered him. How could that be? He'd sworn off women, lest he get involved with another Emily Guilfold—Mistress Leach.

As Mrs. Wadsworth settled Honour in a wingback chair and coddled her, the sound of the women's voices faded as thoughts floated through his mind . . .

He had never felt, longed for, anyone like this before. The arrangement with Miss Guilfold was to benefit their families. She never loved him, nor he her. He'd been committed to her for three long years, until she became of age. Why he and not his brother, who was better matched to her in years and common interests? Yet, in haste she married another merchant's son—Edmund Leach. The man far exceeded her in age and in wealth, or so he thought. But of late, Joshua heard rumors of the Leach family's holdings being in a state of decline. What would she see in the roué? Might she truly love the man? Although Joshua did not love Miss Guilfold, he'd grown to care for her and certainly did not wish to see her taken advantage of. Might she be taking advantage of Leach?

Joshua exhaled and surveyed the room. Gowns, petticoats, and panniers hung from the walls and ceiling. A beautiful mantua was exhibited in a corner unit. Shelves of cloth—some he recognized as coming from Sutton's—laces, buttons, and accoutrements were set out with precision. He turned toward the windows flanking the front door and beheld the fabric and decorations that were strewn about the windowsills. Mrs. Wadsworth's displays ruined. A broom leaned against the wall by a pile of broken glass and litter. Glass panes were smashed, looking as though the icy rocks had been thrown at them with harmful intent.

He spun toward Mrs. Wadsworth, who stared back at him, a frown planted on her face, fists upon her hips.

"What you see here is how it is in every shop—your father's surely, he having such great windows," she said.

"Yes, I know. Our building was in shambles. Shards of glass everywhere. Repairs have been underway since dawn."

Mrs. Wadsworth blew out a big sigh, and her eyes watered. "The glazier cannot attend me for another four days. With glass no longer imported due to the heavy taxes, I know not if there is enough to replace it. I should be as fortunate as your father."

"Then you shall be. I'll secure the glass and send some of our workers to do what they can for you until the glaziers come. They will likely board up your windows." Joshua's brow furrowed. "It will be too dark for working. We will find a space suitable for you to work at Sutton's for a few days."

"You would do that for me?" She walked toward him and cupped his face in her hands. "You are surely a saint, Joshua Sutton. Just like your mother."

Joshua laughed. "Please don't tell Miss Metcalf." He made a show of shielding his voice, his gaze alighting on her. "I don't want her to think excessively well of me. I have a reputation to maintain, you know."

"Oh, we know of your reputation. All the girls in town swoon over you, but none can have you."

"Nor will any want me, since Miss Guilfold's rejection and the speculation accompanying it." Joshua flattened his lips.

Mrs. Wadsworth waved a dismissive palm at him. "You mustn't allow it to bother you, Joshua. It is nothing more than foolish prattle. You are one of the most outstanding young men in Boston. Do not let anyone tell you otherwise."

"You have not heard then. Miss Guilfold is now Mrs. Edmund Leach. Reverend Cooper officiated her wedding at Widow Lankton's estate yesterday."

"I did not hear the banns cried."

"They obtained a special license."

"I see. Well, be glad of it. Now you are free to pursue other options." Mrs. Wadsworth tilted her head. "Did you hear that, Honour? Our bachelor is available for courting. You'd best join the queue." She placed her hand over her mouth to contain her mirth.

Miss Metcalf was looking at him most uncomfortably when a strawberry-blonde girl came running in and threw her arms around her neck. "Honour! I knew you would come back. I knew it. I said my prayers, and God listened."

Honour kissed and hugged the girl who climbed into her lap. It warmed his heart to see such sisterly affection. Miss Metcalf obviously needed the girl as much as her sister needed her.

The girl flailed her arms around with much emotion, describing the storm as it came to destroy the doors and windows of Mrs. Wadsworth's shop. "And our bedroom window upstairs did not break. God watched over us, Honour, just as you said."

Though the storm was over, the disaster was not. He needn't add to it by lingering here when he ought to return the carriage and see what else he could do to aid his own family. Joshua took slow steps backward and retreated from the store—but his mind stayed on the lovely Miss Metcalf, who had already stolen a piece of his heart.

3

Joshua stood in stony silence listening to his father's tirade. "You mean to tell me you have invited the mantua makers to use our building? We have little enough usable space as it is. Haven't we done enough for her already?" Father shook his head vigorously. "While you were out on your errands of goodwill this morning, your brother took inventory of the storehouse. The flooded storehouse."

"I know, Father. I organized it myself this morning and left the men under Andrew's direction." Naturally, he had to practically pull his brother out of bed by his nightshirt to do so.

Joshua's father paced from one end of the office to the other, hands clasped behind his back. "You should have stayed to see the task through. Andrew reports that most of the inventory is at best partially damaged. All that imported cloth—ruined!" Father peered out one of the broken windows. "When are those glaziers going to come repair this broken glass?"

"This afternoon, sir."

Father craned his neck toward Joshua. "Then how will I get any work done?" He turned again, rocking back on the heels of his buckled shoes.

Joshua leaned against a large oak table in the center of the room and addressed his father's broad back. "Sir, the cloth has been in storage for nearly a year, since the Non-Importation Agreement last autumn. It became musty and mouse infested . . ."

"I thought I told you to get a cat," Father murmured.

Joshua continued, "And now it's water-damaged. We could not have sold it in that condition when the embargo lifts in January next—if, in fact, it does. We should have disposed of it months ago."

"Why did our customers have to boycott our textiles? I paid the duties before I signed that agreement with the other Boston merchants. I have lost on both ends!" Father pounded his fist into the air.

Joshua squeezed the edge of the table, attempting to remain calm. It would do him no good to succumb to his father's volatile mood—the same demon he endeavored to tame in himself—yet the vigor in his speech rose a notch. "There are rumors from the Sons of Liberty about a movement to extend the embargo. Even if nothing comes of that, many patriots will continue to boycott merchandise coming from England."

Father twisted toward Joshua. "Do not raise your voice to me. I'm as good a patriot as the next man. But the consequences of refusing to comply with the Townsend Acts, thereby not paying Britain for the expenses of the French and Indian War, are wearing on me. I lost my father in that war. Is not that enough? Must I now lose my business?"

Joshua tightened his jaw as he met his father's bulging eyes. He loathed when Father became like this, an occurrence more frequent over recent months. Mayhap Father needed a blood-letting to restore his humors. Or a stiff tankard of syllabub, though he doubted either would help. Joshua took a deep breath to temper his growing exasperation. Why couldn't he see reason?

"Father, I am merely trying to explain the situation. With all due respect, I am not the one who is yelling."

"Then alter your tone." Father turned back and planted his hands on the windowsill.

Joshua hung his head and exhaled a grunt. "I believe 'tis my message you dislike." Joshua braced himself for another round. "Father, I have been trying to get you to see this since last fall when we received that last shipment." Joshua clasped his hands behind his head, staring at the water-damaged ceiling and the bucket below catching a drip. "I told Andrew to spare what was salvageable and distribute it to the needy with some bars of lye soap. Perhaps they can give it a good washing and find it useful still."

"Hmmph. Did your mother instruct you to do that? Now I have to pay for soap? Why not hire a laundress do it for them? Better yet, we shall hire them to do their own work."

Joshua stared, dumfounded.

Father wagged his finger. "Your munificent mother is too generous for her own good . . . and mine."

On cue, Joshua's mother entered the office. "Did I hear you mention me, my beloveds?" She pecked Father on the cheek and smiled at Joshua. "We mustn't forget whether the fabric is sold or offered at no cost, it is still British merchandise, and some may not accept it. Do not presume the poor have lower morals than the rest of us. Many are folks who have simply fallen on difficult times. Patriotism should pay no heed to one's status." She eyed Father sharply.

"A philanthropist, and now a politician." Father scratched the rolls on his gray wig.

"As a matter of fact, dear, I belong to the Daughters of Liberty."

"What, pray tell, is that?"

"Had you paid more attention to my affairs, Mr. Sutton, you would know I've been attending gatherings with the ladies of our colony who are standing for our freedoms. It is an organized effort to become more self-sufficient and less dependent on King George."

"How do you go about it, Mother?" Joshua asked, eyeing her demure stance, hands cradled at her waist.

Mother poised her chin as if addressing a full audience. Perhaps she endeavored to recruit them. "You know we make our own teas from plants grown on our own soil. You are also aware women weave their own cloth and often get together in a cooperative effort to do so. Why, last month a group of us spun for a parson's wife and had a grand day of it. Now she has plenty of thread for her weaving."

"And putting me out of business in the doing," Father muttered under his breath.

"That is not true, dear." She walked to the large desk and flipped through the ledger. "Our accounts have suffered little, all things considered. Women sell their homespun to us, and customers are eager to purchase the non-boycotted fabric we keep on our store shelves, as well as carding supplies which are exempt from the Agreement." She turned to Joshua. "It was wise of you to advise us to make those purchases and to keep a greater amount of inventory in the shop. Others have forfeited much, yet we have not suffered nearly so, despite the good cause of taking a stand against the king."

"The 'good cause' is going to bring me to ruin." Father walked over to the desk and sat, pointing a firm finger at the open ledger. "Despite your claims, dear, our profit is lower than last year's, because we purchased an excessive amount of cloth we are unable to sell."

"You are looking at our losses, not our gains," Mother said. "We are doing better overall than in previous recent years. Customers respect us for not selling British goods, and have rewarded us with their patronage. Don't you see?"

"Father, the situation at hand has been wrought by the flooding. It could happen anytime, embargo or not." Joshua cocked his head toward one parent and then the other. "You both have valid points. In the past we've maintained such a large surplus to entice our customers we've placed ourselves at an extraordinary risk. I propose in the future we proffer a sufficient selection of textiles, but refrain from hoarding such enormous stores. At least while tensions with England are so high."

"When haven't they been?" Father miffed.

"Not like this, dear," Mother chimed in.

Joshua crossed his arms. "We've long maintained a steady clientele on the basis of quality supplies and by virtue of our talent as tailors. Let us take our stand as business owners and as Whigs and not allow the tyrant king to intimidate us."

Father and Mother looked at Joshua with chagrin—and pride?—then faced each other and shrugged.

Mother rested her palm on Father's wide shoulder. "You know, he has a point."

"Olive, whose side are you on?"

Joshua held his arms out, palms upward. "We are in this together, are we not?"

Father leaned back in his chair. "Joshua must have inherited his good head for business from his old father. Though I am not managing well presently." Father retrieved his handkerchief and patted droplets of sweat from his furrowed brow.

Joshua stepped closer, meeting his father's worried gaze. "You are a fine businessman, one of the best in this city. But we are trying to recover from unexpected trouble. It is taxing on us all."

"Good heavens. Do not speak of taxes, taxing, or anything else stressful." Mother tossed her head back, though how she kept from toppling over from the weight of her high coiffure, Joshua could not fathom. Women wore such peculiar styles. He thought for a moment of Miss Metcalf with that collapsible taffeta contraption of her own. Though he had to admit, she would be lovely in most anything.

Father cleared his throat. "I sincerely beg your pardon, son. I should not have lashed out at you. You are going above the mark to help, and not only that, you seem to find the time to be benevolent to others." He patted Joshua's hand, that being about the limit of affection Joshua expected to receive from the man. "How does that young woman you rescued fare?"

"Well enough. Though the hail sorely assaulted her."

"She is the new mantua maker?" Father asked.

"She is a quilter," said Joshua. "And very apt at her skill."

Of course, Father needed to get his two shillings in. "Margaret would not have needed another quilter if the embargo were lifted. She could have purchased some of the quilted Marseilles from France we paid such heavy duties on."

"There is nothing to be done about it now. We had to place the order for the Marseilles. Though I must say, I have a preference for hand-quilted cloth myself," Mother said.

"Yes, darling, but I suppose the new quilter will be let go come the new year when the agreement ends. Mrs. Wadsworth can hardly afford to keep her."

His mother tilted her chin. "Why must you be so overbearing where it concerns Margaret? She is your cousin's wife and you promised to protect her interests while her husband is at sea."

"Nevertheless, I am concerned about Joshua's interests. I hope you do not intend to give your heart away to the girl. You will only be hurt again." Father's countenance sombered.

Was Father remorseful about pressuring him to marry Emily only to have it turn out so dreadfully? The Guilfold family's shipping enterprises would have proved to be a great asset to Sutton's Clothiers, though at Joshua's expense.

"I already discussed the topic with him this morning, Mr. Sutton." Mother eyed Joshua teasingly. Joshua hadn't considered Miss Metcalf's employment in Boston might be temporary. Did she have plans for her future? The thought of Miss Metcalf alone and unemployed, after learning of her woeful circumstances, racked him with concern. She'd entrusted him with her deepest thoughts and fears. Did he dare risk hurting a woman so vulnerable?

Father drummed his fingers on the desktop. "I suspect it might be best to allow Mrs. Wadsworth and her girls to work here where they can have some decent light. You said they were boarding up all her windows?"

"Yes, Father." *All but one.* Joshua recalled Honour's little sister exclaiming how God was watching over them during the storm and kept their bedchamber window from breaking. He hoped God was watching over her even now.

Mother placed her hand over Father's drumming fingers. "That is gracious of you to provide them with the space. It should only be for a few days. Moreover, we need to support the smaller shopkeepers to keep this town thriving."

"Let us hope we will thrive as well." Father's stomach issued an audible growl. "Is it dinner time already?"

"Yes, we are having a fine meal of veal pie today. We shall also try a new tea. It is made from the four-star loosestrife grown in my garden. They call it 'Liberty Tea.' They served it at the spinning party, and it is every bit as good as any British tea I have ever tasted."

"Liberty. Hmmph. If this is liberty . . ." Father flattened his lips, stifling further comments. He patted his protruding belly and stood. "I hope the coach is parked nearby."

"Right outside the building, dear. Joshua returned it in a timely fashion so that Redmond could take me to my Daughters of Liberty meeting this morning."

Father shook his head. "What will females think of next?"

"Come along, Father. We shall never know until we taste some of the tea ourselves." Joshua shook his head in mirth and donned his frock coat.

"Do refrain from encouraging her, son." Father waved his hand. "Eh, mayhap it will relieve my headache."

"I hear it has a calming effect. Let us hope so." Mother draped an arm over Father's arm. Her drawstring purse swung, reminding Joshua of Miss Metcalf's missing workbag.

Indeed, a little calm would be nice. But first he had an important task to attend to. Joshua hastened past his parents and faced them, taking backward steps as he spoke. "If you will pardon me, I have an important errand to see to. Please do not wait dinner for me."

He jogged toward the exit hearing Father say, "Where is he off to now?"

Mother responded in her melodious tone, "Heaven only knows, but I suspect it might have something to do with that charming quilter."

Honour wrapped a cloth strip around the remaining lock of Temperance's reddish-blonde hair. "There, all ready for the night with a head full of curls, waiting for the morrow."

Temperance hopped off the bed and faced her older sister. "What will happen?"

"When?" Honour smiled at the imp of a girl in her white night shift and bare feet and placed her sleeping cap over her rag-laden head. Sitting on the bed, Honour picked up the hairbrush and ran it through her own dark auburn locks.

"Tomorrow, when we go to Sutton's Clothiers." Tempe jumped on the bed and knelt behind her sister. She took the brush from Honour and continued with the grooming.

"Mrs. Wadsworth, Maisey, and I will go there to work. You will go to your dame school, as you usually do. When I pick you up from school we shall return to Suttons where you shall do your chores for Mrs. Wadsworth, as you always do."

"I will straighten the fabrics, sort the tapes and notions, hunt for dropped pins and buttons, dust and tidy the room, sweep the floors, empty the waste, la, da, da, da, da," Temperance said, in a whimsical cadence.

"Exactly. The same tasks, but in a different place." Honour winced. "A little gentler, please. My head is sore yet, pumpkin."

Tempe threw her arms around Honour's neck.

"Have a care, Tempe."

"Oh, Honour, I didn't mean to hurt you! I meant to hug you." Tempe whimpered.

Honour reached up and tugged her sister's arms close. "It was not so bad, but please be gentle. Your brushing is so thorough, I think you lengthen my hair every time."

"Is that why your hair is so long and pretty?" Temperance laughed and fell back on the straw-filled mattress.

"Hush now. We mustn't disturb the others in their bed chambers."

Temperance said in a loud whisper, "Maisey disturbs us with her snoring."

"Temperance Metcalf. Do not speak ill of Mrs. Wadsworth's apprentice," Honour chided.

"I thought she was a quilter, like you are."

"Maisey is a quilter and an apprentice mantua maker. She is learning all the tasks involved in making gowns." Honour twisted her hair into a long tail and wound it into a ball at the nape of her neck. She donned her ruffled nightcap and tucked it beneath the dimity cotton.

"Will we be staying at Suttons' Clothiers overnight?" Temperance traced her finger along the swirly acanthus leaf pattern on the indigo bed quilt.

"We only need daylight from their workspace whilst Mrs. Wadsworth's shop downstairs is boarded up. We'll come home as usual for our supper, Bible reading, and then off-to-bed-we'll-go!" Honour turned around and tickled Tempe's waist, and another round of quiet giggles escaped. Their eyes both widened with mirth, and each pressed a finger to one another's lips.

With a kiss on Temperance's index finger, and one on her forehead, Honour pulled down the coverlet and Tempe jumped under the cozy bedding.

Honour blew out the Betty-lamp on the small bedside table and climbed under the whole-cloth quilted counterpane, so exquisitely designed by their mother and salvaged from the ship. Honour had wrapped it around Tempe and her—providing comfort and protection—while hiding beneath the stairs that horrific day on their journey to the British American colonies. Although the American frigate had intercepted the attacking French pirate ship, the buccaneers had seized most of their belongings, save a few trunks of clothing. The frigate took them aboard and brought them into Boston harbor, but she was informed their cargo either hadn't been spared or had been seized by customs. How grateful she was for this beautiful remnant of her mother's love and care, and the skill her Mum had passed along so Honour had the means to provide for her young charge.

"Time to say your prayers, Tempe," Honour said softly.

Temperance let out a big sigh. "Heavenly Father, I thank Thee for Thy bounty, and for keeping Honour safe from the storm. Please heal her aches and pains. And please let the bachelor, Joshua Sutton, choose Honour for a wife above all the ladies who fancy him. In Jesus' name I beseech Thee, Amen."

Honour gasped . . . then uttered a silent "Amen."

4

Honour sat in the light of a sunny window, needle in hand, quilting a length of golden calamanco. The glazed sheen of the satin-weave wool appeared as smooth and glossy as silk, though its substance would provide the warmth needed for the garment's purpose. She stuck the dull point of her bodkin into the bodkin case, which dangled from her chatelaine, along with her worn pincushion and tape measure, though her tiny scissors remained absent. She sorely missed her workbag, which held her more substantial sewing tools.

From the holes she'd pricked in the worsted wool backing, Honour stuffed bits of fleece batting into the serpentine pattern to produce a raised effect and highlight the elegant design. The repetitious sequence neared completion, and the end of the project drew nigh. Soon she would receive the bonus wages promised her for the extra hours worked.

A light breeze drifted through the opened window of the workspace Joshua's family provided for Mrs. Wadsworth over Sutton's Clothiers. Though August had just begun, the cooler weather would be upon them soon. Temperance would need new boots and a wool cloak by winter. Mum had planned to purchase items such as these in America, to save duties on the cargo, but now the responsibility to provide them fell upon Honour. Perhaps she could barter for some wool and set aside money for the boots. Mrs. Wadsworth gave Honour as many hours as she could afford, providing meals and lodging above the mantua shop, but not much more. Tempe shared a bed-chamber with Honour, ample despite the shared bedstead, and her employer graciously provided Temperance chores to compensate for the additional meal expense. Their basic needs were met, but for how long?

Honour worked more batting into the design. Her finances were dwindling. The guineas she'd claimed from her dear Poppa's coin purse had enabled her and Tempe to get settled in Boston. She worked hard to make arrangements for Tempe's schooling, a matter of utmost importance to their parents. How different Honour's life was now than in England. Honour had a proper education at a prestigious finishing school. She'd learned how to read and write. Poppa had taught her to cal-culate along with the boys. From Mum, she learned the finer skills required of an upper middling class female. Honour enjoyed many leisurely occasions by the fireside of their fine home quilting for her dower chest, while Mum tutored her in decorum and Christian character.

"The Lord has a grand design for your life," Mum would say, "be faithful to trust His handiwork, even when the pattern isn't clear." Honour had tried to make sense of her lot, a situa-tion greatly altered from the hopes she and her family had for life in New England. But, try as she might to find a new pattern emerging, she found it not.

She went to retrieve her tiny scissors from her workbag only to remember that it remained lost. She had to rely on borrowed items for her quilting until she found it, hoping that she would not need to purchase a replacement. Yet, though the bag was lost, as sentimental as her attachment to it was, Honour was grateful that her skill remained and enabled her to provide for herself and her sister.

"May I borrow your small scissors, please?" Honour asked Mrs. Wadsworth's apprentice.

"Surely, but have you not your own supplies?" Maisey handed the scissors to Honour.

Honour took a snip of some batting. "I misplaced my work-bag the other day and have not yet discovered where it is."

"The pretty one your mother gave you, with the small compartments?" Maisey asked.

"Aye. I hope I shall find it soon." Honour frowned and set to more stuffwork.

"I hope you shall. Mrs. Wadsworth is keen on her workers being responsible for their own equipment. She is anxious enough being absent from her own shop. I'm sure she appreciates the Sutton's kindness, but she cannot afford to lose customers while away."

"I will continue to search. 'Tis very dear to me."

"I do not mind being here myself, near the handsome Sutton men, especially Joshua." Maisey gave a sassy grin.

As Honour placed the scissors on the table she raised her eyebrows, tempting Maisey to continue.

"Word is that Joshua Sutton is now an available bachelor. He was attached to Emily Guilfold for years, but she unexpectedly married another man." Maisey leaned closer and whispered, "By special license."

"I had not heard. I know little of the Suttons." But Honour knew enough of Joshua to realize he was kind-hearted. Was that heart now broken for love lost? Although, when she had shared her thoughts with him on the topic, he had not responded in kind. Would she ever have a chance to meet with him again? Perhaps he was merely extending compassion to her as a distraction to the pain he now bore from his ended betrothal.

"To be sure, the girls in this town will be lining up to have him measure their gowns, rather than letting Mrs. Wadsworth drape them for a proper mantua," Maisey said.

Honour's eyes widened at Maisey's vulgar insinuation.

"Moreover," Maisey whispered, "He was seen carrying one woman through town the other day, and kissing another in a carriage the next." Maisey turned the sleeve she was working on right side out and smoothed out the wrinkles. "At least someone is garnering his attention . . . or shall I say affections."

Honour chided herself for paying heed to her coworker's ramblings, eager though she was to learn more about Joshua Sutton. But what she did not expect was to hear herself included in the account—or so she thought—even if it was incorrect. A nervous chuckle burst forth.

"'Tis no laughing matter. This is the biggest news since the British occupied the city last October!" Maisey clucked her tongue. "If we cannot have him for ourselves, at least we might get an occasional gander at his handsome face while we're here. Perhaps you might like to go downstairs and borrow his scissors next time. I'd be happy to do the asking for you." Maisey broke into throaty giggles, but stifled them when she looked up to see Mrs. Wadsworth sauntering toward them with decisive steps.

"Maisey, I will not abide your prattle, even if you speak a truth. Although, I must say, I have misgivings about the content of your report. I do not know where you come by such news, though I do have my suspicions, Miss Hubert."

Mrs. Wadsworth turned to Honour and winked. "Do not believe a thing she says, Honour."

Now Honour knew why Mrs. Wadsworth was not forthcoming when Maisey asked how they had fared during the storm when she'd been away. There was enough to tell her regarding the damage to the shop and Honour getting caught in the storm, but any further detail involving Joshua Sutton was best left unsaid to the gossip-prone worker.

"I will not have you repeating any of that heresy, Maisey Hubert, or I shall be fitting you for a gossip's bridle."

"There is no need of the brank for me. I'll speak no more of it. But you cannot stop me from dreaming." Maisey patted her chest, feigning a lovelorn heart.

"Allow me to remind you both," Mrs. Wadsworth continued, "as workers in my shop you may have the occasion of hearing reports and opinions shared by some of my patrons. What you may hear is to remain strictly confidential." Mrs. Wadsworth tapped Maisey lightly on the head with her thimble. "I will not have gossipmongers coming from my place of business."

Honour nodded. "You may count on me, Mrs. Wadsworth."

"Yes, Mistress," Maisey answered, inflecting exaggerated amiability. "Though I see no harm in keeping it within our walls. It helps pass the time."

Mrs. Wadsworth shook her head and uttered a long sigh. "You may pass the time with the tasks I pay you to do. If you wish to manage your own business someday, you would be wise to learn proper decorum. Sharing falsehoods tends to harm the one doing the sharing as much as it does the subject."

"I shall make an effort," Maisey pledged.

To what? Comply with Mrs. Wadsworth's wishes? Continue spreading rumors? Despite Honour's attempts at friendship with her fellow worker, the discomfiture she felt at Maisey's impertinence was just another awkward stitch in the quilt of Honour's inability to truly trust her.

"How are you girls coming along on Widow Lankton's quilted traveling suit?" Mrs. Wadsworth patted the edges of her coiffure beneath her linen cap. She adjusted her work apron and stepped closer to peruse Honour's and Maisey's handwork.

"I am putting in my last stitch now," Maisey said, tying a final knot. "There. It is done!"

"Hold it up dear and let me see," Mrs. Wadsworth said eagerly.

Maisey held up the top portion of the gown, a glimmer of pride on her rounded cheeks.

"It is lovely." Honour admired the quilted caraco jacket. The partially open front, from waist to thigh, would display the petticoat worn as its companion, now sitting in Honour's lap as she worked on the coordinating piece.

Mrs. Wadsworth carefully retrieved the garment from Maisey's grasp and walked toward the light of the window. She inspected every stitch through a small magnifying lens as she uttered a variety of hmms, ahhs, and mm-mms. "Maisey, if you intend for the sleeves to stay attached to this gown, you must pay heed to a smaller stitch, particularly around the shoulders. We must ensure the quilting shan't unravel. Please redo the sleeves."

Mrs. Wadsworth handed the jacket back to a pouting Maisey and turned her scrutinizing eye toward Honour. "How are we coming along with the quilting for the petticoat?"

Honour pulled a waxed strand of satin thread through the fabric draped over her lap. "I am nearing completion. The border has a few more pattern repetitions, and then it will be ready for Maisey's fine hand to assemble and sew the petticoat." Honour glanced at Maisey and offered her an encouraging smile.

"May I?" Mrs. Wadsworth asked with open hands.

Honour relinquished her work to her employer, who laid the length of quilted cloth out on a large worktable.

Mrs. Wadsworth leaned over, examining the meticulously stitched quilt. This had been one of Honour's most extravagant pieces yet. The border of the cloth showed frond and scroll work betwixt a floral pattern, this being more elaborate than the rest of the quilting with a repetition of geometrical designs. Honour's heart fluttered as she awaited the verdict.

"The motif is gorgeous, and your needlework is outstanding. You have an exceptional skill, Honour Metcalf."

After having spent months on its quilting, Honour sighed with great relief. "Thank you, Mrs. Wadsworth. I do hope Widow Lankton will be pleased at our handiwork."

Mrs. Wadsworth glanced back at Maisey. "Let us hope that Widow Lankton will approve of the finished product."

A *tap, tap, tap* sounded at the door. "Good afternoon, ladies."

Mrs. Wadsworth turned and greeted the silver-haired woman, with coiffure high upon her brow, entering the room. "Good morning, Mrs. Sutton. How nice of you to come by."

"Do you find your new accommodations satisfactory?" Mrs. Sutton asked, approaching the worktable.

"Indeed we do. The room is more than adequate for our needs and provides a generous amount of lighting," Mrs. Wadsworth said.

"Very good." Mrs. Sutton looked at the table displaying Honour's handiwork and let out a gasp. "What have we here?"

"This is quilting for Widow Lankton's new traveling suit," Mrs. Wadsworth said.

"It is stunning, Eunice will look lovely in it. This quilted pattern is beautiful, I have never seen anything to compare. So much nicer than machine-loomed quilted material they are making in Marseilles, France now. Though some prefer it, I do not."

Mrs. Wadsworth nodded. "I must agree with you, Olive."

"But it is neither here nor there, and literally not here while we have the embargo in place." Mrs. Sutton placed the back of her hand against her forehead. "I'd best leave that topic alone, although it does present the opportunity to tell you, Margaret, the next Daughters of Liberty meeting will be held at my home in a fortnight." Mrs. Sutton looked at Maisey and Honour. "You girls are welcome to join us."

Mrs. Sutton eyed Honour with curiosity. "I do not think I have had the privilege of making your acquaintance."

"This is Miss Honour Metcalf, of late from England. She is my new quilter," Mrs. Wadsworth said. "And the talent behind this quilt." She smoothed her palm over the calamanco.

"Talented, indeed. Mayhap Sutton's can contract you to quilt some of the children's and gentlemen's garments we make—if you could use the extra work." Mrs. Sutton eyed Mrs. Wadsworth. "With your permission, of course, Margaret."

"I think we might arrange something," Mrs. Wadsworth said.

Honour smiled at Mrs. Wadsworth and then addressed Mrs. Sutton. "I would be happy to consider it, madam. Thank you."

Mrs. Sutton planted her hand against her cheek, perusing Honour. "You have made quite an impression on my Joshua. Now, I see why. Talented, pretty, and kind."

A warm blush rose in Honour's face, and she lowered her lashes.

"Did you enjoy the ride in our coach the other morning when Joshua drove you home from the parsonage after your unfortunate incident?" Mrs. Sutton continued.

Honour looked at her and smiled. "Aye. It is a lovely carriage and the ride was most pleasant. Thank you for your kindness."

Mrs. Sutton tilted her chin, beckoning her to say more.

"And Mr. Sutton."

"I have three Mr. Suttons, my dear. Please call him Joshua or I shall be utterly confused."

"Would you thank him—Joshua—again for me please." Heat rose beneath the modesty piece tucked into Honour's upper bodice.

"Certainly. We are happy to know you are all right."

Honour dared glance at Maisey and shrugged.

Maisey's eyes big as saucers, she mouthed, "Josh-u-a?"

Mmm, yes, Joshua . . . his Christian name. And he had called her Honour.

Hopefully, Maisey would abide by Mrs. Wadsworth's rule of confidentiality and not let rumors take flight—like Ben Franklin's electrically charged kite—it was Honour Metcalf who had recently been found in the company of the bachelor Joshua Sutton.

This is where I found Honour huddled in the street. I am sure of it. Joshua had already scoured each side of Marlborough Street the other day and now was at it once more. He walked over the cobblestones on the side of the road, looking over and under fences, behind watering troughs, between buildings, underneath steps . . . ah, he missed this one. He bent down and looked behind the wig-maker's porch, finding nothing but dead leaves and a small porcelain curling rod which looked like an old bone. Joshua stood and kicked the bottom step and groaned.

The low tone of Reverend Cooper's voice met Joshua's ears. "Are you missing something, Mr. Sutton?"

Joshua spun around, surprised to see the parson there. "Good day, Reverend Cooper."

"Is it?" the clergyman asked.

"Hmmph. I am not certain. What I am looking for is like trying to find a bodkin in a bundle of straw."

"Our omnipotent God knows where it is. Have you inquired of Him?" the reverend asked.

"No, sir, I cannot say that I have. Does He care for the trivial things in our lives when He has much weightier matters to concern Him?"

"His concern is for you, son. Moreover, your lost article, which is important to you."

"It is important to a friend, and thus to me. The item was lost during the hailstorm. I believe it may have fallen into the street, but by now, everything has been cleared away. I fear it is lost forever."

"Should you like to tell me what it is, I will be happy to help you find it."

"I am searching for Miss Metcalf's embroidered work satchel."

"Ah, then, we are making progress."

"Are we?"

The reverend shuffled over to a nearby bench and patted the seat beside him. "Sit."

Joshua sat beside the clergyman, who today wore his black parson's frock. How peculiar he seemed at times, but always generous, strangely insightful, and naturally pious.

"Tell me, how is the young lady? Better, I trust."

"I do hope so, though I have not seen her since I took her home from your manse a few days ago."

"I see."

What did he see?

Reverend Cooper peered from beneath his wiry eyebrows. "God is in the business of finding lost things. Coins, sheep, His beloved children."

The man apparently sensed that Joshua was looking for more than Honour's bag.

"Dear Lord, we beseech Thee to aid us in locating Miss Metcalf's workbag. We seek Thy direction and ask for the item's safekeeping until it is discovered. Please care for Miss Metcalf according to Thy will. Bless this young man as he endeavors to become more like Thee. Amen."

Joshua echoed, "Amen." *Methinks.*

"Well, then. I shall be on my way. I have an appointment to keep. Be sure to let me know how it turns out." The clergyman stood and ambled away.

"Good day, sir. Thank you." Joshua scratched his head, bewildered at the reverend's classification of help, and pondered the duplicitous meaning in his sermonizing prayer.

Then the soft, melodic voice of another caught his attention. "Why, Mr. Sutton. How good it is to see you."

Joshua turned and beheld Honour, paused along the walkway behind the bench. How strange she should appear at precisely this moment. "Miss Metcalf, what a pleasant circumstance. How do you fare? You are looking lovely." Lovely, indeed, in a gown of green and peach striped calico, showing off the beautiful light of her fair skin and dark auburn hair spiraling onto her shoulder, beneath her straw Bergère hat.

"I am much improved, thank you," she said, her eyes smiling as she talked. "I intended to thank you for your kindnesses the other day, but before I had the chance you had disappeared from Mrs. Wadsworth's shop."

"I thought it best to leave quietly while you were enjoying being reacquainted with your sister. She is an adorable thing, isn't she?"

"She is. The little imp." Honour giggled.

"Temperance is her name?"

"Aye, it is. In fact, I am on my way to fetch her from Mistress Hollister's dame school. After doing so, I shall continue my search for my workbag by inquiring within some of these shops along this side of the road. I scouted the opposite side yesterday and found nothing."

"I have also been looking, to no avail. Yet, I have it on good word it shall turn up soon."

Honour tilted her chin. "Do you? Whose word might that be?"

"The Almighty's."

"He informed you of its whereabouts?" Honour asked.

"Not exactly, but Reverend Cooper assures me God is interested in this matter," Joshua said.

Honour made several attempts to speak, though nothing came out. At last, a word erupted. "Really?"

Joshua shrugged. "It is what the man said."

"I take it that you believe him." Honour smirked and dimples on each side of her pretty mouth blossomed.

"Why shouldn't I?" Joshua asked. Had she no faith or was she jesting?

"You children, skedaddle! I shan't be having urchins with dirty hands touching my merchandise. Go on now!" The shrill voice of the keeper of Carter's Millinery rose above the normal din of passing wagons, carriages, an occasional horse, and a bustle of people walking by.

"Now there is one place I have not looked." Honour consulted the small watch pinned to her bodice. "I may have time for a quick stop before I continue on my way."

"May I join you?" Joshua asked.

Miss Metcalf hesitated for a moment, and smiled. "Certainly, Mr. Sutton."

Joshua offered Honour his arm as they crossed the street together. "How are you finding the conditions for working in my father's building? Is the space ample?"

"It exceeds our requirements and provides a great measure of light to sew by. How generous it was of your family to accommodate Mrs. Wadsworth's need." Honour looked straight ahead. Did she feel awkward about being seen with him?

"I am glad it has helped." They approached the millinery shop, and Joshua held open the door. "After you, milady."

"Why, thank you, kind sir." She nodded, then lowered her gaze as she stepped inside to the jingle of small bells hanging over the doorway.

With no one immediately present to inquire of, Joshua and Honour wandered around the store looking over shelves and displays in search of the bag.

Mrs. Carter, the shopkeeper, stepped behind a counter. "Is there something I may help you with?"

Honour faced the older woman, Joshua standing near. "Good afternoon. My name is Honour Metcalf and—"

"I know who you are," the cantankerous proprietress said.

"I came in search of a workbag," Honour continued.

"How much do you plan to spend?"

"Why, there it is!" Honour pointed to the bag sitting on the shelving behind the counter.

"There what is, Miss?" Mrs. Carter glanced over her shelves.

"My workbag. I misplaced it during the storm the other day and thought I might never find it. I have been searching all over." Honour extended her arm. "May I see it, please?"

The store owner planted her fists on her hips, "It is not for sale."

"I surely hope not. As I said, it belongs to me." Honour kept her tone in perfect poise, though she tapped the toe of her shoe against the planked floor.

"You may look at it and if you have the coin. Mayhap I shall consider selling it to you." The contrary woman placed the satchel on the counter.

Honour picked it up and held it snuggly against her middle. "I told you this is the very bag that I have been looking for. It is already mine."

Mrs. Carter narrowed her eyes. "You refuse to pay for it, eh?"

"I do, but mayhap—"

The storekeeper came out from behind the counter and hollered, "Thief!"

5

Joshua stepped in front of Mrs. Carter, blocking her from the door. He stayed his hand over the woman's arm, untouching. "Miss Metcalf is no thief."

The irate shopkeeper jerked away from Joshua as if he'd attempted to accost her. "Move away, or the sheriff will hear my testimony that you've acted as her accomplice."

In disbelief, Joshua stared into the woman's possum-like eyes, and tried to appeal to her sensibilities, assuming she had some. "I am nothing of the sort, Mrs. Carter. Please be reasonable and return Miss Metcalf's property to her."

"Do not speak to me in a harsh manner, Mr. Sutton, or I shall refrain from making purchases from your father's business," she snapped.

Joshua's eyes darted at Miss Metcalf, who remained by the counter, her face tense with concern. Mrs. Carter looked back at Miss Metcalf, glaring.

"Mrs. Carter," Honour pleaded. "I have a young sister I must get from Mrs. Hollister's dame school. I came to see if, perchance, you had my satchel. I see that you do and would like to have it back, please."

The woman's face contorted. "Without paying. That is an act of thievery. We will see what the sheriff has to say about that." Mrs. Carter crossed her arms over her rotund bodice.

The door opened and Joshua stepped back, astonished. Reverend Cooper entered the millinery shop to the surprise of all. Joshua met his gaze in earnest, hoping the minister could read his silent plea for intervention.

"Reverend Cooper," Mrs. Carter said. She donned a smile, and her inflection changed instantly. "Is there something I may help you with today?"

"I happened by when I someone call out. Mayhap I can be of assistance." The reverend's rich voice held an air of authority. His eyebrows curved in varying degrees as he beheld each of them in turn.

Mrs. Carter's eyes flitted toward the thick black tome tucked beneath Reverend Cooper's arm. "Why . . . Why, yes. This woman is trying to steal my merchandise."

Reverend Cooper looked about the shop seeing no other, save Mrs. Carter's assistant who remained timidly in the corner. "You are referring to Miss Metcalf?"

"It is whom she claims to be. I know her as Mrs. Wadsworth's new quilter. I also know quilters earn precious little, especially from the frugal Margaret Wadsworth. Each time this one patronizes my store she carefully counts each and every coin she removes from her purse."

"There is no crime in that," Joshua said.

"Hmmph." Mrs. Carter dismissed Joshua's comment and looked down her long nose at Honour. "She attempted to take something valuable from my store without paying for it. Can you not see she is nothing more than a common criminal?"

All eyes turned toward Honour. "I find nothing wrong with Miss Metcalf's appearance," Reverend Cooper said. "It is not by the outward appearance one should be judged."

"I beg to differ, Reverend Cooper. How a woman dresses is evidence of her true nature. God's Word says so, does it not? Women are to dress circumspectly, without being showy."

"Mrs. Carter." Reverend Cooper chided, and pursed his lips.

The proprietor's ire rose. "She wears the attire of a fine lady. Do you not agree, Mr. Sutton? You know about such things." Mrs. Carter glanced at Reverend Cooper meeting his disapproving gaze. "As a tailor, I mean."

Joshua regarded Honour's gown. It had not escaped his notice, despite Miss Metcalf's vocation, she was well-attired in the latest fashions. He refrained from replying, for he knew not what Mrs. Carter was insinuating.

"Finery, for sure. The fabric, trimmings, her accoutrements. Why, the purse she is claiming is of the highest style." Sarcasm dripped from Mrs. Carter's tongue. "Miss Metcalf could never afford to own such fashions with her meager earnings as a quilter. She must have attained them by *alternative* means—by deception—just as she attempted to acquire this!" The woman waved the satchel in front of all.

The parson scratched his wig. "So then, you have seen her with this satchel before when she made purchases in your shop. Did it look like this?"

Mrs. Carter closed her eyes and huffed. "I cannot be expected to recall each of my customer's purses."

"Though you amply stated you had taken notice of hers." Reverend Cooper looked at Joshua, lifting his overlong eyebrows. "Mr. Sutton, do you recognize this bag as belonging to Miss Metcalf?"

"No, sir." Joshua frowned. "I have never seen it until now."

"How do you know this bag belongs to her?" the reverend asked.

"She told me she had lost her workbag during the hailstorm. Thus the reason we came into Carter's Millinery today.

I have been assisting Miss Metcalf in locating it and we have searched most everywhere else along this street. It meets her description of it precisely."

"Yes, and I saw you looking for it myself." The reverend acknowledged Joshua, then turned toward the accuser. "How did you come by this bag, Mrs. Carter?"

"I do not recall, it must have come in on a shipment from England long ago."

Revered Cooper rubbed his chin. "So, you are neglecting the Non-Importation Agreement? Have you other items you are selling from England? *The Chronicle* may be interested in this bit of news." The parson looked at Joshua. "Do you not agree, Mr. Sutton?"

"Mr. Mein is eager to print such things," Joshua said.

"Hmmph. It may have come in a shipment from one of the other colonies, I cannot recall. I have done nothing wrong here. I merely asked this woman to pay for the merchandise before leaving the store."

"What was your intent, Miss Metcalf?" Reverend Cooper asked.

"I was not inclined to leave with any of Mrs. Carter's merchandise today. I only wish to claim my personal property."

"May I remind you, miss, that possession is nine points of the law," said the shrew.

"Let us see, then. Mrs. Carter, if Miss Metcalf can prove this item belongs to her can we rely on your good sensibilities to return it to her without cost?"

Mrs. Carter looked at the ceiling and huffed. "Why, if she can prove it."

"Miss Metcalf. Does that sound fair to you?" the reverend asked.

"Aye, Reverend Cooper." Honour's large brown eyes drifted toward the door. She crossed her arms across her stomacher, and her foot set to tapping in quick successions. Her pretty jacquard shoe peeked out from beneath her petticoat.

Revered Cooper held out his hand. "Mrs. Carter, may I?"

The ill-favored jade reluctantly handed Reverend Cooper the bag.

Joshua took in a deep breath, dragging his fingers through his hair. How the sweet smell of the millinery contrasted to Mrs. Carter's demeanor.

Honour's tone remained pleasant, despite her frustration. "The bag was specially made for my mother in England and used for her quilting."

"Oh . . . so she was a quilter as well," snapped Mrs. Carter.

"Aye, madam. She quilted at her leisure along with her tambour work. She was quite adept at it, and her handiwork was admired by many," Honour retorted.

Mrs. Carter turned her nose. *Was Honour from a family of means?*

"You will find the bag has several compartments. The one on the top is where I keep my coin. There should be three shillings inside, no more."

Reverend Cooper passed the bag to Joshua. "Would you please look inside the top compartment, Mr. Sutton?"

"Yes, sir." Joshua lifted the cover.

"What do you find there?"

"It is empty."

Honour gasped. "Someone must have . . . Perhaps they fell . . . Please check the side pockets. On the left, I keep my pins, and on the right, you'll find my needles. The lower drawer on the front hosts my thimbles." Honour's face lit up. "You shall find my silver thimble with my initials engraved on it there."

Reverend Cooper nodded at Joshua. "Mr. Sutton?"

Joshua opened each of the small compartments. "The drawers are empty."

"Empty? Oh, no." Honour shook her head and frowned. "Please look inside. You shall find all manner of sewing supplies."

Joshua opened the front flap of the satin bag. "I am afraid it is empty as well."

Honour pouted. "Empty or not the bag is still mine. Please, can we not settle this matter? I must fetch my sister from school." Honour set her foot to tapping.

Reverend Cooper looked at her sympathetically. "Is there some source of evidence you can provide?"

"Other than sending for Mrs. Wadsworth and Maisey, as they both have seen me use this bag daily." Honour rubbed her temple, and sighed.

Was she still suffering from her head malady? This inquisition mustn't be helping.

Honour's face lit up. "I have been remiss! You shall find my mother's initials, *EM*, stitched onto the lower enclosure. I am so used to its presence that I barely give it heed."

Joshua turned the bag over, and precisely where Honour had indicated, he discovered the carefully stitched letters *EM*.

Honour clasped her hands with glee. "Elizabeth Metcalf. My mother." Honour's eyes misted and she entreated Mrs. Carter with a silent plea.

"Apparently, Mrs. Carter, you were mistaken," Reverend Cooper said. "We shall thank you for returning the workbag to Miss Metcalf."

Joshua handed the embroidered satchel to Honour, and smiled. What an ordeal. He hoped she would begin to feel well now.

He cocked his head. "Do not fret, Mrs. Carter, we shall not report it was returned missing its valuable contents." Joshua glanced and nodded, signaling Honour to agree to this resolution.

Mrs. Carter's mouth parted, then she clamped it shut without a word.

"As I attempted to state earlier, Mrs. Carter, I would have been happy to reward you for finding my bag, yet my coin is now gone. Please accept my appreciation instead."

How Honour could be so gracious after all of this rigmarole astounded him.

The thud of footsteps coming up the steps announced Sheriff Porter's arrival. "Good day, all." The sheriff's gaze shifted from one person to the other. "Mrs. Carter, is there a problem?"

"No, Sheriff, I believe we have settled the issue." Mrs. Carter pursed her lips.

The Sheriff planted his fist on his broad hip. "You are certain?"

"Indeed." Mrs. Carter crossed her arms and looked away.

"Though it is resolved, please inform me of the nature of the problem so I can be assured no one has taken the law into his . . . or her . . . own hands," the sheriff said.

"You see, Sheriff Porter, I mistakenly thought this young woman had intended to leave my store without paying for an item."

He shifted his gaze to Honour. "Is that so?"

"Why, yes . . . I mean, no," the harried shopkeeper said.

"Reverend Cooper? What say you?" Sheriff Porter inquired.

"Apparently, Mrs. Carter mistakenly had an item on her shelf which is the personal property of Miss Metcalf. But we have sorted it out and now Miss Metcalf has her rightful possession." Reverend Cooper tilted his chin, and issued a satisfied nod.

"Mrs. Carter was kind enough to return my misplaced workbag," Miss Metcalf offered.

Sheriff Porter squinted at Honour. "You are new in Boston, miss?"

"Aye. I arrived in the spring. I work for Mrs. Wadsworth."

"As a seamstress?"

"A quilter."

The sheriff eyed Honour's workbag. "It is a fine bag. Something my wife would envy."

"Thank you, sir. It was a gift." Honour smiled meekly.

The sheriff eyed her with suspicion. "Very well. If you are satisfied with the outcome."

"Aye, Sheriff Porter. And thank you, Reverend Cooper for intervening," Honour said.

Sheriff Porter walked toward the door. As he placed his hand on the door handle, he stopped and turned back. "How is it you came to be involved in this matter, Mr. Sutton?"

"I am a friend of Miss Metcalf's and we were searching for the satchel together, sir," Joshua said.

"Do be careful, Mr. Sutton. If this woman continues to be suspect, it could be harmful to your reputation, such as it is," the sheriff said.

The muscle in Joshua's jaw twitched. "I assure you there is nothing suspect about her."

"And I assure you that there is nothing suspect about him," Reverend Cooper defended.

"That remains to be seen." The sheriff shot a glance at Miss Metcalf. "How long have you been acquainted with her, Mr. Sutton?"

"Only recently, sir."

"I see. You are ready to vouch for her character?"

"She has given me no reason to mistrust her," Joshua said. *Or had she?*

"Honour, you found it!" Temperance clasped the embroidered satchel in her small hands as it hung from a long satin cord over Honour's shoulder.

"Aye!" Honour glanced at Mr. Sutton.

Temperance released the bag and hugged Honour around her waist. "Where was it?"

Honour ran her fingers through the light ginger curls hanging from the back of Tempe's straw hat. "We found it in a shop in town. Thus, I was late in coming."

"I wondered what had kept you. Mistress Hollister was growing upset that you were late. I told her not to worry, that you always keep your promises and I knew you would be along soon."

As they walked from the Hollister's house, where Tempe attended the dame school, she squinted up at Joshua with a lopsided grin.

"Do you remember Mr. Sutton from the other day at Mrs. Wadsworth's? He helped me find my workbag today." Honour offered Joshua a shy smile.

"Hello, Mr. Sutton. Are you a knight? Mistress Hollister read us a story about the crusades today and said knights are noble and shiverous helpers."

Joshua pretended to shiver and gave a hearty laugh.

"Chivalrous, Tempe. It means gentlemanly," Honour said.

Temperance looked up at their winsome escort. "Are you a gentleman, Mr. Sutton? My father was a gentleman."

"Some people say that I am." Joshua stepped between the two ladies and offered his elbows, smiling at one and then the other.

Honour tilted her chin. "Why, thank you, sir."

"Thank you, kind gentleman," Tempe said in a grown-up lady's voice.

"What else did you learn in school today, Tempe?" Honour asked, peeking around Joshua at her sister.

"We practiced in our hornbooks and primer. The eighth commandment is, 'thou-shalt-not-steal,'" Temperance recited.

"Truly?" Honour bit her lower lip to contain the odd humor she found in it. She gave her sister a little smile. "How is your needlework coming along, pumpkin?"

Tempe's mouth formed into a wide circle. "I forgot to show you! May we go back?"

"You may show me tomorrow. We must get back to Mrs. Wadsworth's shop, we are already tardy."

"You mean Sutton's Clothiers." Tempe looked up at Joshua again.

"Aye. Mr. Sutton was kind enough to offer to walk us there."

"'Tis no inconvenience as I am going back there myself, and I am glad to have the company of two of the prettiest ladies in town."

Temperance projected her lower lip. "Are you going to court my sister?"

"Temperance Metcalf!" Honour placed her hand against her cheek, glancing into the sky.

"Hmm. I have not contemplated it until now. But it is a rather charming idea." Joshua bent low to Temperance's ear and said overloud. "Perhaps I will consider it."

Honour buried her face in her hands and dared peek out from under them. She tripped over a raised cobblestone, and Joshua reached out to steady her balance. "Steady now. Are you all right?"

"Mortified, is all," she said.

"I was not aware you find me so repulsive." Joshua gave her an exaggerated frown, pressing his hand against his heart. "You wound me, Miss Metcalf."

Honour offered a weak smile. "Forgive me, sir. I meant no offense."

"None taken." Joshua gave her a conciliatory grin, and she tried not to concentrate on his dimples as he did so.

"Now, Temperance, you must never speak of such things in mixed company. It is entirely impolite, even in jest," Honour scolded.

"But Honour, I was not joking," Temperance whined.

The corner of Mr. Sutton's mouth turned up. "Nor was I."

Honour's stomach fluttered. "Perhaps we might discuss this at another time, Mr. Sutton."

"I see no need. Unless, of course, you are otherwise attached."

Tempe's small hand covered her giggles, the tips of her fingers wiggling as they peeked out from her fingerless summer mitts.

Mr. Sutton addressed Temperance. "Miss Metcalf, the younger, are you in any way attached?"

Tempe craned her neck toward Mr. Sutton. "No, sir. I was fond of Willy Sandborn before he was the dunce in school today. I shall not abide his nonsense."

Mr. Sutton suppressed a laugh, addressing Tempe again. "And the elder Miss Metcalf?"

"She was in England, but is no longer," Temperance chirped.

Mr. Sutton nodded, looking from Temperance to Honour. "Then I should like to ask you both if you might accompany me to a picnic, a fortnight from Saturday next. It shall take place at the home of my parents in celebration of my birthday."

Tempe eyed him carefully. "Your birthday? I didn't think birthdays were celebrated in New England?"

"My mother keeps some of her family's traditions from Wales. Does it offend you?"

"We keep birthdays too! I do not see why such a delight-ful event is frowned upon so. God made us, after all," Tempe explained.

Honour shook her head and laughed, eying Joshua over her shoulder. "A topic for another day, you precocious child."

Tempe ran to Honour's side and tugged her arm. "May we attend, Honour? Please?"

Honour's heart melted as she looked into her sister's hope-filled eyes. It had been long since they had something enjoyable to look forward to. Besides, it was the man's birthday . . . How could she refuse? Honour let out a deep sigh. "Yes."

Tempe's eyes danced with mirth. "She said yes, Mr. Sutton! She said yes!"

"Marvelous! I shall call for you at noon on August the twenty-sixth."

Mr. Sutton reached across, resting his hand on Honour's forearm she'd linked through the crook of his elbow. When his thumb rubbed the back of her hand—ever so lightly—a little breath caught in her throat. Sensing his eyes upon her, she looked sidelong, meeting his gaze. One of his eyebrows rose, and his dimple seemed to wink at her. Her duplicitous lips returned a demure smile, before she turned away. Had he truly asked to court her or was he teasing? How dare he toy with her heart!

6

Arm in arm, Honour, Tempe, and Joshua Sutton ambled along Boston's busy sidewalks, continuing toward Sutton's Clothiers. Although the walk to Tempe's dame school was only a mile and a half, closer now from Sutton's, Honour grew fatigued and the faces of passersby blurred. A multitude of thoughts wove through her mind in no distinct pattern. Her life here was nothing like the life of comfort she once enjoyed in England. She had been excited about her family's prospects in the British American colonies, yet her life now in no way resembled her hopes and expectations.

Poppa, an American sympathizer, had looked forward to his future with his business connections in Boston. "We shall have a grand adventure in a land full of promise," he'd said on many occasions. When Honour and Tempe arrived at the port—alone—she had sought out one of father's associates. He generously paid customs for her salvaged cargo, arranged for her family's burial, and set her and Tempe up with Mrs. Wadsworth for their lodging and employment.

When she inquired of Mr. Leach as to how she could repay him, he informed her that she needed only to sign a document releasing her obligation to him, and likewise he to her. But as she finished penning her signature on the parchment, a sense of foreboding had come over her whether she'd given enough consideration to his request. How much of an investment had her father made with Leach and Sons Enterprises? She had signed away her chance at ever knowing.

Her eyes moistened at the thought that she had this very day been accused of stealing—her own property at that. Never would that have happened in England to her well-respected family. How different Temperance's upbringing would be than Honour's had been—never wanting and with parents who cherished her. Honour vowed to do her best to give her sister the love she deserved and instill in Tempe the values their parents had imparted to her.

Tempe skipped ahead, twirling around as she chattered on. "Come along, you dawdlers."

Only then did Honour realize she alone walked arm in arm with Joshua.

"It is impolite to run ahead and to call names, Tempe. Now please come back here with us and be patient." *Us.* Oh, dear. Had she really agreed to attend his picnic?

Tempe pouted, but rejoined them for the remainder of the walk. Soon they turned the corner onto King Street and arrived at the sign of the silver shears. The stately two-story yellow clapboard building housing Sutton's Clothiers was an impressive sight. Its large bay window, newly repaired, displayed beautiful fabrics and a sampling of men's and children's garments.

Honour reclaimed her arm from Joshua's safekeeping, inadvertently rubbing it as she widened the space between them.

"Tempe, go on upstairs. Mrs. Wadsworth is probably wondering what has kept us. Please tell her I shall be along by and by."

Temperance proffered her version of a curtsy toward her escort. "Thank you for walking us back, Mr. Sutton."

Joshua bowed. "It was my pleasure, Miss Metcalf." He turned to Honour, "And Miss Metcalf."

Tempe ran inside leaving Honour and Joshua in front of the store. Honour stared at the beautiful window boxes overflowing with red and purple pansies, trying to collect her thoughts. "These flowers held up fairly well during the storm, I see."

"Yes, though Mother had to refresh them. How are you holding up, Miss Metcalf? You have been rather quiet the way back," Joshua said.

"A bit tired, mayhap." Honour gently touched a leaf.

"It has been an eventful afternoon."

A pair of young women sauntered by, waving their fans in front of their flirtatious smiles. "Good afternoon, Mr. Sutton."

Joshua tipped his cocked hat. "Ladies." He certainly played the gallant.

Honour placed her hand on the railing and took a step up. "I should be . . ."

Joshua covered her hand with his, sending a small shiver up her arm. "I do hope I have not offended you, Miss Metcalf. Have you reconsidered my invitation?"

The wooden rail stood between them like a fence she dared not trespass. She looked toward the window, as if she could see her sister inside. Tempe had already gone through so much in her short life. How could she disappoint her? Although Honour had admired the handsome tailor from afar, her tattered heart needed much mending before she could consider giving it away. She had done so once before and had learned a grave lesson.

Joshua retrieved his hand. "Let us get out of the sun. Mayhap we can continue our conversation inside."

Joshua trotted up the steps and held the door for Honour. The storefront was much larger than Mrs. Wadsworth's Mantua Shoppe and catered to a different clientele. Walls of shelves containing exquisite fabrics in an array of colors and textures greeted them along with countertops displaying fashionable accoutrements, sewing notions, and weaving supplies. "Each time I enter I am newly impressed with the lovely displays." She pointed to a silk brocade waistcoat hanging near some of other garments. "Is that new? It is a handsome piece."

"Thank you. I finished working on it this morning," Joshua said.

Honour tilted her chin and smiled. "You did a fine job. It looks about your size. Does it belong to you?" She blushed as she imagined how handsome he'd look in the fine garment.

"Thank you. Yes, it is mine." Joshua leaned against a counter. "Now, what is troubling you? Do you regret your decision to accompany me to my birthday picnic?"

"Why, no. That's not it at all. Tempe and I are looking forward to attending," Honour said. "Thank you for including her."

"Ah, then. It is the other matter. You do not wish to be courted." Joshua crossed his arms.

Honour narrowed her eyes, and donned a little grin. "Your invitation hardly constitutes a courting relationship."

"No, but it does not exclude it either. Perhaps your status in England would have found me beneath your station. But here in the colonies are we not more equally matched?" Joshua donned a mocking grin and stepped closer. "In fact, some may consider my status above yours. Should you not be grateful for my interest in you?"

The corner of his mouth curled, his dimple appearing again.

Honour met his blue eyes. "Should you not loathe the idea of courting a criminal?"

"You are nothing of the kind." Compassion and sincerity shown in his eyes.

"I do not know what I am here, but a lowly quilter," Honour said.

He took her hands in his. "In some eyes, perhaps. But I know you to be a woman of much talent, and of great worth to God."

"Any talent I may have comes from Him. Yet if I am of worth to the Lord, why must He subject me to hardship—and humiliation—such as I endured today?"

"I know not. But you bore it with much grace. I am grateful your workbag was found, as Reverend Cooper and I had prayed."

"I, as well. But the ways of God often confuse me." *Distress me.* Honour lowered her gaze and sighed.

"Nor do I understand the ways of man. Perhaps today we saw evidence of God's sovereignty, despite human circumstances." Joshua tipped her chin up with his fingertip, encouraging her to smile.

"Why did you want for me to remain silent about the missing contents of my bag?" Honour asked.

"Because. I know Mrs. Carter. The contents could have spilled into the street before she ever laid eyes on your satchel. If we accused her there would only be more trouble. She has some powerful acquaintances," Joshua said.

Honour nodded. "A wise decision then."

Joshua tapped his fingers on the counter. "I had to bite my tongue more than once."

"I dare say Reverend Cooper did the same, but he was such a help. He is a kindly man, and wise," Honour said.

"Let's be glad to put it behind us now." Joshua cocked his head. "Your initials. You mentioned them earlier. What are they?"

"H. E. M.—Honour Elizabeth Metcalf. If you recall, Elizabeth was my mother's name. I was christened with it."

Joshua smiled. "H. E. M., hem. How fitting for a quilter and mantua maker. Quite charming, actually."

"Aye, I think Mum liked the idea. She used to say that God would hem me in." Honour let out a little sigh. "Thou hast beset me behind and before, and lain thy hand upon me."

Joshua tilted his head. "From the Psalms."

"Aye, Psalm 139:5," she said.

"By all accounts, He is indeed doing so." Joshua extended his arm. "May I see your workbag for a moment please?"

Honour handed him the embroidered satchel. Joshua retreated behind the counter and reached into a small bin. He retrieved a small paper-wrapped package of pins and opened one of the side compartments of her bag. You said you keep your pins in here?"

"Yes, but . . ."

He took another small package from another bin. "Needles on the other side." He tucked the package into the other compartment. Joshua held up a small wooden ball, containing a tape measure. "You will need this, too."

"Mr. Sutton, please."

"It is but a small gift, Miss Metcalf." He opened a drawer and held up a medium sized pair of shears and a small pair of scissors. "These should suffice." He tucked them inside the workbag.

Honour smiled apologetically. "You are exceedingly generous and have gone to much trouble already. I shall pay you for these items."

"Nonsense. You need these things for your livelihood, do you not?" Joshua asked.

"Well, yes," she said.

"Then it is settled."

"Mr. Sutton, please allow me to reciprocate by offering my quilting services, if you ever have the need."

"A grand idea. But I thought we were beyond formalities. You must call me Joshua." He set a glass jar on the counter filled with an assortment of beautiful pin cushions. "Choose one you like best."

Honour reached into the jar and retrieved a small rectangle with tasseled corners. "This one is comely, and I can clip it to my chatelaine." To her chagrin, and pleasure, it was from a remnant of the same fabric as Joshua's new waistcoat. She lowered her gaze. Mayhap he wouldn't notice. But when she ventured to peek up again, Joshua was grinning at her.

He glanced at the round pincushion dangling by a ribbon from her waist. "It looks as though it has seen better days."

Honour toyed with her old pincushion. "Aye, it has been much abused."

"If there is anything else you should need, please let me know. It is no imposition to me."

Honour held the satchel close to her heart and sighed. "I do not know what to say."

"Thank you will do." Joshua's dimples deepened.

"Thank you, indeed, Mr.—Joshua. You have turned this day into a delight," she said, her eyes smiling up at his.

Joshua cocked his head. "Does that mean you agree to allow me to court you, Miss Metcalf?"

"We shall see, Joshua. I shall let you know after your birthday celebration." Honour offered a coquettish smile, and slipped toward the exit to make her way upstairs to Mrs. Wadsworth's workroom.

As Honour entered the sunny loft, stifling heat assaulted her. Mrs. Wadsworth looked up from her sewing. "Ah, you decided to join us. You do realize, dear, that you get paid for time actually spent working." The woman flattened her lips. She took her pencil and jotted down Honour's time of return in her small ledger, as Honour frequently saw her do. Although Mrs. Wadsworth was magnanimous, she owed her success to her meticulous and frugal ways.

Honour nodded. "Yes, Mistress." Honour glanced at Maisey and Temperance, meeting their accusing grins.

Mrs. Wadsworth continued to sew, but glanced up again curiously. "How is it that you leave here to fetch your sister from school and return attached to Joshua Sutton?"

Honour's mouth hung agape as she eyed Tempe with disappointment.

Tempe's eyes grew wide. "Mrs. Wadsworth asked me what was keeping you . . . I told the truth. That is what you would want me to do, is it not?"

Honour sighed. She could not compete with Tempe's sassy reply. "Of course. But you must refrain from offering personal information when it is unsolicited."

"It was solicited, for certain," Maisey said. "When I saw Tempe bursting with glee I insisted she tell all. So it is true. You are the one who Joshua carried in the street. And the one he kissed in his carriage."

Honour's face heated. "He did not kiss me."

"How could you keep any of that from me?" Maisey asked.

"It was irrelevant," Honour said.

"You know how I feel about gossip, Maisey," Mrs. Wadsworth chimed in.

"Yes, Mistress." Maisey's grin disappeared. Narrowing her eyes, she hiked her chin toward Mrs. Wadsworth. "You do not appear surprised at this news."

"Oh, I had a suspicion it would be only a matter of time before Joshua laid claim on our Miss Metcalf."

"But Joshua has only recently become available." Maisey pouted.

"He has also recently become better acquainted with Honour. Besides, it is his own business if, and when, and whom he marries," Mrs. Wadsworth said.

"We are not getting married," Honour huffed.

Maisey widened her eyes and grinned. "Yet."

Honour shook her head. "I have not yet agreed to court him. It was merely discussed."

"What about the picnic?" Tempe asked.

"We shall attend the event, and then we shall see," Honour said.

Maisey hugged herself with a dreamy smile. "To be in love."

"I am not in love." Honour sat at her quilting frame and sorted through her things, trying to ignore the prattle.

"Yet," Maisey said.

Honour glared at Maisey until they both laughed.

"I am glad to see Joshua at least helped you find your workbag," Mrs. Wadsworth said. "Now, enough of this tittle-tattle, or there will be no time to attend picnics. Widow Lankton needs to have her gown completed and there is yet much work to do." Maisey's cheerful countenance faded and she turned away, fussing over her work.

"Please do not worry, Mrs. Wadsworth. It is coming along as it should." Readying herself for her afternoon tasks, Honour took the small scissors and the shears from her workbag and tied them onto her chatelaine, near her new pincushion. Now every time she used it she would think of Joshua. Her head still lowered, she could not help but smile.

But when Honour unclasped the top compartment of her workbag, she found three silver coins there.

She gasped.

These were not hers. Joshua must have placed them there when she was not looking. Accepting the sewing supplies was one thing, but she could never take his money.

Coins in hand, Honour stood. She rested her palm upon the worktable as a slight wave of dizziness washed over her. Honour took a few slow breaths and headed toward the door. "Mrs. Wadsworth, I've an urgent matter to tend to—it cannot wait. I beg your leave."

Mrs. Wadsworth shook her head in exasperation. "If you must, but please make haste. You have already lost a great deal of time today."

Honour looked back over her shoulder. "Tempe, you get started on your chores, I shall return in a moment. Mrs. Wadsworth has some carding for you to do."

Honour was about halfway down the steep, narrow staircase when a man's gruff voice bellowed from a room below.

"What did she mean 'courting a common criminal?' I was in the back and overheard your conversation. I should have had the sense to stop it. What do you mean by giving merchandise away? Is she in some kind of trouble with the law?"

"No, Father, you misunderstood what was said. Please, lower your voice, sir."

"Did I not hear that you are courting her?" Joshua's father asked.

Honour's heart pounded as she took another step. The stair creaked and she froze.

The elder Mr. Sutton rambled on. "You were pledged to Emily Guilfold and now that she has married another, you take matters into your own hands and attach yourself to a common quilter?"

"You know nothing of her," Joshua said.

"Nor do you!" his father snapped. "Joshua, if you are doing this to insult me . . . to retaliate for getting spurned. What do you say for yourself? . . . Do not be contumacious with me young man. Where are you going? We are not yet through . . ."

"Yes—we are. We'll talk when you calm down, Father. When I do."

The sound of heavy footsteps came near the stairwell. Honour turned to retreat up the steps, lest she be thought eavesdropping. The hem of her gown caught on a nail protruding from the baseboard. As she leaned over to release herself, a hazy feeling assailed her and she went tumbling into the darkness.

7

Joshua ran to the alcove at the bottom of the stairs at the sound of tumbling, followed by a large thud. There lay Honour in a contorted heap. *O, Lord! Please, no!* "Father, come quickly!"

Joshua dropped to her side. Honour's hair spilled onto the floorboards all around, but he saw no blood. His heart thumped as he placed his fingers on her neck to feel for a pulse. "Praise be God," he breathed.

Father rushed up behind him. "What on earth!"

Joshua lifted his head, imploring his father. "Get some help . . . please, make haste!"

As Joshua knelt surveying her limp body, a child's voice shrieked. "Honour!"

Temperance peered down at her sister from the top of the stairs.

"I'll help her, Tempe."

Mrs. Wadsworth and her assistant appeared behind the stunned girl. The anxious group made their way down the steep stairs. "Be careful, Temperance, we do not want you falling, too," Joshua heard Mrs. Wadsworth say.

The ladies carefully stepped around Honour's motionless body. Mrs. Wadsworth held Temperance back by the shoulders. The little girl sobbed. "Is she dead? She cannot be! She is all I have."

Temperance wilted to the floor and cupped Honour's cheeks. "Honour, please wake up. Please God, don't let her die!"

"The poor girl. She's barely recovered from her other injuries. She must have been lightheaded, though she hadn't complained," Mrs. Wadsworth said. "She shouldn't have exerted herself so these past few days."

The other worker put her hand on Tempe's shoulder, "She'll be all right, you'll see."

Father entered the alcove, catching his breath. "I sent Redmond for Doctor Westcott. It's a good thing I stopped by the shop this afternoon with the landau."

Joshua clamped his jaw, censuring his thoughts. It was no time to place blame. As the afternoon sun streamed in through a window, something shiny glinted on the floorboards. A shilling. And two more. Honour must have been on her way down to return them. He should have known she'd not accept the money from him, proud as she was. If anyone were to blame, it was himself. He was the cause of her fall.

Joshua's heart sank. He lifted her arm and began to pat her wrist. "Miss Metcalf, Miss Metcalf, can you hear me?"

"Try my vinaigrette." Mrs. Wadsworth reached into her pocket and handed him a small silver container. Joshua opened the egg-shaped trinket, containing a mixture of perfume and vinegar, and waived it near Honour's nose—without effect.

"It is safe to move her?" Joshua asked his father.

Father clutched his jaw and shook his head. "I do not know, but she cannot stay here."

Tempe's silent tears streamed down her freckled cheeks. Joshua grabbed her small hand and gave it a gentle squeeze, and she sniffled.

"Let's take her to the parlor. Please step back everyone." Joshua scooped Honour up and carried her to his family's lounging room, located behind the large gallery of the store. As he made his way past the long counters and display tables, Father waited for the doctor by the front door. A nosy customer peeked over Father's shoulder. He instructed her to return another day and latched the door. Joshua never thought he'd hear such words on his father's lips.

Joshua lay Honour on his mother's velvet chaise, where mother reclined on many long days spent at the store. The ladies entered behind him.

Honour's arm slipped off the couch. Mrs. Wadsworth picked it up and rubbed her wrist and patted her hand. "Come now, Honour. Wake up, child, wake up."

As Joshua looked down at Honour's still form, the feeling of helplessness overwhelmed him. He could not lose her now, so soon. He had only just begun to feel what it was like to care for a woman this way. Someone his heart chose.

Mrs. Wadsworth proceeded to straighten Honour's clothing, and the ribbons of her chatelaine dangled at her side. She picked up the shears and let out a gasp. "Blood!"

Tempe winced.

Mrs. Wadsworth untied the shears and smaller pair of scissors from Honour's skirt. "Let me get these away from her. We need to see where this blood is coming from."

"I'll go see if the doctor has arrived," Mrs. Wadsworth's apprentice said as she hurried from the room.

With trepidation, Joshua scanned Honour for a telling sign of red, when Tempe burst out, "Beneath her stomacher!"

The V of Honour's embroidered insert gracefully decorating her bodice concealed a blotch of crimson seeping through the folds of fabric at her waist.

"This way." Father ushered the doctor into the room, the apprentice following.

"Hello, Doctor Westcott. We've discovered a wound that is bleeding." Joshua pointed to Honour's waist.

The doctor approached Honour and set down his black leather satchel, leaning over Honour inspecting her thoroughly. "We need to apply pressure to the wound. Mrs. Wadsworth?"

"Yes, doctor." Honour's employer stooped down by her side.

Joshua handed Mrs. Wadsworth a clean handkerchief from a nearby drawer.

"Like this. We need some more clean cloths . . . and fresh water," the doctor instructed.

"I'll get some," Father said.

"'Tis Miss Metcalf again," Dr. Westcott said grimly.

"Again?" the apprentice asked.

Mrs. Wadsworth turned to her worker as she pressed on Honour's injury. "Yes, Maisey. She was injured in the hailstorm while you were away."

"Mr. Sutton rescued her then, too," Tempe said.

"She didn't say anything about it. Why must she be such a martyr?" Maisey asked.

Joshua glowered at her and shook his head in disbelief. He didn't care if she saw him.

"She did not wish anyone to know of her ordeal. Now do you see why I disdain gossip? Partial truths tend to spread about, regardless of one's desire for privacy."

"Thou shalt not bear false witness. That is the ninth commandment." Tempe looked at Honour and pouted. "I forgot to tell Honour we practiced that one in school today, too."

"Who is the child?" Doctor Westcott asked.

"Her sister," they all said at once.

Doctor Westcott frowned. "Has the girl anyone else?"

"No. Their parents and brothers were all . . . It is only the two of them." Joshua sighed.

"Everyone needs to step out of the room," Doctor Westcott said. "Mrs. Wadsworth, please remain while I examine her. I need you to loosen her stays so her breathing is not restricted. And I will need to get to the wound."

Joshua's face reddened as he exited the room. Maisey and Temperance followed chattering about whether Honour would be able to recover from being stabbed with scissors. As they went to the storefront, Joshua's father looked at him with worried brow. "How is she, son?"

"Doctor Westcott is examining her now." Joshua's mouth drew into a grim line.

Father placed his hand on Joshua's shoulder. "I know the Great Physician is looking after her, as well."

Tempe sidled up to Joshua and clung to his arm. He looked into the girl's frightened eyes and offered a weak smile. He certainly hoped that God was watching over Honour. If not, what would become of her little sister? What would he do without the woman who had claimed a piece of his heart?

Honour woke beneath the comfort of a soft counterpane, but it was not her own. As she pulled herself up, a dull pain pierced her abdomen and she drew in a sharp breath. She looked about the room, with fine baroque furnishings and lavish draperies at the windows. Where was she?

"It is about time you awoke. We thought you had decided to sleep forever. Though we prayed you would not." The melodious voice of Mrs. Sutton carried across the room. She rose from her tall desk and ambled toward Honour. "Try a sip of this, dear. Dr. Westcott said it will relieve the pain."

Honour took a sip of the bitter herb tea. "Mrs. Sutton, why am I here?"

"You took a terrible fall down our stairwell. The shears hanging from your chatelaine stabbed you in the abdomen in the process. You also obtained a concussion." Mrs. Sutton frowned with concern.

Honour groaned as she rubbed her neck.

"Your neck is quite bruised . . . and all sorts of pretty colors. And your right thigh," Mrs. Sutton said.

My right thigh? She saw my thigh? Had anyone else seen it?

Honour closed her eyes and took in a slow breath, willing this to be merely an unpleasant dream. *Lord, please help me.* Instead, the aches all over her body made her keenly aware she was living a nightmare.

"My sister? Where is she?"

"Not to worry, dear. She is in good hands. Mrs. Wadsworth has been taking fine care of her these past few days."

"Days?" Honour's gaze darted around the room looking for . . . a clock? What would that tell her? How confused she felt. "How long have I been here?"

Mrs. Sutton took a cool cloth and wiped Honour's brow. "This is your fourth day."

"Four days? But what about . . . my work . . . Tempe's school . . . ?" Honour started to sit up, but Mrs. Sutton gently laid her hand upon her arm.

"My Joshua has been seeing to that," Mrs. Sutton said.

"He has?"

"He is this moment retrieving her from school."

Mrs. Sutton dipped the cloth into a porcelain bowl and wrung it out. "Temperance did not want to leave your side for the first two days. She was beside herself with worry." She continued, gently patting Honour's neck. "We decided that the best thing for her was to keep her regular schedule. So she comes with Mrs. Wadsworth and Maisey each morning to see that you are well, and Joshua brings her to school and back again. They should arrive shortly."

"I am relieved Tempe has been well cared for. I would never want her to miss school. She is a bright child," Honour said.

"Precocious she is. Charming, too. I think my husband has taken a liking to her." Mrs. Sutton smiled as she straightened Honour's covering.

Mrs. Wadsworth peeked through the door and made her way near. "Honour! How good it is to see you up. You had us all exceedingly concerned." She took Honour by the hand. "How are you feeling, dear?"

"I certainly have felt better. I hear my head has taken another battering. And I managed to stab myself with my shears." Honour pulled her hand over the covers, close to her wound.

"Dr. Westcott says that your first head injury contributed to your fall, thus making your condition worse. But it was the fall down the stairs that nearly broke your neck. If it hadn't been for your stays, those shears might have gone clear through." Mrs. Wadsworth turned toward Mrs. Sutton and chuckled. "Armor, for females!"

"Ow . . . I guess laughing isn't something I should do until I heal." Honour's smile faded.

"You said Dr. Westcott had seen me? It is the second time I have seen him recently. I don't know how I shall afford it."

"Sutton's Clothiers will pay your bill for this injury. My husband insists," said Mrs. Sutton.

"I do not know what to say. It is exceptionally generous."

"Dear, girl. It was our negligence that caused the fall. Joshua found a nail protruding from the baseboard lining the stairs. Although, Joshua chooses to blame himself."

"Why ever would he do that?" Mrs. Wadsworth said.

"That boy carries the weight of the world on his shoulders. He had given Honour those new shears only moments before and feels he somehow contributed to it."

"'Tis nonsense. Your son is a fine young man, but he takes too much responsibility for things," Mrs. Wadsworth said.

"You'd never know it by his amiable countenance, but he indeed takes life too seriously at times," said his mother.

"I owe him so much," Honour said. "I owe you both as well. Mrs. Wadsworth, how are you getting along in my absence?"

"Maisey is picking up the slack. But she hasn't quite the skill you have. Her stitches are not as fine, overly long. Please keep this confidential will you? Pity she does not heed my instruction better. She is contracted as my apprentice, but if truth be told, I wish you'd come along a little sooner."

"Oh, dear," Mrs. Sutton whispered. Mrs. Wadsworth let out a tiny gasp.

Maisey was standing in the doorway, her mouth ajar. She turned and ran.

8

Joshua took long strides up the stony pathway toward the brown clapboard house to fetch Temperance from Mrs. Hollister's dame school. About to grab the wrought iron door knocker, the door swung open and Joshua met the austere face of Tempe's teacher. He lowered his hand and offered a tentative smile. "Good day. I'm here to retrieve Temperance Metcalf, on behalf of her sister."

"Her sister. Yes, I should like to have a word with you about her." Mrs. Hollister's face scrunched into a forced smile beneath her lappet cap.

Joshua tilted his head in interest. "Go on."

Mrs. Hollister clasped her hands, working her thumbs so hard he thought they might spark. "Given Miss Metcalf's recent infirmity, it concerns me she will not have the means to continue to pay for Temperance's schooling. She is already a week in arrears and then some. I have given her extended grace on countless occasions. I have great concern she will be encumbered even more henceforth. I have other students waiting for a space to open up so I may serve them—students whose parents are of stable means."

Joshua crossed his arms. "This concerns me how?"

"You are her friend, are you not?" Mrs. Hollister planted a hand on her hip.

"Yes, but I've no knowledge of Miss Metcalf's financial matters," Joshua said.

"I have just enlightened you, Mr. Sutton." The caustic woman jutted her chin.

"So you have."

Mrs. Hollister continued, "As you informed me yesterday, there is no way of knowing how long her recovery may take, it seemed prudent to alert you to the tentativeness of Temperance's situation here."

"Perhaps I can settle her debt and ensure you I will take financial responsibility until Miss Metcalf recovers."

"That is most kind of you, Mr. Sutton. As a man of means, I suspected you might offer to help." Mrs. Hollister feigned a smile.

"I suspect you would. What is the fee?"

Mrs. Hollister's mouth contorted. "She was going to do some quilting for me, but now I see it is not possible. It was a timely request and now I must find another quilter." So Honour not only worked for Mrs. Wadsworth, but bartered her services to help meet her obligations, just as she'd offered to repay him for the sewing supplies. She must work her fingers to the bone.

"How much does she owe, Mrs. Hollister?"

Mrs. Hollister held out her palm. "Five shillings, three pence per week."

Joshua handed her a half guinea. "We are settled then for the remainder of the week."

Mrs. Hollister took the coin and pushed it into the folds of her calico gown, deep within her pocket. "I expect her to return the material I gave her for quilting."

"I'll see to it. I'd like to get Temperance now." Joshua planted his foot on the threshold.

Mrs. Hollister held up her palm to halt him. "There is another matter, Mr. Sutton."

Joshua exhaled. "What is it, Mrs. Hollister?"

The woman threw her shoulders. "It has come to my attention Miss Metcalf's character has recently come into question."

Joshua glowered at her, incredulous. "Whatever it is, you are surely mistaken."

"A most reliable source has made me aware of Miss Metcalf's recent attempt at thievery. I could scarcely believe it, but when the father of one of my students came to me out of concern, I had to pay heed. You see, the influence on Temperance by Miss Metcalf's questionable character, may in turn affect her classmates." Mrs. Hollister issued a labored sigh. "He threatened to pull his daughter out of my school. I fear it is only a matter of time before other parents complain."

Joshua's ire rose. "Your sources are grossly misinformed." How quickly Mrs. Carter had maligned Honour's character. Joshua eyes darted beyond Mrs. Hollister's shoulder, hoping to catch a glimpse of Tempe. He had to get her out of here.

"There was a little incident . . ." Mrs. Hollister began, but a cacophony of discord erupted from inside the house.

Mrs. Hollister turned, hurrying to her keeping room and Joshua followed. In the corner of the room, a cluster of children of varying ages yelled and teased.

"Liar. Liar."

"You stole it. You're a thief like your sister!"

"You're going to jail!"

"Tempe is a thie-ief. Tempe is a thie-ief."

"Children, children . . . order!" Mrs. Hollister cried out, to no avail.

A russet-haired boy teased, "Pert-Miss-Prat-a-pace!" And Mrs. Hollister promptly snapped her iron thimble upon his skull.

Another boy saw it and laughed out, "Thimble-pie!"

"Enough!" Joshua shouted. The startled children turned around with wide eyes. As the boys and girls stepped back, Joshua's stern gaze dropped to see Temperance tottering on a small one-pegged stool with tears flowing down her cheeks.

"I had to put her on the unipod, she was caught with something that didn't belong to her," Mrs. Hollister said.

Joshua squatted down in front of Temperance, who sat balancing on the small one-legged stool. "Is that true?" It broke his heart to ask, but he had to settle this now.

Temperance sniffled, wiping her tears with the palm of her hand. "Sally dropped her kerchief and I tried to hand it to her . . ." Sniffle. "But her brother said I stole it."

Joshua lifted Tempe to her feet and the stool toppled over. He pulled her to his side, and addressed Mrs. Hollister over the onlooking children. "Did you ask her why she had the kerchief?"

"Uh, the consensus was . . ." Mrs. Hollister tumbled over her words and let out a huff.

Joshua scanned the children's faces—some ashamed, one crying, others pouting or frowning. He stared at Mrs. Hollister. "Let it be understood by all of you that Temperance Metcalf was attempting to do a kindness. Neither has her sister stolen anything as I am her witness." Joshua took Tempe by the hand and they left the room.

As they made their way to the front door, Mrs. Hollister chased after them. "Mr. Sutton, Mr. Sutton. Temperance, dear—"

Joshua turned and faced Tempe's schoolmistress. "She is done here. Good day, Mrs. Hollister. I believe you have some children who need attending to."

As Joshua and Tempe walked briskly down the path, Mrs. Hollister called out, "Make sure Miss Metcalf returns my fabric!"

———

"Honour! You are awake!" Temperance ran to Honour's outstretched arms. Pulling her close, she felt a tug in her belly, a small price to pay for the love and comfort of her little sister.

Honour gently withdrew and took in Tempe's sweet face. "You have been crying. Whatever is the matter?"

Joshua entered the parlor and strode toward them, looking as handsome as she had dreamed. "She is all right now. A little matter at school, but it is all straightened out now."

He glanced down at her sister, and placed his hand on her shoulder. "Right, Tempe? We shall tell her about it later. The important thing is Honour is awake."

Joshua smiled at Honour. "How are you feeling? You had us all worried, you know."

"Aye. So your mother said. She has been so kind, taking good care of me. When she explained what happened to me I could hardly believe it." How Honour managed to fall and sustain such injuries stupefied her. She should have taken more care. Worries of Tempe, her schooling, Honour's employment, and their well-being beset her like the stiches of a carefully sewn quilt unraveling before her.

"My head is still rather fuzzy, but overall I think I shall recover." She hoped. Though the pain in her neck and head and everywhere else racked through her body.

Joshua seemed to notice her strain to look up at him and knelt by her side. "I feared I might lose you before we even started our courtship."

Honour grinned. And blushed. "Why Mr. Sutton, you don't expect to get out of it so easily do you?"

She blushed some more. "You have caught me unawares and I haven't even a fan to hide my blushing."

Temperance ran to a side table where she retrieved a small pierced wooden fan and handed it to Honour. "Here, Honour. Now you may blush properly."

Joshua chuckled. Honour started to laugh, but winced in pain, grasping her stomach. Her eyes closed and she took shallow breaths. When she opened them, Joshua and Tempe were looking at her with concern. "I am all right."

"Your wound?" Joshua asked.

"Aye," she said.

Joshua squeezed her hand. "I am afraid it is my fault. Could you ever forgive me?"

His hand felt cool, strong like a tailor. But his gentle tone and heartfelt appeal pricked her heart. "Joshua. This was nothing of your doing. Please, there is nothing to forgive."

Joshua nodded humbly.

"Promise me you won't dwell on it," she entreated. She closed her eyes for a moment, still holding his hand.

"You have my promise," he said.

Honour opened her eyes and smiled at Temperance, who was fanning her. Concern laced Tempe's brow. "You look peaked and your brow is moist. Have you a fever?"

"Mayhap a slight one, but I shall be all right. Mrs. Sutton informed me I might suffer one for a few days yet. It is part of the healing process until my humors are fully restored. But I dare say I find nothing humorous about it." Honour's lips curved to reassure her sister.

Tempe grinned and continued her fanning ministrations.

"Now tell me, Tempe, how has school been? Have you learned more commandments?"

Tempe looked up at Joshua with a frown. "Thou shalt not bear false witness." Honour suspected a secret was held there, but felt too weak to ask.

"We should sue her," Father said.

"Whatever for?" Joshua asked, meeting his father's glower.

Father's eyes narrowed. "She defaulted on your betrothal."

"Ha!" The sound escaped Joshua's lips before he could stop it. "I beg to differ, Miss Guilford—"

"Mrs. Leach, you mean," his father interrupted.

"Yes, Mrs. Leach, did not default anything. We were not yet betrothed. We merely had an understanding. Rather, our parents did," Joshua said.

"It was understood by both of our families for how many years?" Father asked.

"Three." Joshua sucked in a deep breath. "But that is neither here nor there. She chose the man she wanted to marry and that is that." If, in fact, she truly did desire to marry him. Joshua couldn't help but wonder if she might have been pressured into it.

Father paced the floor. "I am attempting to salvage your reputation, Joshua. The circumstances of her hasty wedding have given rise to speculation."

"That's most unfortunate for her. As you said it is only speculation, and based on nothing substantial," Joshua said.

Father cocked he head. "Time will tell."

"What do you mean by that? If you are implying—" Joshua shook his head in disbelief.

"Surely you've heard the rumors, son. And now, they have come to my ears. Even worse, your mother's." Father grimaced.

"I assure you there is no basis for them. Emily has always been the picture of propriety for as long as I have been acquainted with her. Simply because she is charming, does not mean she ever flaunted herself or acted indecently," Joshua said.

Father looked at Joshua in earnest. "She has never played the temptress? Tell me son and I will believe you."

Joshua raked his fingers through his hair. "Father, please assure Mother she must ignore the hearsay. I have never acted untoward to Emily . . . nor she to me. As for her relationship with Mr. Leach, I cannot discern her motivation, but I am certain she had her reasons. Can we not just accept it?"

"I will tell your mother and do my best to put a halt to the rumors. But I must caution you given these uncertain times, you must strive to keep your reputation intact by every measure possible. These things affect our business relations. The citizens of this city are already up in arms over the constant looming of the redcoats, watching our every move. We cannot afford to fall under any suspicion the Suttons are any less than honorable in their pursuits." His father straightened the knot of the stock at his neck. "Have I made myself clear?"

Joshua stiffened. "Of course, sir." But what would happen when word spread Honour Metcalf had been accused of stealing?

9

Her fever is rising."

The gravity in Dr. Westcott's voice gave Joshua a sinking feeling in his gut. "What does it mean?"

"I'm afraid she has a serious infection which I am not sure can be controlled at this point. Her wound is festering and I've tried every poultice known to medicine. Yet . . . are you certain she has no family?"

"She has me." Mrs. Wadsworth, wiped her tears with the corner of a tatted handkerchief.

Dr. Westcott turned to Honour's employer and nodded. "You had best prepare the girl and make arrangements for her continued care. An almshouse perhaps?"

"She'll do nothing of the sort. She will live with me, as my own daughter," Mrs. Wadsworth declared, and looked up at Joshua, entreating his approval.

Joshua nodded. "It would please Honour to know that, but I'm not giving up on her yet."

The physician continued, his countenance grave, "I know it is hard to hear, Joshua, but you should prepare for the worst. I have seen soldiers die from less severe wounds. In all honesty, I am mystified how she remains alive."

Joshua couldn't believe what he heard. How could this be God's plan? He had finally found a woman he could give his heart to, and what? He was losing her when their relationship had so recently commenced? He squeezed his fist into a ball, willing away the doctor's fate-filled words.

Joshua gazed at the doctor, imploring him for a thread of optimism. "Yet there is hope?".

"There is always hope. Her life is in the Lord's hands. But the natural course of things often leads to—"

Joshua strode from the parlor, slamming out the back door of the store.

"No! No, no, no!" Tears streamed down his face and his vision blurred. He hung his head and prayed. *Mighty Father, please allow her to live. Honour has so much to live for, so much to give. Temperance needs her . . . I need her. Oh, God, please. Suffer her not to die.*

A firm grip on his shoulder startled him out of his deep meditation.

"Joshua." The deep tenor of his father's voice proffered comfort to his grieving heart. Then his father extended his other arm, and tugged Joshua into his embrace. "My son. You love her."

"Yes, Father. I do."

Honour reclined in a comfortable chair, enjoying the bright sun through the newly glazed window of Mrs. Wadsworth's Mantua Shoppe. Everyone said it was a miracle she had lived; she had remarkable strength to pull through. And they gave praise to God, for His tender mercies. For His watchcare over her during her time of need.

How was it that the Almighty One had seen fit to allow her to live, not only now, but when the ship was attacked? He had spared her life then also. It wasn't as though she wanted to live, not without her Mum and Poppa and her brothers. But in God's providence He spared her for Temperance's sake. Then she recalled how Joshua had rescued her during the hailstorm. She had thrice survived. *Oh, Lord in Heaven, thank you! I have been protesting when I should have been praising Thee.*

She took a tiny stitch as she worked on the last bit of quilting for Mrs. Lankton's traveling suit—long project, finally drawing to completion. It was gratifying Mrs. Wadsworth allowed her to finish it in these remaining days of her convalescence. It would have been so disappointing not to complete it herself when she'd labored over it for so long. How good it felt to be sleeping in her own bed, under her own indigo quilt, snuggled beside her precious sister. A lump formed in Honour's throat. It would have been awful if Tempe had lost her too. So much grief to bear for a young soul. But now Honour knew God would always watch over Tempe, as, in fact, He had been doing.

Mrs. Wadsworth brought a tea tray and joined Honour at the window. "Here, dear. Why don't you set that down and take a moment of respite." Mrs. Wadsworth continued to fuss over her—mother her—and it touched her so. Mrs. Sutton had been the picture of grace and kindness. But Maisey . . . she had withdrawn from Honour, casting little more than an occasional glance her way. What had she done to offend Maisey?

"I hear you have a picnic to attend on Saturday," Mrs. Wadsworth said. "Temperance has been talking of it all day."

Honour took a sip of her hyperion tea. "Aye. I told her we would go, providing I continue to feel stronger. Joshua assured me of a restful and enjoyable time. He thought getting out would do me good after these past few weeks of being cooped up."

Mrs. Wadsworth peered at Honour over the rim of her teacup. "He has certainly been doting on you."

"He has. Quite a friend he has become." Joshua had indeed been attentive to her. He also paid particular attention to Tempe, taking her on occasional outings since Mrs. Hollister had canceled school for a couple of weeks. Honour was glad of his watchcare as she was not comfortable with Tempe out on her own while British soldiers stalked about and occasional riots occurred in the streets. Tempe usually returned with a candy stick or piece of chocolate to share.

"Friend? Is that all?" Mrs. Wadsworth asked, arching an eyebrow, and snapping Honour from her musings.

Honour glanced down at the quilted fabric lying on her lap. "Aye. Nothing more."

Though Honour had grown exceedingly fond of Joshua and been keenly aware of his devotion to her, he'd made no declaration of anything more than friendship. Joshua remained the perfect gentleman, refuting any lingering fears of him ever being cavalier in his relationships with women.

"I have been invited to the birthday picnic also," Mrs. Wadsworth said. "It will do me good to go, but mostly I look forward to seeing you enjoy yourself."

"You are such a dear, Mrs. Wadsworth," Honour said.

Mrs. Wadsworth stood, smoothing her apron. "Now I must return to work after this refreshing visit."

"And I must finish this quilt. I expect to have it done before the day is through." Honour smiled. How good it was to be occupied with a task she truly enjoyed and to be paid for it. The world looked brighter, she was grateful, and she was alive. Now if Joshua Sutton would notice her as the woman who was fast falling in love with him.

Come Friday it occurred to Honour she had no gift for Joshua's birthday. Without having to pay for Tempe's dame school for a few weeks, mayhap she might afford a small trinket; something to show her appreciation to Joshua for all of his kindnesses to her and Tempe. Mrs. Wadsworth and Tempe agreed to accompany her to Greenleaf's Mercantile where she had once admired a handsome carved wood needle case in the shape of a cod, so fitting for a Boston tailor. Mrs. Wadsworth had first protested, but Honour convinced her a brief outing to the nearby store would do her good.

As Honour perused the wooden display trays at the mercantile, a silver thimble caught her eye. She picked it up under the watchful eye of Mr. Greenleaf. "Is there something wrong?"

"This thimble reminds me of one I used to own, 'tis all." She was sure of it. It was her own silver thimble, embossed with pomegranates and bearing her initials. The gift she received from her parents upon her last birthday at nineteen. Their final gift to her, save her new life in America, though she sometimes considered the latter as a burden.

"You may purchase it for a guinea," Mr. Greenleaf said.

A guinea? It was worth so much more! Yet as much as it sickened her to lose it, she hadn't the energy to endure another argument over her property. Nor did she wish to further risk her reputation, which was of more value, as her parents had taught her. "No, thank you, sir. Though I would like to purchase that needle case, the fish."

Tempe smiled with excitement. "Joshua will love it!"

Honour peered down at her sister. "Joshua? Don't you mean Mr. Sutton?"

"He told me that I must call him Joshua, as his father is Mr. Sutton," Tempe explained.

"I see," Honour said. He'd told her the same, so she supposed it was acceptable since it was at his request, though she preferred Temperance practice proper decorum.

The storekeeper wrapped the needle case in a piece of old newsprint. "A fine choice. Is there anything else you need today?"

Oh, yes, she thought. But she would restrain herself until she saved enough to redeem her thimble, providing no one else purchased it before she had the opportunity to do so. No one would accuse her of stealing again. She scarcely believed she'd been accused in the first place.

Honour handed Mr. Greenleaf her money and placed the trinket into her embroidered workbag. "Tempe, please tell Mrs. Wadsworth to take her time browsing, I am going to rest outside. Please stay here in case she needs assistance carrying her purchases."

Honour sat on the bench and took in a deep breath of the warm August air. She watched pedestrians amble down the street and occasional conveyances pass by, though nothing as elegant as the Sutton's shiny carriage. From a distance, she made out Boston Common, dotted with hundreds of white tents belonging to the king's soldiers. Then a woman's high pitched voice caught her attention, mixed with the deep intonations of a man. Were they quarreling? She hoped the woman was safe.

Honour followed the muffled voices to the alley between the mercantile and the adjacent building. She stood out of view, not wishing to presume too much or intrude on a private conversation. Suddenly, the din surrounding her quieted and the voices became clearer. Honour's core bounded to attention upon hearing, "Mr. Sutton . . . you have it all wrong!"

"Mr. Sutton now, is it?"

"It is only proper. I am now a married woman."

The man's voice cracked. "*We were to marry.* Why did you spoil our plans?"

"I had no choice. My father has aligned himself with Tories and found favor with the Leach family. The connection will save his business. They required an immediate marriage. Please understand, I had to do my part. I could not bear to see my parents suffer any longer."

The man groaned. "Does he treat you well?"

"Fairly."

"Do you love him?"

"I shall in time."

The man's voice became stilted. "Then I wish you the best. But please know this. I love you, Emily, and I always shall."

Honour peeked around the corner. The wounded suitor pushed the woman against the wall and placed an overlong kiss upon her married lips. Honour pivoted around lest she be caught spying. Her hand flew to her chest and she tried to ease her pounding heart. Heavy footsteps upon the brick path faded into the distance and the woman erupted in loud sobs.

The woman cried inconsolably. Honour didn't care how much Mr. Sutton claimed to love her, he had no right accosting her with a kiss. She dared look around the corner again . . . coming face to face with Emily Leach.

"Pardon me. I should have been more careful." Mrs. Leach blinked back tears.

Honour stayed her hand near Emily's arm. "Please, let me help you."

"Nothing can be done," the woman sobbed.

"Would you sit with me a moment until you have calmed."

"That is kind of you, miss—"

"I'm Honour Metcalf, recently from England," Honour said, as a British officer in red uniform and pointed helmet happened by.

"Isn't everyone these days?" The woman sniffled into her handkerchief, joining Honour on the wooden bench.

"Mayhap they are—" Honour offered a tentative smile.

"Emily Leach," she said extending her hand.

Honour shook Emily's trembling hand. "Should you like to talk, I am happy to listen. Sometimes it is easier to share one's problems with those unfamiliar to us." Hadn't she done the same with Joshua? What a mix!

"I suppose it is. Those closest to me do not seem to care to hear how I feel." The woman sighed deeply. "I have recently married, under the pressure of my parents, but the man I once cared deeply for has not accepted it."

"Oh, dear. It must be difficult for you."

"By chance we met and he escorted me to the alley to confront me about it. He was quite upset and I cannot say I blame him."

Honour looked at her compassionately. "He shall accept it in time . . . he must."

"He kissed me farewell. I was stunned and know not what to do." Emily's eyes widened. "Please keep my confidence. My husband must never know."

Honour looked at her compassionately. "How distressing this must be. Life is challenging at best sometimes. This I understand. I assure you, I shall never tell a soul."

Mrs. Wadsworth and Tempe exited the mercantile carrying several packages. "Honour, there you are. How are you feeling?"

Honour looked up. "I was tired so I thought it best to sit, but I am well."

"I'm glad to hear it." Mrs. Wadsworth acknowledged Emily with a nod. "Good afternoon, Emily. I understand congratulations are in order. Your Aunt Eunice told me you have recently been wed and returned from your wedding trip."

Emily donned a polite smile. "Yes, I have. Thank you, Mrs. Wadsworth."

Mrs. Wadsworth glanced at Honour. "I see you have met my quilter. She has recently quilted a stunning suit for your aunt."

"How lovely. And who might this be?" Emily's face brightened as she glanced at Tempe.

Honour smiled. "This is my sister, Temperance. Tempe, this is Mistress Leach."

"A pleasure to meet you, Temperance."

Tempe nodded. "'Tis nice to make your acquaintance."

"It has been a fortuitous circumstance meeting Honour today." Emily cast Honour a small smile. "She has proved to be a fast friend."

Mrs. Wadsworth smiled. "We should be getting along, if you are ready to go, Honour."

Honour smiled at Emily. "Perhaps we shall see one another again."

"Honour, you will remember my request?" Emily asked.

"Most certainly," Honour said. "I shall keep you in my prayers."

Emily and Honour clasped hands in agreement and fond parting.

As Mrs. Wadsworth, Honour, and Temperance strolled down the brick sidewalk Tempe tugged on Honour's sleeve, craning her neck. "Is she the lady Joshua almost married?"

"How do you know about that?" Honour asked. "Oh, never mind."

Mrs. Wadsworth interjected. "They were not betrothed, Tempe, but now she is married to Mr. Leach, so it is of no consequence."

Except to Honour.

10

"Ladies, your carriage awaits." Joshua held open the door of the carriage, the portrait of a perfect gentleman. The dark blue tones of his new waistcoat complimented his gray-blue silk and linen frockcoat and breeches, making his eyes look bluer still. Honour's eyes locked on his but for a moment, and as he dipped his chin ever so slightly, her heart quickened. When she averted her eyes, she caught a glimpse of the knowing grins of Tempe and Mrs. Wadsworth.

He handed the dear lady and Tempe up as Honour looked on. Why hadn't he allowed his driver to see to the task? Her errant thoughts of Joshua found kissing in the alley twisted her emotions into a ball of tangled threads. She should forget about the incident, instead it left an imprint in her mind like the pattern of her bridal quilt now lost to her forever.

Yet she wondered . . . what would it be like to be kissed by him? Alas, she would never know. The pain of it stung afresh.

"Honour? Are you ready?" he asked.

"No, and I never shall be," she wanted to say. But as she stared at the open-topped carriage she willed herself to step forward. "Yes, thank you." She accepted Joshua's sturdy hand, but stiffened when he braced her back as she ascended the small metal steps. Honour found her seat opposite Mrs. Wadsworth and Tempe, the pair leaving no choice but for Honour to sit at Joshua's side.

Perhaps she should have said she was not feeling up to the picnic today. It wouldn't have been an entire fabrication. Although she was well enough physically, her heart and mind were in great distress. Yet her actions concealed the fact she did not wish to go. But all was made right as she looked over at Tempe beaming with excitement, reaffirming Honour's decision not to disappoint her precious sister.

As the group settled comfortably into their seats, Mrs. Wadsworth addressed Maisey, who watched them from the door of the mantua shop. "We are off to the Sutton residence. I thank you to keep an eye on things."

Maisey nodded. "You may count on me, Mistress."

"This will be a good opportunity for my apprentice to manage the shop in my absence," their employer said. "I trust you will have a quiet day and all will go well."

Maisey donned a smile. "Enjoy your picnic." But when Mrs. Wadsworth turned away, Maisey's eyes connected with Honour's and a hint of something less felicitous appeared. Honour smiled as she waved goodbye. She hoped Maisey was not hurt being left out of the party, though it occurred to Honour that Maisey was not as well-acquainted with the Suttons. Maisey returned a weak wave, smile lacking.

"Home, Redmond. We've a party to attend," Joshua directed his driver, who was clothed in impressive livery.

"Yes, Master Sutton." Redmond snapped the reins and the carriage rolled forward with a clop, clop, clop of the horse's iron shoes against the paving stones.

Tempe smiled brightly, waving at Maisey as they drove away.

"Have you any word on your husband, Mrs. Wadsworth?" Joshua asked.

"It has been nigh on six months." Mrs. Wadsworth trailed her fingertips across her neckline as she often did when thinking of her husband. "After all these years, you would think I'd become used to his long absences, but alas, I am not."

"I pray he returns soon and with a good bounty," Joshua said.

Honour offered an affirming nod. "I thought you might wear your pearls today. The ones Captain Wadsworth gave you."

"I had wished to, but the clasp gave way. I shall have to get it repaired." She sighed.

Tempe frowned. "Ohh . . ."

Mrs. Wadsworth squeezed Tempe's hand. "That is all right dear. I still possess them. Sometimes the things we hold dear need a little repairing now and again."

"Like Honour? She needed repairing and now she's better."

Everyone's laughter burst forth.

"Indeed." Mrs. Wadsworth laughed again.

Joshua turned to Honour with a grin.

Honour certainly knew not how she remained so fond of Joshua, while she struggled with his secret. Though her sensibilities betrayed her, perhaps in time her heart would also mend. Was his in need of mending too?

"Uncle Joshua!" A plethora of giggles resounded as Joshua's young nieces ran toward him and danced around him in a swirl of ruffles and lace.

Joshua pivoted around and seized the girls with tickles. As they twirled away, he caught hold of the leading strings flowing from the back of their small gowns. "I've got you now, and you've someone to meet."

He turned back, laughing. "Miss Temperance Metcalf, please meet my nieces, Abigail and Sarah. And, girls, this is Tempe's sister, Miss Honour Metcalf. You know Mrs. Wadsworth."

The girls proffered their best curtsy. "Good day," they said in unison.

Honour smiled demurely, and rested her hand on Tempe's shoulder. "'Tis a pleasure for us to meet you both."

Tempe offered a shy smile before casting her eyes down at her small shoes. Was she fearful of being teased by children again? He hoped his vivacious nieces didn't intimidate her. It would be nice for her to have some new friends.

Tempe glanced up and Joshua animated his expression. "Sarah has a young brother tottering around here somewhere in his pudding-cap. Perhaps you girls can find him. He likes to be entertained by watching the girls play with their hoops."

Sarah and Abigail took Tempe by the hands and led her away over the grassy lawn of the estate. Temperance peered back over her shoulder, but quickly turned around and the trio skipped away, the colorful ribbons of their straw hats streaming in the air behind them.

Mother approached and took Honour's hands in hers. "Welcome, ladies. Honour, it is good to see you looking so well, and rather lovely at that."

She tilted her chin. "Don't you agree, Joshua?"

Joshua regarded his mother and stole a sidelong glance at Honour. "Lovely, indeed." In fact, he could hardly keep his eyes off her. For a moment, he allowed his eyes to rest on the ruched satin ribbon adorning her neck, the shade of the petals of his mother's impatiens plants. Dark auburn curls graced her shoulders, resting on a scarf of gossamer—the tinge of coral on her cheeks and lips pleasing enough to kiss. Did Honour realize what a beautiful woman she was?

"You are making the girl blush," said Mrs. Wadsworth.

Honour looked around the group, her cheeks tinged pink. "It is good to be well. I thank you all for your care and generosity, and for your prayers in my time of need."

Her sweet demeanor attracted him to her all the more. The past was gone, today the start of something new—he would reveal his affection for her and hoped to mark the beginning of their courtship.

"Let us join our daughters and their husbands under the tent. Though I haven't yet seen your brother." Mother glanced at Father with a frown.

"He was off tending to some business or other this morning, though I told him to leave it to another day," Father said as he joined the group.

Mother said, her inflection rising. "Hopefully he'll grace us with an appearance. Come along, we have a grand feast about to be served for your birthday, son."

Platters of food graced a long table clad in white linen. A bit extravagant for a family who tempered luxury during such times, but mother insisted the special occasion, to her, was akin to the King's Birthday! After Father offered a word of thanksgiving and a blessing for Joshua, they partook of a bountiful meal. Salmon pie, breaded oysters, fresh asparagus, kabobs roasted on the spit—his favorites!

"Mother, you have outdone yourself in preparing this fine menu."

"I wished to serve mutton kabobs instead of beef, but all the sheep are being spared for wool for homespun," Mother said.

Joshua dabbed at his mouth with his napkin, stood and stretched. "Everything was delicious. My hearty thanks."

"Later we shall have cake and ice cream with raspberry sauce. Now 'tis time for gifts," said his sister, Deborah, bouncing her little son on her lap. The girls clapped, and Matthew copied in turn.

Matthew crawled down and tottered around. He made his way to Honour, extending his tiny hands. "Up."

Honour glanced at Joshua, concern laced across her brow. "Oh, I should love to hold him . . . though I'm not sure that it is wise with my injury."

Joshua scooped his little nephew into his arms and sat at Honour's side.

"What a handsome fellow you are." Her smile so bright, it was apparent she adored children. She certainly was an excellent caretaker of her sister. Honour played peek-a-boo with him and he let out a belly laugh.

Joshua nuzzled the toddler's neck and made embarrassing blustery noises against his soft skin. Oh, to win the woman's heart, he'd do anything to impress her. But the truth was, he adored his nephew and nieces. What would it be like to have a family of his own?

Matty promptly found Joshua's queue of hair and tugged the tie right out. *A toy! So much for good impressions.*

Deborah's husband let out a hearty laugh. "You might get used to it, Joshua. You may have a son of your own one day."

"Take him, dear, so we can give Joshua his presents," Deborah said.

Instead, his other sister retrieved Matthew from Joshua's arms. "I'll hold him for a while," Anne said. "I need get in the practice again, for we shall have the blessing of another child come spring."

Sighs and smiles abounded. Brothers-in-law exchanged happy nods. Mother took a step closer to Father, and he pulled her close, a rare display of affection. Yet, Joshua could tell there was no loss of love between them even after all of these years. Joshua's gaze glided toward Honour, her eyes already lit upon his face. What dreams lay within her heart?

"The gifts!" Abby and Sarah said.

"May I?" Tempe asked.

Honour nodded and reached into her pocket, retrieving a small parcel.

Temperance handed it to Joshua. "This is from me and Honour."

Joshua untied the cord securing a swatch of cloth. He opened it, smiling.

"A needle case," Tempe said.

He regarded the beautifully carved wood of the needle case fashioned into the shape of a cod. "Thank you, both of you," he said, peeking up at Honour. "I will treasure it, and think of you both each time I use it."

Tempe's face beamed. The joy he saw there was a gift in itself. How fond he'd grown of the sweet girl.

Matthew made a funny shriek and Joshua noted the little pudding head was gnawing on his black ribbon quite heartily. "Ah, and I shall make use of this cord to repair my hair, as I should not wish to take Matthew's new toy from him." Joshua handed Tempe the needle case for a moment and raked his hair back, tying it back in place.

Everyone passed him presents, which humbled him to receive—a brass shoe horn from Deborah and her family, silver buckles from Anne's family, and Mrs. Wadsworth gave him a fine handkerchief.

Father cleared his throat. "Please accept this gift from your mother and me to commemorate your five and twenty years as our beloved son." Father handed him a piece of folded parchment.

Joshua carefully opened the paper. The din quieted as Joshua read the document. He looked up at his parents in astonishment.

"An early inheritance, call it what you must, but we are gifting you shares in our holdings on this occasion of your five and twenty years."

"I do not know what to say . . ." Joshua swallowed back the lump forming in his throat. This gift was more generous than he could have ever expected, especially during such demanding times. "I sincerely thank you."

Mother dabbed at her eyes, and Joshua stood and embraced her. Joshua extended his arm toward Father, who heartily gripped his hand. "We are proud of you, son. You have earned it."

Joshua longed for this moment. To receive the blessing of his father. To have earned the respect of the man whom he most admired and the means to plan for his own future. A future he yearned to share with a woman he loved.

"Hello, the house!" Andrew entered under the canopy. "Birthday greetings, brother."

"So good of you to join us, at last." Joshua said as Andrew clapped him on the shoulder, a bit of rum wafting from his brother's breath.

Andrew angled his posture toward Honour, and made an elaborate bow. "Ah, you must be the famous Miss Metcalf. I don't believe I've yet had the pleasure."

11

Joshua held out his elbow, flashing his dimples at Honour. "Would you care to take a turn about my mother's gardens with me, Miss Metcalf?"

She appreciated his removing her from the uncomfortable introduction to his brother. Introduction or confrontation? Perhaps one and the same, though she could make little sense of it. "I appreciate the diversion, thank you." How could one brother be so different from the other, or were they? So alike in looks, the two, but Andrew's crass tone held an air of resentment and something more. Though they'd never met, he directed it at her. How had she offended him? Was he merely protective of his brother? Had Joshua confided his feelings about her to him? Mayhap Andrew felt that she was not good enough for Joshua, she a simple quilter. Yet she and Joshua had settled the issue, hadn't they? Their situations evened out, or else it did not matter. It mattered not to her. But now she must guard her heart against the wiles of the brother whose passions were misaligned.

Honour cast her gaze at the carefully plotted pathway laden with crushed seashells. As they ambled along, she fixated on her damask mules and his buckled shoes, their steps moving in tandem. She intentionally altered her gait, to avoid being so painfully synchronized with him. But try as she might, their strides resumed perfect harmony. She considered their ease of conversation, his anticipation of her needs before she even spoke them. There was no denying the kindred rapport she shared with Joshua. At least, that was what her heart believed.

Yet the truth of it was, he was not all that he appeared to be. Perhaps she was merely a distraction to him for love lost. His attempt at forgetting his unrequited feelings for Emily Leach. Honour might even be willing to allow it, if it meant she could gain a piece of his heart. For he had already claimed hers entirely.

How could she ever reconcile his love for Emily with her own desire for him to return her feelings of ardor. What kind of man would profess his affection to a married woman with his lustful kiss? How unlike the Joshua she had come to know and admire.

The light in Joshua's bright blue eyes pierced through her unwelcome contemplations. "How pleasant it is to enjoy one's company, even with thoughts unspoken."

She wanted only to cherish this time spent with him in this splendid setting. This day she intended to consider his antici- pated request of courtship, though she remained uncertain. "I find it pleasant indeed. It has proved to be a lovely day."

"A lovely day for a lovely lady," he said.

She smiled beneath the shade of her wide-brimmed Bergère hat. "Your mother's gardens are magnificent."

"Yes, they are her pride and joy."

"My mother had a beautiful garden, but not so carefully plotted out. She had an herb garden, and her flowers all grew together in a riot of blooms. Quite different, but lovely all the same. She enjoyed spending time tending it, as I see your mother does." Honour paused her steps and pointed to some leafy plants. "I do not recognize those plants."

"That is loosestrife, and there is hyperion. They are for Mother's Liberty teas."

"Mmm. She served me some while under her care."

"Did Mother also serve you a course in her ideals as a Daughter of Liberty?"

"Aye, she did. I enjoyed listening to her perspective. My family sympathized with your plight in the colonies, thus being partly why we removed to America."

The sun caught the highlights of Joshua's ash-brown hair, so neatly gathered into its tie. "May I ask how these sentiments transpired?"

"It is a mystery. My father used to receive anonymous packets with American newspapers and handbills. At first, he thought it ridiculous, but after time he was won over. He used to read them aloud to our family, but only at my begging." Honour proffered a pert grin. "I found the ideas quite revolutionary."

"Ah, a progressive thinker."

"I see no reason the colonies should be subjected to tyranny," Honour said. "Mrs. Wadsworth has explained to me the unjust hold the king has on the economy, as it affects business owners like herself. I've often wondered how it might have affected my father's business ventures. He was taking a great risk."

"He was, and I admire him for it," Joshua said as they continued along. "Sutton's has suffered considerably since the Revenue Acts were implemented. But we do what we must for the greater good, such as supplying local textiles and tailoring homespun." Joshua leaned closer. "I dare say some of the ladies in town dreadfully miss their imported chintzes and silks."

Honour laughed. "I must agree. But I give the majority of ladies credit for their commitment to the cause of liberty."

Joshua's eyebrow arched and his mouth curved into an attractive grin. Was he impressed with her views? Or that she dared to speak of them? "Enough about politics. 'Tis too fine a day for dreary thoughts."

"I find them inspiring," she said, halting.

Joshua toyed with the single curl draping over her shoulder. "As I find you."

Honour lowered her lashes, then glanced up demurely.

He took Honour's hand in his. "You must be fatigued. Come." He led her to the arbor where the cooing of doves from the nearby dovecote filled the air. "Honour—I must confess, there is something weighing heavily on my mind. Something you must know, since you are now well. Please sit with me."

Her heart quickened. Was he to tell her about his feelings for Emily? Would he tell her he was mistaken in his love for Emily and his heart only belonged to her?

Then she noted the concern etching his brow, she longed to smooth it away. "It cannot be all that worrisome."

"It concerns your sister," he said.

"Temperance?" Honour squinted with confusion.

"Her schooling." Joshua pushed his hair away from his face. "You see, when I was taking her to Mrs. Hollister's the woman confronted me with the matter of your outstanding debt."

"Which I intend to pay once her dame school resumes," she said with a defensive lilt.

"Temperance will not be attending Mrs. Hollister's dame school anymore."

"Why ever not?"

Joshua stood and paced a few steps away. He faced her again. "She has not been attending school for the past fortnight."

Honour attempted to stand, but Joshua stayed her with his hand. "Why was I not informed? How did this come about?"

"You were far too ill to concern you with it at the time," he said.

She squeezed her hands in her lap. "But I am fine now."

"Thus the reason I can tell you about it. I could not allow another day to go by keeping you in the dark."

"By all means, enlighten me." Honour pushed back her wide brim, staring into his face.

"You see, Mrs. Hollister was not only concerned about being paid, but she had learned about the accusation of stealing from Mrs. Carter." He winced as if regretting this disclosure.

Honour's lips parted, but she spoke not.

Joshua continued. "A few of the parents were threatening to dismiss their children from her school."

"That is preposterous. I did nothing wrong!" she whined.

"I know that. I tried to convince her of it, Honour, truly I did. But when Tempe was mistreated by the other children—"

"Mistreated? What happened?" She clamped down on her lower lip.

Joshua sat again. "They teased her mercilessly. A boy even accused *her* of stealing one day when she picked up his sister's handkerchief for her. Mrs. Hollister was disciplining Tempe in the corner when I arrived. While I was settling the debt, the children assaulted Tempe with their teasing again. I found her in tears and immediately put a stop to it."

Honour's palms flew to her cheeks, her eyes glistened with tears threatening to spill.

Joshua blew out a deep breath. "She has not been back since."

At last she spoke. "Poor Tempe . . . I cannot believe I was not available to comfort her or deal with this dreadful situation myself."

"I did what I could in your stead." The muscles in Johsua's jaw pulsed.

Honour stood. "You paid my debt. You took my sister out of school without telling me." She stepped away, spun back around. "Who else has been keeping this secret? Everyone, mayhap! I do not teach my sister to lie, and I abhor that you required her to do so." Honour stomped her foot. A twinge of pain pricked her abdomen, her hand protectively covered the spot.

Joshua stood and escorted her back to the bench. "Here, sit."

She reluctantly acquiesced.

"We thought it best to withhold the knowledge from you given the gravity of your health." He raked his hand back through his hair. "Honour, you almost died."

The intensity in his face almost made her believe he truly cared. But she felt betrayed, deceived, abused, and knew not what to think. She cupped her cheek, shaking her head in dismay. "Now I must make new arrangements for her schooling, find someone else to barter with. If I can locate another school mistress in need of quilting.

"Joshua, my debt to you has now increased and I don't know how I shall ever repay it. Yet, upon my honor, I shall." Her voice became raspy. "My honor. As if that holds significance."

He knelt by her side. "It does, and you do." He reached for her hand, but she pulled away. Yet his ardent profession continued. "Honour, you owe me no debt. I am a man of some means, and it has pleased me to help you in small ways. I detested seeing Tempe mistreated. I am quite fond of her . . . and even more so of you."

"It is no small thing to me to provide for her." She looked down at her lap to regain her composure, but the wealth of her turmoil erupted most unbecomingly, too fatigued to restrain it.

"I do not believe this is how one treats someone whom they are fond of, Mr. Sutton. Your skills in this regard are most lacking."

Honour rose and Joshua followed suit. He looked down at her with intensity, his blue eyes a storm of emotion.

Her lips parted as she took shallow breaths, and allowed her eyes to close for a single moment. As she opened them again, Joshua's lips hovered above her mouth . . . and she . . . blurted out, "Even Emily Leach would agree."

Joshua snapped back his head, palm pressing against his forehead. "What does *Emily* have to do with this?"

Honour bit her lip and released a diminutive breath through her nose. "I am referring to your disrespect toward the weaker sex. You have taken advantage of our vulnerabilities. I have seen it with my own eyes."

"Seen what?"

She stiffened her resolve. "I do not have the liberty to say."

"So much for your sublime ideals," he protested.

"I have taken an oath of confidentiality," she said.

"This conversation is preposterous. I only intended to inform you of what I had done on your behalf, out of my sincere—"

Three giggling girls came running toward them. "It is time for cake!"

Honour frowned apologetically at Tempe. "I'm afraid there will be no cake for me. I am feeling rather poorly."

"As am I, but I shall not disappoint my guests." Joshua marched off, but turned back and said, "I will have Redmond bring you home when we are through, Miss Metcalf."

As Honour watched Joshua and the girls walk back to the canopy, a shower of tears sprang forth. She hadn't expected her courtship to begin and end in the same moment.

Joshua took long strides across the lawn. He should have never left Honour in the garden. But as he approached the arbor he heard his brother's voice, accosting her with sarcasm.

"I find you here in tears, a tiny willow, weeping," Andrew said, leaning against the wooden structure.

"Leave her be!" Joshua called forth.

Heart to his chest, Andrew feigned compliance. "I would never intrude on your ladylove, though you have staked no claim on her. A nasty habit you have."

Joshua perused his mean-spirited brother's disheveled state. He caught Honour's attention as their eyes met. "Please ignore the *shabaroon*. He apparently began his own celebration at the tavern this morning."

Andrew cocked his head back. "I heard the news of your shares."

"You shall receive yours in due time, you've only two years more until you reach your majority," Joshua said.

"In the meantime, will you get all I desire?" Andrew gawked at Honour as he hovered over her.

The pulse in Joshua's temple throbbed. "What has gotten into you, man?"

Andrew pulled a blade from his frock. He inspected it from each side as it glinted in the sun. He touched the sharp point with his fingertip, piercing his skin.

A small drip of blood streamed down his finger.

"What . . . are you mad?" Joshua stepped forward.

Andrew pointed the blade at Joshua, halting him. "No, forgetful. I did not yet give you your present. It is your birthday, is it not?"

Andrew stared at the knife a moment longer with glazed eyes then handed it to Joshua, the tip stained in crimson. "Go

116

ahead, take it. You have wounded my heart and now you shall have my blood, as well."

Joshua clenched his jaw and released a tight breath. "I know not what the meaning of this is, but we will settle the matter another time. Not in the presence of Miss Metcalf."

"She is privy to my secrets already. What is the harm?" Andrew sneered.

Joshua's head spun toward Honour, a mass of confusion crossing her strained face.

"She weeps for you," Andrew condescended. "As do all the young maidens, save one. Yet, you've managed to ruin her, too."

"I don't know what you speak of. Go, Andrew. We will discuss this later. I'm going to see Honour home."

"Yes, you do that, brother," Andrew said and he trailed his finger across her chin.

She turned away.

"Move away from her!" Joshua stepped closer. He needed to get her away from here. Away from him.

But as Joshua approached, horror crossed her face. "Joshua, look out!"

Joshua twisted around as Andrew slammed into his chest. The intensity almost knocked the wind out of Joshua, but he girded himself for the fight.

Joshua pulled back with force, but Andrew lurched forward and grabbed the knife.

Their bodies locked, and Joshua thrust the knife in Andrew's fist downward.

Honour sprung toward them screaming, "No, stop! Stop!"

"Get back, Honour!" Joshua panted, throwing back his arm, attempting to shield her. But Andrew was unrelenting and came at him.

Honour grabbed Andrew's sleeve.

Andrew's elbow jammed up.

Joshua rammed into his brother with a swift blow, crushing him into a bed of sage.

Andrew stumbled up, but Joshua held him back with tight fists, Andrew's strength waning. His brother's face paled and contorted as he stared past Joshua.

Joshua spun around, and beheld Honour lying on the ground—the knife at her side, a smear of scarlet staining her gown.

—ಌಌ—

A myriad of faces hovering over her awakened Honour out of her slumber. The images dissipated as her eyes grew accustomed to the bright moonlight streaming into the room. She intuitively looked toward the window at the cry of the night watchman in the street below, outside Mrs. Wadsworth's shop. "Four o'clock, and all's well."

But all was not well. She felt completely out of sorts.

Honour clutched the quilted counterpane, the weight and texture of it bringing assurance she was no longer dreaming. The dream, a remembrance from the afternoon at the Suttons. She'd been knocked to the ground. Or had she fainted? Either way, she was lying on the ground looking up at the concerned onlookers gathered around her. Upon sitting up, Tempe had clung to her with all her might, crying inconsolably. Joshua and his father helped her to her feet, worry etched deep into their brows.

"We thought we'd near lost you again," Mr. Sutton said. "Thought you'd been stabbed a second time."

It had taken a few moments to realize what he referred to, but then she recalled the knife, the fight.

Joshua took steps back, as Deborah and Mrs. Wadsworth tended to Honour. Aye, all was well . . . save her broken heart. And Joshua's.

She failed at romance, failed at providing for her sister. She failed her parents.

Tempe's soft breathing as she lay by Honour's side continued to bring sobering thoughts. What would become of her if Honour had met her demise? She should be grateful people cared enough to protect and provide for Tempe and her when she could not. People like Mrs. Wadsworth, the Suttons, Joshua.

Honour's finger traced the familiar pattern of the quilt so imbedded in her memory. Thoughts of Mum's instruction to her children to heed God's Word for direction in their lives made her want to remain under the comfort of her mother's quilt forever. But it was not to be. What she could do, is follow her advice. Honor her.

Tempe stirred, and Honour stroked her hair with feather light touches. She pondered the lessons that Tempe learnt in school, her lessons of the commandments.

Honour thy father and mother; that it may go well with you and that you may enjoy long life on the earth.

That was God's promise to her even now. *Thank you, Lord. You heard my prayer before I uttered it. Aye, you heard my heart.*

Honour breathed a deep sigh, and tucked the quilt under her chin. She would honor their parents, by loving and providing for Temperance. It would be her focus, as purposeful as every stitch in her mother's quilt. As for her bridal quilt, it was long gone, and so were her selfish notions of romance. There was no room in her life for it, nor for Joshua Sutton.

12

Joshua picked up the needle case from his chest of drawers, rubbing the grain of the carved fish scales. 'Twas no small gift he received from Honour and Temperance. Any expenditure was surely a sacrifice from Honour's meager savings. He pulled the cod's head off the wooden trinket. It was a fine case for his bodkins and he would cherish it—especially now.

He looked inside the hollow container and there he found a slip of foolscap with something scrawled on it.

> Inside this fish, an answer find.
> Have your wish, love is blind.

He read it again. This message, Honour had intended to let him court her. She loved him? She loved him.

Until Saturday.

Joshua groaned. He set the needle case down and read the lines again. He pounded his clenched fist down on his high dresser. Everything was in a royal state. From Honour's anger about his interference in her personal matters, to Andrew's drunken diatribe, to Emily's influence over it all. Though he highly doubted Emily had any indication of the hold she still had on his life.

She needed to know. Rather, he needed her to know. Apparently, she was the one who held the key to the mystery of his ruined relationships. How had she become so entangled in his affairs?

Joshua threw his banyan robe onto his bed, and grabbed a fresh shirt from a drawer. With haste, he tucked the muslin into his breeches, resolving to decipher the riddle this very day. His sanity depended on it.

Foregoing his breakfast, Joshua set to his mission. A short time later, he found himself stomping down the steps of the Leach brownstone without answers. "The mistress is not home at present. She is out making morning calls," the Leach butler informed him. Must he chase *Mrs. Leach* all over town? Perhaps Emily was visiting her parents, or her Aunt Eunice. To Mrs. Lankton's he'd go.

The long walk did him good, gave him a chance to cool down. The faint scent of the salt breeze drifting off the harbor filled his nostrils. The day was fine with a hint of autumn color embellishing some of the ivy clinging to brick buildings and wrought iron fences.

A band of the 29th Regiment of Foot filled the sidewalk. One of grenadiers bulled into his shoulder as they passed. Joshua turned, spying him elbow his comrade for the implied humor of it. Was Joshua every man's fool? He whooshed out a deep breath and refocused his steps.

"Reverend Cooper!" Joshua came face-to-face with his pastor as he crossed Brattle Square.

"Joshua, what a pleasant surprise to see you on this fine day." Reverend Cooper adjusted his black felt brim and smiled.

"Fine, but not so pleasant," Joshua said. "Pardon me, I am afraid I've misplaced my cheerful demeanor."

The reverend lifted his eyebrows. "Care to tell me about it? I can walk with you a while."

"Seems you often find me with extra knots in my thread." Joshua cast a sardonic grin.

"What is troubling you today, son?" Reverend Cooper asked.

"What isn't?"

"All that bad?"

"I am afraid so."

"Miss Metcalf?"

"How did you know?"

The reverend grinned. "Intuition. Revelation. Both. Besides, when a fellow like you is so forlorn, it usually concerns a lady. Something you and your brother appear to have in common."

Joshua angled his chin. "My brother?"

"I ran into Andrew this morning. I found him a bit out of sorts as well." Reverend Cooper raised his wiry eyebrows.

"That, he is. I don't know what has gotten into him. He has become a reckless dolt." Joshua rubbed the tension from his taut neck. "Forgive me, I should not speak ill of him. I am greatly concerned for Andrew. He is not acting like himself."

"Your heart is heavy for those you love," said Reverend Cooper.

Joshua's eyes locked on the reverend's compassionate gaze. "God knows. Yet nothing is going right."

"Do you recall my text from yesterday's sermon?" the minister asked. "'Let us not become weary in doing good, for at the proper time we will reap a harvest if we do not give up.'"

"From Galatians," Joshua replied.

The minister smiled. "Ah, you were listening."

Barely. Joshua had been so distraught over the events of the day before that he could hardly pay attention. He was painfully aware of Honour's absence. Mother had inquired of Mrs. Wadsworth regarding Honour's health. She was assured that

Honour was returning to health, though they thought it best for her to remain home and rest rather than become taxed from the long walk to the meeting house.

"I tried to be of service to Honour while she was indisposed, yet she was offended by my actions. Perhaps I overstepped in my desire to win her heart," Joshua told the reverend.

"Oftentimes our exuberance overshadows our good intent," Reverend Cooper said as the pair turned the corner.

Joshua swallowed. "I truly care for Honour."

The reverend clasped his hands together. "I have no doubt that you do."

"Yet she somehow has come to the conclusion that I am one to mistreat women, though I have only shown her kindness. While my brother believes I am one to trifle with the ladies, robbing him of the pleasure in the process." Joshua kicked a pebble.

"Sometimes one matter gets confused with another. The answer may be simpler than you think. Have you asked your Heavenly Father about it?"

"These past two sleepless nights." Joshua sighed.

Reverend Cooper slowed his pace. "Has He shown you what step to take next?"

Joshua stopped, realizing he'd arrived at his destination. He looked up at Mrs. Lankton's impressive house, just beyond the ornate iron gate.

Joshua placed his shoe upon the granite step. "This one."

⎯⎯⎯

Honour reached for the scrap of paper fallen behind her bedside table, the piece of newspaper Mr. Greenleaf had wrapped around Joshua's gift. She sighed deeply as she thought of how she'd ruined his birthday. She should have heeded her inclination to not go at all. As it was, she became totally unraveled at his explanation of what transpired while she was incapacitated, things Joshua tried to rectify on her behalf. And she had berated him for it.

A tiny shiver jolted her as she recalled the vile manner with which Andrew had treated her. Why did he treat her like an object of scorn? There were no secrets between them. She had just met the man. How unlike Joshua he was in demeanor, yet so like him in looks. When she had seen him walking near the garden, she'd called to him thinking him Joshua, planning to apologize for her outburst, for her ungratefulness. But then Andrew came to her. Honour buried her face in her hand, felt the tension of her warm brow beneath her palm.

She bit down on her lip, recalling how Andrew had baited Joshua with that dreadful knife. The thought of the brothers fighting pained her so, though she now understood Joshua was protecting her. Didn't they know how blessed they were to have one another? Her own brothers were dead. *Thomas. Wesley. How I miss you both.* Honour collapsed against her bed and wept.

Some moments later, she sat on the edge of the bed, wrinkled paper still in her hand. She opened it, scanning the words out of curiosity. The diversion failed to last when she fixated on a small advertisement.

> Publick Notice per Commissioner of Customs
> A number of trunks, recently seized by the Admiralty. Diverse goods, linen white-work, English gowns. Unclaimed items to be sold at public vendue.
> Inquire of the Printer, Mein & Fleeming, Newbury Street, Boston, Massachusetts.

She could scarcely believe her eyes. English gowns, linen white-work. Could they be her missing belongings? She must find out before others lay claim to the items at the auction. A bit of hope, at last. She whispered a prayer. *Dear Lord, if the items are mine, please return them to my hands.*

Honour made her way down the stairs, exercising caution as she went. She entered the front room of the mantua shop hearing Mrs. Wadsworth and Tempe engaged in conversation.

"Temperance, dear. Please drag that basket of rags out to the sidewalk." Mrs. Wadsworth pointed to the large basket of unusable cotton and linen remnants in the corner of the shop. "*The Boston Gazette* advertised the printer's pickup is today."

"What does he do with them all?" Tempe asked.

Honour entered the room. "'Tis what the printer sends to the papermaker to make rag linen paper."

"Everything must be made in the colonies." Mrs. Wadsworth planted her hand on her hip. "Although, Mr. Mein, *The Boston Chronicle's* publisher, would certainly have no scruples about importing paper from England. He is a blatant supporter of the crown and delights in mocking those who do not."

"Why is it bad to get things from England? I came from England." Tempe looked at Honour. "We both did."

Mrs. Wadsworth wagged her finger and smirked. "But we did not have to pay taxes for you to be imported."

Tempe's eyes widened. "Ohhh . . ."

"Is that so? I wasn't aware Mr. Mein is a Tory." Honour nibbled her lower lip. "He owns the lending library we subscribe to."

"I cancelled my own account," Mrs. Wadsworth said.

Honour crossed her arms. "As shall I."

Tempe crouched to drag the basket of rags, but then straightened. "Is that a boycott? Is it because he is a boy? If he was a girl, would they call it a girlcott?"

Honour and Mrs. Wadsworth laughed. "No, pumpkin. 'Tis because he supports unfair taxation. Do you remember Poppa talking about it sometimes?"

Tempe opened the door and pulled the basket toward her. "We came to America for Poppa's business and to stand with the colonists." Tempe's lip quiver. "That's why they died. It's so unfair!"

With one last tug of the basket to the sidewalk, Tempe allowed the door to slam behind her, the doorbells jangling as she did. Honour looked back toward Mrs. Wadsworth with a frown. When she turned around, Tempe was gone.

Honour rushed outside and looked down the street. Tempe was nowhere in sight. Honour's chest constricted with fear and she spun in the opposite direction.

At the sight of Tempe, Honour's hand flew to her chest and she drew in a deep breath. A smile crept across her face as Tempe skipped toward her, hand in hand with Joshua's nieces.

"Honour! Look who came to see us!" Tempe cheered.

"Abigail, Sarah. What a nice treat to see you girls again so soon." Honour restrained her panic and met the girls as if nothing had gone awry. The thump of her heart began to resume its normal pace.

Joshua's eldest sister greeted Honour with her lovely smile. "Good morning, Honour. We have come with good news and hope you and Temperance will agree."

"Hello, Deborah. 'Tis a nice surprise to see you and the girls." Honour glanced toward the shop door where Mrs. Wadsworth was peeking out at the group of them.

"Do come inside, ladies . . . and young ladies," Mrs. Wadsworth called to them.

Honour allowed their guests to enter the mantua shop first. She tugged on the long pair of fabric pleats streaming from the back of Tempe's calico gown, and held her back. "Temperance

Metcalf, if you ever run off again without so much as a 'by your leave', I shall have to tie you up by your leading strings. Is that understood?" Honour scolded in a hushed voice.

"Aye, Honour." Temperance scrunched her nose.

Honour slid her fingertip down Tempe's pert nose. "And none of that." She pulled her sister to her side for a quick hug. "Now, let us see what these tidings are about."

When they entered, Deborah was talking to Mrs. Wadsworth. "I shall come by soon with my homespun, and schedule a fitting. I should have thought to bring it today, but we had another matter on our minds." Deborah turned toward Honour. "Shall we tell her, girls?" Abigail and Sarah squeezed Deborah's hands with glee.

"Your news. You have made us both curious." Honour smiled at the girls.

"Anne and I have hired a tutor, at the bequest of our parents, and there is room for another student. We hope you will allow Temperance to join Sarah and Abigail in their schooling—unless you have other arrangements in place, of course. It would require no tuition and your only expense will be for a few supplies." Deborah continued her invitation, "Mother insists that the girls learn to cipher and measure. She allowed Anne and me to sit with our brothers whilst they were tutored in mathematics and wants the girls to benefit similarly. Of course, Father grumbled about it then, but he has slowly changed his ways—largely due to her skill at reckoning his accounts proper."

Honour could hardly believe the conversation unfolding before her.

Deborah parted her lips and paused. "You don't object to mathematics, do you?"

Honour rested her finger on her chin. "Well, no. I encourage it. It proves useful in sewing and quilting."

Tempe tugged on Honour's sleeve, looking up from beneath her long eyelashes. Honour smiled widely. "How could we decline such a generous offer? I am exceedingly grateful."

Dimples, much like Joshua's, blossomed at the corners of Deborah's mouth. "Wonderful! We shall have the three brightest girls in Boston!"

Mrs. Wadsworth clasped her hands and glanced heavenward with a generous smile. Honour agreed. This was an answer from God.

"May I have a moment privately?" Deborah asked.

"Certainly," Honour said.

Mrs. Wadsworth corralled the girls. "I've some fashion babies to show you. Follow me." The older woman led the girls away to see the Pandora dolls, dressed in examples of high fashion—from before the embargoes—while Honour and Deborah retreated to a corner.

"How are you faring?" Deborah asked in hushed tones.

"I am well. Thank you," Honour said.

"That is good to hear. We have all been concerned for you. Please accept my family's sincere apology for the appalling behavior of Andrew and Joshua."

"Joshua did nothing but defend me. I regret that I became unnecessarily upset with him."

Deborah touched Honour lightly on the arm. "I do not blame you for being upset. You were hurt. And how is your heart?"

Honour released a little breath and clamped down on her lower lip.

"As I thought." The corners of Deborah's mouth turned down. "He is hurting also."

Honour discerned Deborah meant that knowledge to bring Honour comfort, but who was Joshua hurting for? To whom did his heart belong?

The bells on the door jingled and Maisey entered.

"How did Mrs. Lankton like her gown?" Mrs. Wadsworth asked her.

"She was most pleased, Mistress." Maisey handed her employer a letter.

"Good. A reply to the note I sent with you." Mrs. Wadsworth said, turning the square piece of parchment one way and then the other.

"She has invited you for tea at noon." A knowing hint laced Maisey's face. Had she read the missive?

"And you know this how?" Mrs. Wadsworth asked, carefully breaking the wax seal.

"Mrs. Lankton told me so. She sent me back in her Boston chaise," Maisey said with a cheeky grin. "It awaits you . . . and Honour."

Honour placed her palm against her breast. "You must be mistaken."

Maisey whispered something in Tempe's ear, and she giggled.

Honour narrowed her eyes at them. "Something seems a bit fishy here."

The pair exchanged mischievous looks.

Mrs. Wadsworth waved the letter. "It says so right here. We have both been invited for tea and she has sent her chaise for us."

Mrs. Wadsworth's eyes sparkled as she looked at Honour. "This is turning out to be an extraordinary day for you, don't you agree?"

A feeling of warmth surrounded her. "Indeed, it is."

"You shall have a lovely time," Deborah said. "Why don't I take Temperance home with us and you can enjoy a day or two to yourself. Abby is also spending the night and the girls will have a grand time."

Temperance pursed her lips at Honour. "How can I refuse a face like that?" Honour squeezed Tempe's chin and gave her a kiss.

"Thank you, sister. I shall be a good girl," Tempe said.

"I know you shall. Go on now and gather your overnight things." As Tempe skipped away, Honour called after her. "Be careful on the stairs."

Honour smiled at Deborah. "I appreciate your kindness. 'Tis a fine idea."

At last, a day that held promise.

13

Joshua paced from one side of Widow Lankton's finely furnished parlor to the other. If he wasn't careful, he'd wear a groove into the well-planed floorboards.

Widow Lankton entered the parlor, followed by a female servant who carried a garment in her arms. "Joshua, dear, how pleasant to see you," Emily's aunt said.

"Good morning." Hands clasped behind his back, Joshua dipped his head in a short bow. "I have come to call on Mrs. Leach. I was told I could find her here today. Your housekeeper informed me she has not yet arrived and has allowed me to wait for her." Joshua glanced toward the window.

"By all means. Do you care for some refreshment," she asked.

"Thank you, no." Though he felt a slight rumble in his belly, he was far too anxious to think about food—though if he imbibed, a sip of rum might calm his nerves.

Joshua eyed the familiar-looking garment. Hadn't he seen that in Mrs. Wadsworth's workspace above Suttons? "What have you here?"

Widow Lankton handled the exquisitely quilted sleeve of the garment. "Mrs. Wadsworth's apprentice delivered it only

131

moments ago, thus my reason for my tardiness in greeting you. The peculiar girl became rather distracted by your presence when she heard you enter. You apparently have an effect on the ladies. Though my niece has confused me on that matter," the dowager sighed.

Joshua straightened and focused on the quilted gown. "This is exceedingly well done."

"A great deal of time and talent went into the making of it," she said.

"I agree, emphatically." Honour's impressive handiwork was a privilege to behold.

The widow addressed her servant. "That must be getting heavy in your arms. You may put it away, but please take care."

Widow Lankton's rose water perfume was giving Joshua a headache. He took a step back, allowing the maidservant to pass.

The elderly woman ambled over to a small table set with silver service. She poured herself a cup from a silver urn and lifted it, tilting her head. "Coffee?" she asked. She noted his refusal, and asked once more, "Are you sure?"

"The aroma is enticing. Perhaps I shall, thank you." He accepted the handleless porcelain cup. As the widow settled upon her chintz settee, he consumed his drink with several sips and resumed his pacing.

Widow Lankton peered at him over her tea bowl. "I do not know what is keeping Emily, but you are making me a nervous wreck."

The elderly lady turned her opposite palm toward a comb-back Windsor chair. "Do sit down, Joshua."

Joshua paused at the window once again. He peered past the drapes, hoping Emily would return from her outing. He proceeded to the highly polished black chair.

"Have you seen Emily since her marriage, Joshua?"

"No, I have not."

Widow Lankton smoothed her sacque-back gown, a fine Indian chintz Sutton's had fashioned for her before the trade sanctions. She patted the back of her gray coiffed wig, piled high upon her head and topped with a petite lace pinner cap. "Have you come to offer your congratulations . . . or mayhap your regret?"

"I only regret Emily hadn't spoken directly to me about her plans before she wed Mr. Leach. I would have assured her I wanted her to marry for love and perhaps she would not have taken such a hasty course." Joshua's mouth tightened. "We were ill-suited for one another and I should have been clear about the mismatch sooner."

"Is that why you were dragging your feet for so long?" Widow Lankton was not in the habit of mincing words.

Joshua shifted on the hard chair. "That, and the fact that she was not yet of age. She still is very young yet, barely ten and eight."

Widow Lankton placed her palm against her cheek and gazed down. Of course. He should not have mentioned Emily's age, though it was of consequence. "I regret I was unable to welcome one of the Sutton boys into our family as a nephew. But the matter is done, and the new Mistress Leach is settling into her new life."

An awkward silence filled the space.

Joshua stared at the ornamental design of his new shoe buckles.

"That is a fine pair of buckles," Widow Lankton said.

"A gift," he said, looking up. "From my sister Anne."

"How nice of her. How is Anne?"

"She is enjoying motherhood." Joshua's neck warmed, and he loosened his neck handkerchief. "You should ask mother about Anne's news."

Widow Lankton clasped her hands and smiled. "Indeed, I shall," she said knowingly.

"How is your mother?" his hostess asked.

"Well, thank you."

"I am pleased to hear it." The woman took another sip of her coffee.

Joshua did not know if he could survive either another lull in the conversation or more of this excruciating discourse. But he opted for one over the other. "Is she happy? Emily, I mean."

"One can hardly tell." Widow Lankton angled her straight posture toward the door. "I believe she is here now. You may ask her yourself."

Emily presented at once, all ruffles and ruches, her panniers filling the doorway, despite her petite figure. "Aunt Eunice, forgive me for having been detained." Her head pivoted in Joshua's direction. "Joshua!"

As Joshua jumped to his feet, the chair scraped against the floorboards. He bowed. "Emily . . . Mrs. Leach."

Emily glided into the parlor. "There is no need of formality with me, Joshua. For heaven's sake, we were once almost married."

"About that—"

Widow Lankton rose. "I have company to ready for, so I shall leave the two of you to your privacy. Emily, I will be in the other room, have you need of a chaperone, though I trust Joshua to maintain all propriety." The lady regarded Joshua with a mix of warning and concern.

Emily circled about the room. She met Joshua's gaze and arched an inquisitive eyebrow.

Joshua squeezed out the insincere words. "Please allow me to offer my best wishes on your marriage."

Emily cupped her hands loosely in front of her waist. "Thank you. Although by the grimace on your face I am not sure you mean it."

Joshua took a few steps away and halted. He found his resolve and spun around. "I am concerned about your hasty decision to marry Mr. Leach."

"I had nothing holding me back. You and I were not officially engaged."

"But it was understood."

"Joshua, you never wanted to marry me. You were only pleasing your parents, as was I."

"And have you pleased your parents now?"

"I have." She cast aside a somber glance. "Very much so."

Joshua eyed her attentively.

"It was a matter of necessity."

His eyes widened. Were the rumors true? Did Emily *need* to get married?

"Oh, dear." The color is her face heightened. "Nothing like *that.*

"It was a business arrangement between families, and more beneficial than the one previously intimated between our own," she said. "Father would have lost everything if we hadn't acted immediately." She retrieved a handkerchief from her pocket as a mist of tears pooled in her eyes.

"I wish you had told me." Joshua's brow tensed.

"Father forbade it. He wanted no chance of the scheme being interrupted," Emily said.

Joshua released a deep breath. "That is why you obtained the special marriage license."

"It is," she sniffled, and turned to rest her hand on the mantle.

Joshua had incorrectly assumed her coquette ways, her flirtations with he, and Andrew at times, were simply a young girl seeking attention. Her attempt to make light of a future she had little control of. "I hoped you could marry for love. I planned to tell you that, and encourage you to pursue a life you were worthy of." He moved beside her and gave her hand a gentle squeeze. "You are a sweet young woman, I see how loving you are. You sacrificed much for the benefit of your parents."

"Someone had to. I couldn't bear to see them suffer over-long." She hesitated, letting out a little sigh. "Truth be told, Mr. Leach shall never love me. At least I know you would have tried."

"Perhaps in time, he will learn to—"

"He detests me. It is a marriage in name only." She turned toward Joshua, the light inside her fading.

It pained him to see her so distraught. He never held romantic affection for her, but yes, he would have tried to love her, had she been his wife.

"I will never be with the one I truly love, all hope is gone." She wrung her hands and pulled them to her chest, tears streaming down her cheeks. "I have forsaken him, destroyed him, yet he loves me still."

Joshua tipped her head up, and stared earnestly into her face. "Who, Emily? Who?"

She collapsed against his chest in racking sobs, trembling. "Your brother."

———⊷∞⊶———

"This way," the manservant said. "Widow Lankton and Mrs. Wadsworth shall join you shortly." Honour stepped into the parlor of Widow Lankton's grand home.

She sucked in a deep breath, clutching the folds of her gown, utterly shocked at the scene before her. Joshua's arms enveloped Mrs. Leach, who huddled against his stalwart form. He stroked her hair and spoke in low murmurs as ragged breaths permeated the space between them.

Joshua pulled away, spinning his head toward her. Horror bolted across his face.

Emily stepped back, smoothing her rumpled gown. "Miss Metcalf!" She briskly wiped her flushed face.

"Honour!" Joshua called after her as she fled from the room.

She exited through the front door and ran around to the rear yard. She ran past the gardens to the refuge of a weeping willow. Honour tripped and collided against the old tree, the rough bark pressing into her palms. She turned and girded her back against the pillar, attempting to catch her breath. Honour burst into tearless sobs. She crumpled to the ground, hugging herself as moist drops streamed down her cheeks. How could Joshua engage so inappropriately with a married woman? Yet, this time Emily returned his affections. She pounded the grass with her fists.

Her long tendrils hung loose around her face, and she brushed them away from her eyes, lifting her head. Long, willowy branches dangled to the ground, surrounding her beneath the shelter of the tree. Andrew's words mocked her. "Like a willow, weeping." Did he feel sorry for her? For himself? "I would never intrude on your ladylove . . ." he'd said to Joshua.

Ohh . . . Andrew was jealous. He loved Emily, but could not have her because of Joshua. Neither could Joshua have her for his own.

Yet, Joshua claimed her, despite it. The very thought of it made her nauseous. Pain gripped her middle. Her whole being longed for him, though he caused her such agony. She let out a deep sigh, finding his name upon her lips. "Joshua."

"Honour."

Joshua emerged through the tangle of willow, coming toward her without reserve.

He held her linen cap in his fists, the black ribbons dangling, and clutching it as if it were his last hope. His earnest gaze pleaded with her. "You must allow me to explain."

She shook her head. "Must I?"

Joshua reached to her to help her up, but she jerked away. "I was only comforting her."

"Aye, I see she found great comfort in your arms." Venom spewed from Honour's lips. "She has a husband for that, does she not?"

The muscles in Joshua's jaw pulsed. "My brother loves her, not I."

"I realize that, but I saw you kissing her. Apparently you have no qualms with impropriety."

Joshua raked his hand through his hair. "On my honor, I was not kissing her."

"Honor? Hmmph! I do not want to hear you say the word . . . or my name."

He lowered himself to the ground, leaning on one knee. "Please. Believe me."

"My senses do not deceive me." She looked at the ground, toying with some willow fronds. "I saw you kiss her the other day in the alley. I heard you profess your love to her." Honour cast her gaze up. "Emily asked me not to tell, but it matters not now." She eyed him cautiously, as he drew nearer.

His voice grew raspy. "It was him."

"Him? It was Andrew?" Honour's eyes widened.

Joshua nodded.

"He sounded, he looked—" Thoughts rushed to her of the times she noted their similarities. Could it be?

Joshua's mouth curved into a tentative grin. "We are brothers. People often confuse us." He stroked the side of her face, tracing his finger beneath her chin. "But you shall never confuse me with him again."

"Never?" she whispered.

"Never." He pressed his lips below her ear and gentle kisses found their way to her mouth.

She accepted the tender affection he offered her as he moved closer and slipped her into the cradle of his arms.

He whispered her name, "Honour . . . Honour . . . Honour."

He deepened his kiss and she felt his warm hand at her waist. She winced. He drew back.

He looked deep into her eyes with an ardor she'd never known. "Do you believe me now?"

Her gaze locked on his—entreating, affirming.

Joshua pulled away from her, the strain of it like the taut threads on a loom. He rose, carefully bringing her with him to her feet, though she could scarcely feel the weight of them. "Come, the others shall be worried. But I am glad Emily convinced them to let me find you on my own."

Honour smiled demurely, feeling lightheaded.

Joshua reached for her hand, but she froze.

"Joshua—" Honour bent forward clutching her abdomen and moaned.

"Honour, what is it?"

"My wound." She pulled her hand away from her skirt, her palm soiled with blood.

14

Streams of color encircled Honour, swirling by like the ribbons of a maypole. Visions of Mum, Poppa, Thomas, and Wesley, dancing by to the tune of a fiddle, waving as they went, faded into the sweet faces of Temperance, Abigail, and Sarah. Soon Maisey and Mrs. Wadsworth joined them, along with Mr. and Mrs. Sutton, Deborah, Anne, their husbands, and Andrew and Joshua. The country dance continued, and smiles all but disappeared, except for those of Andrew and Joshua, with Emily now joining them. Hand in hand they gamboled around the pole until Joshua reached out for Honour. As she took his hand, the others stole away, leaving Honour with Joshua, alone in a glorious whirl of warmth and laughter. The ribbons transformed into the wispy branches of a weeping willow, surrounding them with fronds of joy. Joshua took both of her hands in his, and the pole disappeared, nothing separating them at last.

Honour's eyes fluttered open and the scene was gone. She met the concerned gazes of Mrs. Wadsworth and the Widow Lankton, who sat nearby with needlework in their laps. "I was dancing," Honour said, her voice barely above a whisper.

"There shall be no dancing for you, for some time yet," Mrs. Wadsworth chided.

Widow Lankton tucked her chin. "Heavens no! You'll not move from that bed until the doctor gives his consent."

"For how long?" Honour asked.

Honour tried to sit up, but Mrs. Wadsworth called out, "Stay!" She went to Honour's side with a few short steps, holding her hand out above Honour's covers. "You must lie still, dear, as to not reopen your wound."

Honour instinctively glanced toward her abdomen and felt the light weight of something atop her incision. Mrs. Wadsworth pulled back the bedcoverings and adjusted the lawn shift Honour wore for modesty. How strange it felt to be in bedclothes in midday, in the house of someone with whom she was little acquainted. How long had she been here?

"Thank the Lord Widow Lankton's housekeeper grew some Lady's Mantle in the doorway garden. The woman made an astringent with some fresh root to help stop the bleeding," Mrs. Wadsworth said. "Now let's see how it's doing. We may have to exchange the Lamb's Ear for some new."

"My housekeeper, Mrs. Hall, is quite adept at medicinal herbs, Honour, dear. Her swift ministrations kept you with us until Doctor Westcott arrived. He was pleased with the results."

"You lost a good amount of blood." Mrs. Wadsworth carefully pulled off the large silvery leaf. "We shall need to replace this. It looks clear of infection, but care must be taken to allow the wound to heal completely."

Honour arched her neck daring to take a look. "It was foolish of me to run. I managed to trip, but did not know I had reinjured myself until—" Had she really been embracing Joshua underneath the willow tree?

"Doctor Westcott found an abscess. 'Twas little you could have done to avoid it. He gave you some new silk stitches. He expects you to recover in a fortnight," Mrs. Wadsworth said.

Honour's sleepy eyes widened. "A fortnight? What am I to do until then?"

"You shall stay right here in my guest chamber and recover, my dear," said Widow Lankton. The elderly woman set her tambour work down and stood from her wingback chair. "I shall fetch the housekeeper so she may change your dressing."

Mrs. Wadsworth drew the covers over Honour with care, looking down at her with a meek smile. "You had us all very worried."

"Tempe?"

"She doesn't know. She has been safely at Deborah's the past two days. When we sent word, the dear replied not to worry. She will keep Temperance as long as necessary and only tell her what happened when it is fitting," Mrs. Wadsworth said.

"Two days?"

"Yes. You have been asleep most of the time. The doctor felt it best to keep you from moving. You were a bit restless so he administered a tincture of laudanum, which we continued to give you at regular intervals." Mrs. Wadsworth returned to her seat by the hearth.

"Mrs. Wadsworth?"

"Yes, dear."

"What was our purpose in coming to Widow Lankton's on Monday?" Honour asked.

Mrs. Wadsworth picked up her stitching. "We never got around to it, did we?"

"No, we did not." Honour recalled they'd hardly arrived when she discovered Joshua and Emily together. Relief filled her to know Joshua did not love Emily. Joshua's heart belonged to Honour, and hers to him. Honour sighed.

"Honour?" Mrs. Wadsworth's voice interrupted Honour's thoughts.

"Mmm, aye?"

"Why don't you close your eyes again?" Mrs. Wadsworth said.

But before Honour could answer, she was drifting back to sleep, with the name of her beloved dancing delicately upon her lips. "—Joshua."

Joshua stretched his measuring tape the length of Father's back. Then he wrapped the marked tape around his father's expanding girth. "Mother, was right, sir. You've need of a few new suits."

"Bah, the laundress must have used hot water," Father muttered.

"You have said yourself, I've a good eye." Joshua took another measurement, and marked it down.

"That you do. I taught you well." Father chuckled. "So why not let out the seams, use an old suit for a pattern. I haven't the time for this."

"They have been let out enough already, sir." Joshua turned the knob of the rounded wooden case, rewinding the tape measure. "You do not want to continue going around town with puckered clothing. 'Twouldn't make a good impression for a master tailor and clothier."

His father faced him. "Egad, continue? We are running low on our textiles, I cannot afford to spend them on myself. I shall let you and Andrew play the macaroni. The pair of you have already garnered the attention of all the maidens of Boston." Father tugged on the collar of his waistcoat. "I was quite the dandy when I was your age, you know."

Joshua cracked a grin and glanced down at his father's plump middle. "'Tis what I have to look forward to, eh?"

Father grinned and patted his belly. "'Tis all that good food your mother serves me. By the by, how is that young woman of yours fairing since her reinjury?" He frowned. "Pity, that. I have taken a liking to the girl . . . and I know you have."

Joshua's lips tightened. "I sent a note with Redmond and a request that he discover how she fares today. She has been unconscious the past two days, and they have done everything they could. Doctor Westcott says the outcome is promising, providing an infection doesn't set in. The thought of it drives me mad and I hope Redmond brings word that I may see her soon."

"Well, do keep me informed." Father crossed his arms. "Now about the matter with your brother. Have you made amends?"

"He has been avoiding me . . . and I him, truth be told. Yet I'm certain we will work things out. 'Tis not our first scuff."

"He is back in the workshop with the table monkeys sewing by the window. Awfully melancholy, but he won't speak of it to me. Mayhap you can get to the bottom of it." Father whooshed out an exasperated groan.

"I will speak to him." Truth was, Joshua had already discovered what ailed his younger brother, yet he knew not what to do with it. 'Twas a weighty matter, indeed.

Father put on his frockcoat, buttoning the brass buttons. "Be sure to take it to the Lord first, son. 'Tis always the way."

Joshua nodded. "All right. I shall do the same before I cut the bespoken cloth for your garments. Reverend Cooper says it is also a good thing to take the small matters to the Lord." Joshua picked up the tape measure, and shrugged. "Small, or large. I'll do the same."

"You'd better pray for your soul with that remark." His father chuckled. "I am glad to see you in good spirits, although Honour is unwell. Has something else transpired between you?"

"We have become closer." Though Joshua did not truly know how she felt about him, she had willingly accepted his affection. What relief to have the misunderstanding concerning Emily resolved.

"Now that John Hancock. There's a man who is in a sad state of affairs," his father was saying, stirring Joshua out of his thoughts. "John Mein has published in his newspaper the ship manifests of those he claims are ostensible non-importers, including Hancock. Mein states that he imported linen when it was Russian duck, an exempt textile."

"After Customs raided Mr. Hancock's ship last year, you would think they'd had enough of him," Joshua said. "Mein has made Hancock out to be a hypocrite. He is nothing of the sort. The man wholly supports the cause."

"He's a member of the Body of Merchants and a leader of the Sons of Liberty, thus the reason he is a target. The Sons of Liberty are up in arms." The color of Father's face heightened. "Beware, Joshua, beware."

Mr. Hancock's problems were far greater than his own and would affect the Patriot cause. They would all suffer for it. Joshua glanced toward the workshop. He had some mending to do.

Joshua entered the large workroom. The balmy space smelled of textiles and men's sweat. Filled with tables of every size, bolts of fabric leaned against the walls and filled the shelves. Apprentices and journeymen of various skill levels were busy cutting, pining, sewing, fitting, ironing, and other sundry tasks.

He went to a large cutting table near Andrew, who, slipshod, sat cross-legged atop his window-side perch to keep his work from getting soiled. Joshua laid out Father's original suit coat pattern on the large sheets of rag linen. He read the measurement notations he had taken and began making adjustments to the pattern with a piece of chalk.

He cast a sidelong look at Andrew, who happened to glance up from his stitching. "When you are a master tailor in another year or so, I will pass the task of sewing for Father to you."

"Hmmph, I think not!" Andrew shook his head and grinned.

"What are you working on?" Joshua asked.

"Breeches. For Mr. Hollister," Andrew said.

"The schoolmistress's husband?"

"Aye."

Joshua stared down at his patternmaking, recalling his encounter with the wench. He recalled the poor way she and the students treated Tempe. It relieved him to have her away from there and would soon start school with his nieces. The girls would probably begin working on samplers. Had the sampler that Tempe made at Mistress Hollister's dame school ever been returned to her? Girls treasured their samplers, and maybe she would want to continue working on the one she had already begun. What had the schoolteacher said . . . she would see Temperance received her sampler when Honour returned Mrs. Hollister's quilting fabric?

His gut suddenly felt hollow. He'd forgotten to tell Honour what Mrs. Hollister had said. He doubted Honour had returned the cloth yet. He would talk to her about it, and gain approval rather than provide unsolicited help. She may now understand his motives, but he intended to earn her trust and respect.

A lad scurried beneath his brother's table and picked the "cabbage," scraps of fabric lying about. Andrew looked up at

Joshua and their gazes merged. "About your birthday, Josh. Can you accept my apology?"

Joshua's chest constricted as he sucked in a deep breath. He waited for him to say something about Honour. Was he sorry for that? Joshua picked up the large shears and slapped the flat of the blades across his palm.

"Whoa! Easy there, brother." Andrew's eyes lit with alarm, though he kept his voice low.

Joshua looked at the scissors and shrugged, and shook his head. Did Andrew think Joshua would hurt him? "Calm down."

Andrew ran a hunk of wax over some thread. "What say you? Friends?"

"That depends," Joshua began. *Oh, Lord, how am I to do this? Sometimes he is like a stranger to me.*

Love him as yourself.

Joshua's own thoughts weighed heavy upon him at times; no doubt his brother's did also. He had to know what Andrew was about, and love him in spite of it.

Most of the workers remained occupied on the far side of the room, so Joshua continued. "I mean . . . I hoped you might apologize for harming Miss Metcalf. I know you cannot be such a cad that it doesn't concern you."

"I meant to." Andrew's face grew wan. "I feel terrible that she got in harm's way. It was my fault. Mother now tells me she has been hurt again."

"She will be all right. She has to be. Her little sister will be all alone if Honour does not recover." Joshua gripped the edge of the worktable and hung his head.

"Egad, you love her."

"Yes." Why was he telling Andrew this, now? Although Andrew could be a serpent at times, he cared deeply for those he loved and often put his own needs aside. Is that why Andrew never let on he had developed feelings for Emily? He would have allowed Joshua to marry her, if their parents desired it, letting the eldest brother marry first so Joshua's inheritance would be part of the marriage bargain. He loved Joshua that much. He loved Emily even more.

Joshua walked over to Andrew. "You've got to know something."

Andrew swiveled around and sat on the edge of his table. "What it is it, man? Do you forgive me or not?"

Joshua spoke in a hushed voice, glancing about the room. The apprentices and other workers were gathering their things to leave for the day. "I do, Andrew. Let us put it behind us. But you need to know that I never loved Emily. I was planning to talk to Mother and Father about it before we heard the news she'd wed. I had no idea of your feelings for her."

Andrew gawked at Joshua, intensity burning in his eyes. "How do you know then, now?"

"I went to see her. I needed to know what the secrets were about. She confided in me that you loved her," Joshua said, "and still do."

Andrew's eyes harbored unyielding turmoil. "Nothing can be done about it. I must forget her. Though it will prove to be my undoing." Andrew's jaw clenched.

"It does not have to be. Would it give you any comfort to know she loves you? She married out of pressure from her parents. She doesn't love the man, nor he her."

"To know she is doomed to have a miserable life. No, it gives me no comfort. I know she loves me. It is why it is tearing me to shreds." Andrew grabbed a remnant, and tore it with his fists, his eyes glazed with moisture. He hopped down from the table and trudged away.

Joshua slammed his fist on the table. He doubted there were any words that could untangle this state of affairs. He tidied up Andrew's work area, as his own needed little straightening. He exited the room, his heart heavy for Andrew, and Emily, and Honour. Nothing had changed from the way he felt days before. His relationships were in complete disarray.

Father greeted Joshua in the storefront, getting ready to lock up. "How is that pattern coming along?"

"I am still working on it. There are yet adjustments to make."

15

Sun streamed through the glazed window panes of the bed-chamber, casting a ray of morning light upon the floorboards. Honour marveled at the lovely room with fine furniture and lavish draperies. Indeed, everything from the crewelwork fabric garnishing the canopied bedstead in which she lay, to the exquisite flocked wallpaper opposite the blue-gray painted panels of the mantle wall, made her feel every bit like royalty. Honour once enjoyed the benefit of a fine home in England, while not nearly as grand. Yet, she now lived in quiet modesty in Mrs. Wadsworth's pleasant, but humble home—the home of a reluctant subject of the crown.

Where might her hostess's sympathies lie? If Widow Lankton was a Tory and their ideals were at odds, could Honour continue to accept the hospitality the woman of affluence so graciously offered? Honour smiled inwardly as she now knew her own leanings sincerely lay with the Whigs. These were not merely her father's values, but they had become her own—she was a true Patriot.

As Honour continued her ruminations, she surveyed the room, noticing a small framed silhouette of a gentleman set upon an elaborately veneered chest of drawers. She assumed the inky profile was that of Mr. Lankton, a wealthy merchant. Mayhap the bureau had been imported from some far-off land by the widow's late husband. The dower widow had wealth in her own right, Maisey had informed her one time, and thus maintained full privileges to her grand home and fortune. It was rare for a widow to not marry again, if not for financial gain, for help and companionship in these difficult times. Had the widow been happy in her marriage, or had it been arranged for her those many years past?

What would be the circumstances of Honour's own marriage someday? Thoughts of Joshua entered her mind, though she had not yet agreed to court him—unless kisses under a weeping willow counted. She'd been told he had inquired of her condition every day and promised to pay her a call when she was able to receive visitors. Honour felt her strength returning and hoped to see him soon. She also missed Tempe, yet Honour was certain her sister was enjoying the time spent with friends. It was good Tempe could have a few days of leisure, though Honour could scarce afford it, having missed so much opportunity to earn her wages. And now she was indisposed once again.

Widow Lankton appeared in the doorway. "It often happeth, that the very face sheweth the mind walking a pilgrimage. Penny for your thought."

"Sir Thomas Moore." Honour smiled, glancing up at Widow Lankton. "Good morning. I suppose I was rather lost in my musings."

Widow Lankton crossed the floor and took her seat by the fireplace with her needlework in hand. "I trust you have been looked after this morning by my housekeeper?"

"Aye, she has cleansed my wound and managed to freshen me a bit." How sweet the cloth dipped in the basin of lavender water felt as it washed over her, the scent reviving her from several days of the laudanum-induced haze. Widow Lankton's housekeeper had helped Honour into a clean shift and loose-fitting short bed gown and petticoat Mrs. Wadsworth had sent. The maidservant also came to brush and plait Honour's dreadfully tangled hair.

"You do look improved." The widow's eyes crinkled with a smile. "You have some color restored to your face. How are you feeling, Honour?"

Honour toyed with the loose braid hanging over her shoulder. "I believe I am improving, too, though I still feel terribly weak. Yet, my pain has lessened and I sense my wits returning to me, enough to set my thoughts to worry."

"'Tis difficult to have one's normal activities interrupted. Perhaps we might remedy it when Mrs. Wadsworth comes by later. We've a little something to discuss with you lest you grow overly restless."

A servant girl entered with a tray of breakfast. She pulled a small table close to the bedstead and set the tray down. A steaming cup of coffee, an egg, and toast with strawberry jam tickled Honour's appetite. 'Twould be nice to have something more than broth.

"We'll see how you do with this, miss," the maidservant said.

"Thank you," Honour said, before the girl slipped from the room.

"You go right ahead, dear," Widow Lankton said. "I have already broken my fast this morning, though I dare say it was a tad more plentiful than what you have been served. Yet you must take things slowly if you wish your health to be fully restored."

"Hmm. It shan't be easy." How difficult it would be to stay abed until her wound completely healed, but she could not risk her well-being on account of Temperance. Concern about her livelihood and the burden her absence must be causing Mrs. Wadsworth nudged at her. But it gave Honour comfort, at least for now, she and Tempe were provided for—her sister in the care of a fine family, and she in the home of a grand dame—Patriot or not.

Widow Lankton concentrated on her embroidery, quietly encouraging Honour to take her morning refreshment. Honour closed her eyes offering a brief, but heartfelt prayer of thanksgiving for the Lord's provision for Tempe and herself, and for the care and ministrations she received from Widow Lankton and her servants. Someday Honour hoped to repay the graciousness of her hostess.

After her breakfast, Honour read for a short time from a small Bible Widow Lankton left by her bedside. The affirming words of Deuteronomy 31:6 brought refreshment to her heart. *Be strong and of a good courage, fear not, nor be afraid of them: for the LORD thy God, he it is that doth go with thee; he will not fail thee, nor forsake thee.*

The maidservant returned with word Mrs. Wadsworth had arrived, and at Widow Lankton's direction, Honour's employer came up to the second floor bedchamber. "Good morning, ladies. 'Tis a pleasant day to see you looking so alert, Honour."

"Honour tells me she is feeling improved today," Widow Lankton said.

Mrs. Wadsworth smiled at Honour. "I am glad to hear it. As Temperance shall be."

"You told her then?" Honour asked.

"Joshua went to Deborah's and they told her together you had a setback. They assured her you would soon recover and you were enjoying your visit with Widow Lankton," Mrs. Wadsworth said.

"I am, at that," Honour said. "I do hope Tempe will take comfort in that report."

Mrs. Wadsworth sat in the chair opposite Widow Lankton. "Joshua promised Tempe he would bring her to visit once you were improved. Deborah will keep Tempe with her as long as necessary. Of course, I could keep her with me, but I think she would enjoy herself more with Sarah and Abigail."

"Abigail?" Honour asked.

"Yes, she is there too. Abby's mother, Anne, has been feeling rather poorly in her condition," Mrs. Wadsworth said.

"I am sorry to hear it. I shall pray for her," Honour said. "What a wonderful idea for the girls to be with Deborah. I am certain Tempe must be enjoying herself."

"I've no doubt she is. A young girl needs friends, as do we all." Widow Lankton's fingers covered her lips, but the furtive grin she cast Mrs. Wadsworth did not escape Honour's notice.

Mrs. Wadsworth's eyebrow rose. "I wholeheartedly agree."

Honour nodded. "Mrs. Wadsworth, what shall I do about Tempe's clothing? And her tambour work? She loves to practice her quilting."

"You shall do nothing. I instructed Maisey to pack a satchel for Tempe and be sure to include her embroidery frame," Mrs. Wadsworth said. "Tempe did inquire about her sampler, which we couldn't find."

Honour grimaced. "Oh, dear. Mrs. Hollister must still have it."

"Why was it not returned?" Widow Lankton asked, then instructed the maidservant to prepare some tea.

Honour watched the girl take a creamware tea service from the open cupboard beside the paneled hearth. "I . . . I am not sure. It does seem neglectful." Yet she had something belonging to Mrs. Hollister—the fabric she had bartered to quilt for her in exchange for Tempe's dame school. Mrs. Hollister must be holding Tempe's sampler until the fabric was returned. She'd not had an opportunity to quilt it yet. Honour's brow pinched. Joshua had resolved her debt to the teacher, it was he she owed.

"What is it, Honour?" Mrs. Wadsworth asked.

"I have much to attend to. I remembered I have a piece of fabric to return to Mrs. Hollister. Mayhap it is the reason she is holding Tempe's sampler."

"It is unkind of her to do so," Widow Lankton said. "Your sister is just a little girl. How old is Temperance?"

"She is eight. Though she is a very grown-up eight-year-old, as she has endured much in her young life." Honour winced, straining to sit erect.

"Do be careful and stay reclined, you mustn't pull the stitches," Mrs. Wadsworth said. "Is there something I may help you with?"

"No, thank you. It is still painful to move, but I am all right," Honour said.

Widow Lankton accepted the tea her servant girl had poured. "Chamomile," she said. "Would you care for some, Honour? It should have a calming effect."

"Yes, please." The young maidservant whisked to Honour's bedside with a cup and walked away with the breakfast tray, most of which she'd managed to consume.

The ladies sat quietly while Honour reposed upon the feather tick. Mrs. Wadsworth and Widow Lankton passed secretive glances before turning their attention toward Honour. "Honour, dear, we've a matter of importance to discuss. It concerns you and Tempe."

"Aye, Widow Lankton mentioned there was something to discuss." Honour offered a meek smile hoping for no more unpleasantness to come her way. But the words which came next were far worse than Honour could ever have imagined.

Joshua stood in the windowed alcove at the top of the grand staircase, waiting to be announced. Widow Lankton had instructed the housekeeper to bring him up when he arrived. They'd not told Honour, wishing to surprise her with his visit. He hoped she wouldn't mind. Did she desire to see him as much as he longed to see her?

Joshua's hearing quickened as Mrs. Wadsworth spoke, and the pit of his stomach tightened with alarm. "Regretfully, Honour, I am no longer am in need of your quilting services." He groaned inwardly. How could this be?

Joshua paced a few steps, working his way closer to the bedchamber door where the housekeeper waited to announce his arrival. Finally, the woman tapped on the door. "Mr. Joshua Sutton has arrived, Mistress."

The women's words tumbled over one another in protest. It appeared he had arrived at precisely the wrong moment, but his mind raced ahead, eager to learn about this untoward turn of events. Honour's familiar voice rose above the colloquy, "Nay. Please allow him in. I wish him near me to receive this news."

As Joshua entered the room, his earnest gaze beheld her at once. Bolstered against a carved headboard upon a layer of embroidered pillows, Honour appeared as a precious stone in its glorious setting. Her face yet wan, her eyes glistened with moisture. He swallowed past the lump in his throat. He'd not seen her since he carried her into the Lankton home the last day he'd been here, and now it took all within him to keep from rushing to her side. But just speaking her name brought him great relief.

"Honour."

"Oh, Joshua."

She extended her slender arm toward him and he accepted her hand. He bent down on his knee at her bedside. Covering her hand with his, he drew her palm to his chest. When he released his grasp, their eyes remained locked.

He blinked back. "You look . . . well."

"Thank you. I am feeling better, yet I have received some distressing news."

He heard a woman cough and spun his head around toward the ladies sitting by the fireplace. Joshua stood abruptly and gave them a slight bow. "Widow Lankton. Mistress Wadsworth. Thank you for allowing me to see Honour." His face tensed. "Yet, what is this news she speaks of?"

"We are pleased you have come this forenoon," Widow Lankton said. "Mrs. Wadsworth was beginning to share some advantageous news with Honour."

"I cannot see how the news is advantageous," Honour said.

"My dear, please allow me to explain the situation," Mrs. Wadsworth said. "Unless you would prefer we do it privately."

Joshua looked down at Honour. "I will step out of the room."

"Nay, please, stay. It would hearten me to have you here," Honour said.

Joshua tilted his head, reassuring her with a smile. "Whatever you wish. Now let's hear what Mrs. Wadsworth has to say."

"Would you care for some chamomile, Joshua?" Widow Lankton asked.

"No. Thank you."

"A seat then?" The widow pointed to a chair by the window.

Reluctant to leave Honour's side, Joshua knew the ladies already extended him a grace when he greeted her in such close proximity. How awkward it was that Emily's aunt was aware of his fondness for Honour, and yet encouraged it. He could only imagine Mrs. Wadsworth had filled her in on the bond between Joshua and Honour, especially since he'd gone chasing after her, at Emily's urging, the day Honour had reopened her wound. He planted himself down and nodded at Mrs. Wadsworth to proceed.

"I informed Honour that I no longer can keep her in my employ." Mrs. Wadsworth's brow furrowed, then donned a sympathetic smile when facing Honour. "I planned to discuss it with you some time ago, but there have been many obstacles to doing so. Yet I do have another prospect to introduce."

"My injuries—I haven't been able to satisfy my workload. I am so sorry to have disappointed you." Honour frowned, wetting her lower lip.

"It is not your fault, Honour. Nor, do I feel dissatisfied with you." Mrs. Wadsworth folded her hands in her lap. "You are an exceptional quilter and perhaps the hardest worker I've known."

"The traveling ensemble you quilted for me is exquisite," Widow Lankton chimed in. "I do not believe I have had the opportunity to tell you or to thank you."

"I appreciate your saying so." Honour smiled politely, though masking concern.

Mrs. Wadsworth leaned forward. "Dear, you must know it is purely a decision of finances."

"I, I'm sure we shall get by." Honour reached for her glorious braid draped over her shoulder, absently gliding her other hand along the length of it.

"Honour, you are not considering selling your hair to the wigmaker? I will not allow it."

The women's faces all darted toward Joshua. Widow Lankton's eyebrows vaulted until the wrinkles on her forehead met the hairline of her own wig. Mrs. Wadsworth tucked her chin, pursing her lips. Honour covered her mouth, astonished at his declaration, though he could not readily distinguish whether she was angry or amused.

"Joshua Sutton, if I wish to sell my hair, I shall. But as it is, I hear the wigmaker is no longer in the market for auburn hair. 'Tis too difficult to powder." Honour glanced up, bedstead canopy overhead, finger pressed to her lips. "Mayhap I shall sell Temperance's hair instead."

Joshua almost jumped to his feet. He narrowed his eyes. "Pray, don't!"

"Nay, Joshua. I shan't, although I noticed your queue is in need of a barber," Honour teased. She altered her position, and a small groan seeped from her mouth.

Joshua leaned forward, "Honour, are you all right?"

"I shall be, if you remember your place." She spoke, seemingly bemused. "I am not your—"

Joshua leaned back and crossed his arms over his waistcoat, as his coat fell to his sides. He cast her an exaggerated sidelong glance, restraining his mirth in the process. "Your?" *Betrothed? Wife?*

"I am not your property," Honour said. "I shall not be told what to do by you."

"May I make a suggestion then?" Joshua asked.

Mrs. Wadsworth and Widow Lankton looked on, entertained by the banter.

Honour's countenance piqued. "What may that be?"

"I recall Mrs. Wadsworth has something 'advantageous' to share with you." Joshua smirked, dipping his jaw. "Shall we?"

"By all means." Honour addressed Mrs. Wadsworth. "Now if Mr. Sutton is through teasing me in an attempt to recover from his *faux pas*, please continue."

Joshua proffered his palm, inclining a bow. "Do forgive me, all."

"Certainly, Joshua." Mrs. Wadsworth smiled. "At least you managed to lighten the mood, for a moment."

"I am glad to have done you the service, at my expense, of course." Joshua said with a grin. "Though I did not wish to make light of Honour's circumstance." He had hoped to prove his sincerest admiration for her, had he now offended her? He secreted a glance in her direction, noting her pensive stare as she rubbed her braid between her fingers. How frightened she must be at the uncertainty of her circumstances, though she had deflected it by paying tribute to his "*faux pas*" and bore it well.

"Now, Honour, Widow Lankton and I have something for your consideration, and hope you'll be pleased." Mrs. Wadsworth's inflection held promise.

Joshua slipped another look at Honour, and gave her a slight grin with the faintest wink of his eye—garnering quite the satisfying reaction as a smile flickered upon her flushed cheeks.

"You see, Honour," Mrs. Wadsworth continued, "it appears Widow Lankton is in need of a companion now that her niece, Emily, has married."

The irony of it took him aback. How would Honour feel?

Mrs. Wadsworth turned to Widow Lankton and nodded. The older woman continued. "I would like to offer you employment and hope you shall accept it. You have already been keeping me company these last days, and I have found it quite suitable. I understand you are from a fine family in England and you come highly recommended." Widow Lankton smiled at her friend.

"I mean not to be contrary, madam, but I believe you have been the one serving as *my* companion these last days, including seeing to my well-being."

"I am confident you will continue on the course to good health and I believe it will be an excellent match." Widow Lankton glanced at the needlework sitting in her lap. "I also find I am once again in need of a quilter and would like to employ you for the task. I intend to gift my niece with a bridal quilt."

The starch in Joshua's neckcloth stiffened. A quilt for the woeful Mrs. Leach. Apparently, Widow Lankton was not privy to her niece's despair, or was trying to encourage the new bride in any course.

"'Twould be a most fortuitous arrangement, don't you agree?" Mrs. Wadsworth asked Honour.

"I am in need of a quilter and companionship and you are in need of employment and a home," Widow Lankton said in her matter-of-fact tone.

"A home," Honour said, her words barely audible.

"Naturally, I would expect you to keep your residence here," the dame said.

Honour absently squeezed the counterpane. "I do not know if I am able to accept your offer, Widow Lankton, generous as it is."

Joshua noted the worry etched on Honour's brow, and it almost undid him. Though no one had yet spoken of it, the question hung in the air. *What would become of Temperance?*

16

Joshua waited impatiently for one of the ladies to speak. Hadn't it occurred to them that Honour could not accept a position until the matter of lodging was settled for both her and Temperance?

"You are not sure if you can accept employment from me? Why ever not, dear?" Widow Lankton asked.

Honour lifted her eyes, her worried gaze traveling from Widow Lankton to Mrs. Wadsworth to him. When he noted the light of understanding upon Window Lankton's placid face, Joshua tipped his jaw toward her, encouraging Honour to regard the woman again. It warmed him to think Honour looked to him for reassurance.

Widow Lankton waved her palm. "Oh my, your sister. I should have made a point of mentioning her from the outset. I certainly cannot separate the two of you. Margaret has explained it would be quite impossible as you are her guardian. Temperance shall also have a room here, as part of your compensation. I've plenty of space and it would be delightful to have a child in this home once again." Widow Lankton pointed to the door at the side of the room. "There is an adjoining room right through that door."

Mrs. Wadsworth clasped her hands together, creating a minute clapping sound. "Temperance is welcome to continue her chores for me a few days a week after school. I can afford a few pennies per week and she might like to earn a little something of her own." Mrs. Wadsworth said. "I'd like to keep my eye on her for a while. If she shows aptitude, mayhap I can take her on as an apprentice in a few years when Maisey's contract has been satisfied, providing there is improvement in our economy. Moreover, I shall miss Tempe, as I will you."

"Now what say you, will you agree to the proposition?" Widow Lankton asked.

Honour's face brightened, her dark brown eyes filling with relief. "Aye, I shall. I appreciate your generous offer, Widow Lankton. And yours, Mrs. Wadsworth. You have both blessed me with your kindness." Honour released a deep sigh, pulling her arms over her injury.

"Dear, you must be fatigued, and perhaps it is time for something for the pain, no?" Mrs. Wadsworth eyed Widow Lankton.

The widow glanced at a small clock on a shelf, "My housekeeper, Mrs. Hall, shall be here ere long to administer her next treatment."

Mrs. Wadsworth stood. "I must take my leave and return to the shop. I will remind your housekeeper on my way out." She went to Honour's bedside and planted a kiss on Honour's forehead. "I shall bring Tempe next time I come. You get your rest now, dear." She gave Joshua a quick glance. "Be sure this young man doesn't tire you."

"Oh, he shall never tire me, Mrs. Wadsworth." Honour grinned. "He is consistently piquing my interest."

Mrs. Wadsworth laid her hand on Joshua's sleeve as she passed to the door, with a hint of warning in her eye.

After she departed, Widow Lankton said, "You may have a few minutes with her, Joshua, and then you must allow her to get her rest. If you please, Honour."

"Aye, thank you," Honour said.

Joshua picked up his chair and brought it to the side of Honour's bed. He leaned forward, his elbows resting on his knees, gazing into Honour's serene face. Neither spoke as several moments passed. His thoughts returned to the time beneath the willow tree when he took her into his embrace. Was she thinking the same?

A faint snore came from behind them and Joshua turned back for an instant, finding Widow Lankton had drifted asleep in her chair. "Does she often do that?" he said to Honour in a hushed voice.

"'Tis a habit of hers," Honour whispered, trying to restrain her mirth.

"It appears everything has worked out well," Joshua said.

"Indeed, it has. I can scarcely believe it," Honour said. "Yet, how odd I shall work on Emily's bridal quilt, after all that has transpired."

"I was not aware you were acquainted with her until the other day," Joshua said.

"Aye, and only briefly, leaving me with the terrible secret which proved to be untrue." She clasped her hands beneath her chin. "Thank you for helping me see the truth, Joshua."

"You needn't thank me for that. 'Twas purely selfish." Joshua chuckled softly.

Honour smiled demurely. "I appreciate your visit today, although I'm sure it was not what you expected."

"I only expected to catch a glimpse of your lovely face, and this . . ." Joshua took her braid in his hand and rubbed his thumb over the silky plait. He breathed in the faint scent of lavender at their nearness. He traced his finger along her hairline. "It does my heart good to know you are well."

She closed her eyelids, but for a moment, then looked again into his eyes. A little sigh escaped her lips—lips he desired to kiss again.

"Before I depart, tell me, Honour, is there anything I can do for you? Anything at all."

Honour's eyes widened. "There is. Would you retrieve my workbag? 'Tis hanging in the cupboard." She pointed across the room.

Joshua rose, retrieved the bag and handed it to her. Honour lifted the lid and pulled out a small piece of paper, handing it to him.

"I intended to see to this matter on Monday, but here it is three days gone by. Would you please inquire about this for me, before it is too late?" Honour asked.

Joshua unfolded the fragment of newspaper marked with tiny black print. An advertisement.

Joshua looked up as Honour spoke again. "I believe these are my belongings, especially my quilt. I fear someone else may claim it and 'twill be lost to me forever." Her eyes darkened with anxiety. "It means the world to me—more than that, it is filled with my mother's hopes and dreams for my future, as well as my own." He squeezed her hand as she went on. "I do not know the expense, but I have some money and you may take it. Inside the top compartment there."

"The expense is insignificant, Honour. You may entrust it to me, by your leave, and we shall figure it out later," he said.

Her eyes entreated his and he looked down at the paper, holding them between his thumbs and forefingers. "*Linen white-work*, he read aloud. He looked up. "Your quilt?"

"Aye." She bit her lip.

As he continued to read the advertisement, his grip tightened. *Inquire of the Printer, Mein & Fleeming.* His pulse jumped. Joshua raked his hand back through his hair and squeezed his queue. *John Mein, that enemy of Patriots and publisher of falsehoods.*

"Joshua?" Honour rasped.

His heart plummeted and his palms grew moist as he looked into her eyes with as much earnestness as he could muster. "Honour, I would do anything for you—except this."

⁃⁃⁃

Tears filled Honour's eyes once again as she tossed her head back against the pillows. She could still hardly believe Joshua had refused her request when she told to him how important it was to her. He attempted to explain, but Mrs. Hall had come to treat Honour's wound and whisked Joshua out of the bedchamber. Honour managed to eat a small portion for the midday meal, but after a dose of laudanum the remainder of the day was spent dozing.

A new day had dawned, and Honour had already received morning ministrations. The questions Honour had about Joshua's refusal assaulted her once again. Did he oppose paying the duties? Of course, he did, but couldn't he make an exception this once? Or would it have hurt him to make the inquiry? At least she would have had the peace of mind of knowing if her belongings were still available, or if another had claimed them.

Honour could feel the tension in her brow and her temples began to throb. The items might have been put up for auction by now, as the advertisement did not indicate a date. She hadn't the time to wait, too many days had passed already.

Honour sat with care and brought her legs over the side of the bed. She rested there a moment, as the housekeeper had instructed her to do when necessity called. She grabbed the bedpost and pulled herself up, her legs wobbly beneath her. Honour released a shallow breath. She glanced down at her attire, such a state of undress in her short gown of calico, and plain petticoat rising just above her ankles. If only she had one of her better gowns or even the one she'd worn here, though that had been stained. How nice it would be to have her gowns from England returned to her.

Honour braced her steps and stared down at her bare feet upon the cool, painted canvas floor covering. How would she ever manage to put on her silk stockings or buckle her shoes? She looked about the room, not knowing where Mrs. Hall had put them. Perhaps they were in the cupboard. As Honour took a step, the tautness in her abdomen made her realize how silly she was. She could never bend to perform those tasks. If she pulled open her wound again, it would surely become infected. No infection had yet set in, but the housekeeper warned her that if it did, her herbal remedies would not be enough and Dr. Westcott would have to return and let Honour's blood. She already was so weakened from her successive blood losses, Honour did not know how she'd endure it.

Honour closed her eyes for an instant and let out a sigh. A wave of dizziness swirled around her. She opened her eyes, trying to regain her bearings, and she started to sway. Honour reached for the bedpost, but it was just beyond her grasp. One more step and she'd be there. She leaned her hand upon the small bedside table, but the weight of her pushing on the corner made it topple. Honour tripped back and fell against the bedstead, clutching the crewelwork counterpane as she slipped down to the floor.

Widow Lankton's maidservant and housekeeper came rushing in. "Good heavens! She fell from her bed. Grab her other arm and we shall get her up. Careful now," Honour heard the older woman say.

The haze dissipated and Honour focused on Mrs. Hall as she inspected Honour's incision. "Get some lint, girl, and herbs for a poultice. I shall have to repack the wound," the housekeeper instructed.

"You fell out of bed, Miss Metcalf," the woman said. "I cannot venture a guess as to how that happened, nor do I wish to." She halted her hand mid-air. "I suggest whatever happened, the episode is not repeated."

Honour clamped down on her lip and looked down. This counterpane was not her own. Nor did she enjoy the comfort of her indigo quilt. And now, she would never have the linen white-work quilt she and her mother had started for Honour's dower hope chest. The risk was too great to her health. But without it, her longings seemed ceaseless, her grief unending.

⚬⚬⚬

Joshua snipped around the pattern of his father's new suit with precise movements. Several weights lay atop the dark green gabardine, holding the pattern firmly in place. The design had been determined, the fabric chosen. The form was fitted, the pattern laid, the first cuts taken—and in a similar manner it resembled his life. The dictates of his family's values impacted every decision he made, and those made on his behalf. And like the pattern weights upon the cloth, the heaviness of his situation bore down on him, constant, unmoving.

The sound of the steel blades sliding together as his large shears cut into the fabric echoed the torment slicing through his conscience. He'd lay his life down for Honour, but could not bring himself to do the one thing she had ever asked of him.

The hurt he'd seen on her face ripped at his heart, still aching over bringing her such disappointment. When she had explained how important it was to her to reclaim her belongings captured by the pirates and now so miraculously reappeared, she held such hope in her eyes. Hope he dashed in an instant when he refused to do her bargaining.

Joshua groaned as the top blade of his shears slipped between the pattern and the fabric. He caught the misstep before he made a costly mistake, just as he did when he denied Honour her request. But he could not risk putting the reputation of his family's business in jeopardy.

How could he subject himself to John Mein at *The Chronicle* when the man so adamantly aggrieved those who supported the Non-Taxation Agreement? An encounter with the newspaper publisher might draw attention to the Suttons, making them a target of Mein's insatiable hunger for discrediting the integrity of Patriot merchants, as he had John Hancock and others. As much as he cared for Honour, he had to protect his family and affirm the values he held firmly to for the betterment of his country.

Joshua exhaled. What about what was important to Honour? She had lost so much—her family, her belongings. It struck him that her determination was not only to reclaim her stolen property but what it represented—her past and her future.

Perhaps an inquiry would not hurt. John Mein would not know Joshua was a Sutton, unless Joshua had to sign for something. And if Joshua did, would there be duties to pay on the cargo? He could no more do so than he could deny that he was a Son of Liberty.

Where was his head! There was no boycott on personal property being transported from England to America. Honour's belongings were not imported to be sold. With no restriction, she had every right to redeem her possessions.

Joshua set his shears down on the worktable, having completed cutting the pieces for the coat. He called over one of the young apprentices. "Take care and put these things away. I have another task to see to."

17

Joshua drove past Hayward Square in his father's coach, nearly missing a loose cow that apparently had been grazing on the common. He came to a stop on Newbury Street in front of the building belonging to Mein & Fleeming. Mayhap he shouldn't have taken the carriage. He did not need to draw unnecessary attention to his presence. 'Twas no crime, but to himself. He was growing to resent John Mein for his hostility toward the Whigs. *Lord, please allow me to keep my peace this day and claim Honour's property, especially her quilt.* Seeming more prudent, he steered the horses across the street to The White Horse Tavern and pulled to a stop. He got down and handed a lad a coin to watch the conveyance until he returned.

Joshua crossed the street and the cry of a newsboy rang in the air. "James Otis beaten at the British Coffee House." He signaled the boy who promptly trotted up to Joshua, "Thursday's edition of *The Boston Chronicle*. Eight pence, sir."

Joshua handed the boy a shilling and accepted the large sheets of newsprint. No doubt, Mein had printed more fallacies of merchants who he claimed were not heeding the merchant's agreement to boycott the Townshend Acts. While both *The*

Boston Chronicle and *The Boston Gazette* both published ship manifests, as even Patriots wished to oust those non-complying with the Non-Importation agreement, at least *The Gazette* did not misrepresent the facts. Joshua scanned the front page of the biweekly newspaper. Now James Otis, who often hailed "taxation without representation is tyranny" was beaten over the head with a cane by the customs official. Otis had retaliated, albeit viciously, in an article he posted in *The Gazette,* defending himself from the slander of the king's customs commissioner who had called him a "malignant incendiary." Political tensions continued to rise. How long would it be until a true war arose between the colonies and the king?

Joshua tucked the newspaper under his arm. He'd peruse the rest of the paper later. Surely Father and Andrew would be interested in reading it as well. He despised putting coin into Mein's pocket, but it served well to stay informed and aware of Mein's slant on matters.

Through the large pedimented door Joshua went, and into the devil's lair. The sound of the printing press from a back room and the smell of ink and sweat permeated the building of Mein & Fleeming, the pair of Scotsmen not only published the newspaper, but also printed and bound books. Tall shelves were lined with books to be sold, with an area set apart for a lending library, the only one in town. Joshua approached the counter where a well-dressed, bewigged man engaged in conversation with another man clad in an ink-soiled leather apron, sleeves rolled back to his elbows. Joshua turned around and leaned against the counter. Mayhap he should leave now.

"How may I help you?" a voice asked in a Scottish brogue.

Joshua turned around facing the better-dressed man. "I came to inquire of the printer."

"John Mein, at your service. G'day to ye."

"Good day. I am here to inquire about an advertisement. To learn if these items have yet been claimed." Joshua handed the man the slip of paper Honour had given him.

"My clerk has gone on an errand, but I will see what I can find out for ye." Mr. Mein went to the end of the counter and looked at the ledger.

Joshua followed Mein and faced him on the opposite side of the counter. The man flipped through the pages of the large ledger and trailed his finger down each page. Mein came to a stop and released a small grunt.

"Do you have the items?"

The publisher looked up. "Nay, they would not be here, you'd find them at the Customs House. Yet, my report is they have already been claimed." Mein's eyebrows rose. "A pirate's prize, I see. Someone was fortunate to discover their goods."

But it was not Honour. "Do you know if they were sold at auction or claimed beforehand?"

"Auction? Nay, the matter was resolved shortly after the advertisement was published."

The feeling in Joshua's stomach soured. Honour never had a chance. Moreover, someone else now owned her possessions. How would he ever tell her?

Mein's eye's narrowed. "Say, are you not one of the Sutton lads?"

Joshua groaned inwardly. How could he know that? "I am. Joshua Sutton."

Mein donned a sly grin, and rubbed his jaw. "A brother, Andrew?"

Joshua exhaled. "Yes." *What had Andrew done now?*

"A Sutton, of Sutton's Clothiers. One of the merchants against the Townshend Acts. Or so I understood." The Scotsman eyed the newspaper under Joshua's arm. "I see you've a copy of *The Boston Chronicle*. Have you read it?"

"I read your article about James Otis."

"'Tis a shame about the man, yet he invited attack, ye know." Mein drummed his hand on the counter. "As did your brother."

"I know no such thing." Joshua clenched his jaw. He'd better hold his temper if he wanted to learn what Mein insinuated about his family business, though he had the feeling it would give Mein great pleasure in the telling. "What do you say of my brother?"

John Mein took a newspaper from a stack of them displayed upon the counter. He opened the pages and laid the large sheet down facing Joshua. Mein's finger landed on an advertisement with a thud.

Publick Vendue, Gray's Wharf:

DISCOUNTED FABRICS received last fall
Fine English Broad Cloths, Velvets, Brocades,
Milled Cassimere, Assorted Irish Linen,
French Marseilles
9 September – 8 o'clock a.m.

Joshua glared into Mr. Mein's icy blue eyes. "How does this concern me?"

"Your own dear brother placed the advertisement." A slow smile emerged on Mein's face. "Does my heart good to see a young man so enterprising, indeed."

"I do not believe you," Joshua said.

"Fie! Would a newspaperman tell falsehoods?"

Joshua fumed as he withheld his retort.

"Ye brother's own mark is here in my ledger." Mein turned a few pages. "Ah, here. See for yourself, lad."

Joshua reluctantly looked at the page. *Andrew Sutton.*

"Ye and your brother have much in common besides your similar looks. Ye were willing to pay for the duties on the English imports you inquired about." Mein held up the cutout of the advertisement Joshua had brought in.

"I sought not for myself. 'Twas on behalf of another, an English immigrant."

"Ah, you *do* support English imports." Mr. Mein sauntered away, laughing. The stench of his twisted humor and accusations saturated the stagnant air, leaving behind its inky threat.

<hr />

A blanket of pristine white enveloped the sky above a meadow enameled with the beautiful shades of graceful summer blooms. 'Twas mother's garden, Honour thought, as she lay upon the feathered bed in the center of the fragrant field. The canopy of white in the heavens above, her quilted counterpane teasing her with the comfort of its blessed covering. A gentle wind whirled around her, increasing in strength. The blossoms tore from their stems into a torrent of flower petals to swiftly disappear. A heaviness kept her from rising, so she held forth her arms, striving to capture the quilted blanket of white, though it remained far beyond her reach. Her arms grew weary until arms stronger took hers in His divine, yet unseen, grasp. Then the downy white feathers from her bed caught up in a gentle breeze and floated down upon her, covering her like a bridal quilt of love. A familiar voice whispered in her ear, *Beloved, you are mine, as are your dreams and longings. You are not alone and never shall be. Trust me.*

Honour awoke from her nap to a strong wind sweeping through the low opening of her window. Rain pelted against the window, but she was safe inside. Her gaze drifted to the foot of her bed where a white counterpane rested atop a wooden chest. Her breathing became rapid with anticipation as she beheld the familiar fabric too far from her to reach.

The maidservant scurried into the bedchamber and pulled the window down against the sill. Honour startled at the sound.

"Are you all right, miss?" the girl asked.

"I am," Honour said. "Though would you please hand me that quilt?"

The girl walked over to the trunk, "'Tisn't a quilt yet, Miss Metcalf, but it looks like the process has begun."

The maidservant brought the folded white cloth to Honour and laid it upon her lap, its heaviness instantly warming her. "I thank you. Could you tell me how this was brought here?" Joshua must have redeemed her white-work quilt for her.

"I cannot say. I truly do not know." The girl hurried from the room.

Honour gently slid her hand over the white linen cloth as if it were a thin sheet of glass. She traced the pomegranate and the fern, scarcely believing that the pattern she beheld was real and not a mere fabrication from her memory. The familiar feel of the fabric beneath her fingertips sent warmth all the way to the core of her being. It exuded home and her mother's love. And promise of love to come.

Honour blinked back tears when the tap on the door announced Widow Lankton, behind her Emily Leach.

"Are you up for a short visit, Honour? My niece has come to discuss her bridal quilt." The ladies came to Honour's bedside and gazed down at the white linen. "It is lovely, is it not?" Widow Lankton said.

Honour looked up. "Aye, it is. Do you know who brought it?"

"Emily brought it with her," Widow Lankton said. "I had my housekeeper bring it up while we had our midday meal.

She found you sleeping so she left it in the room, and here we see you have found it."

"Oh, yes, and I am quite pleased." Honour smiled in relief.

"I am glad to hear it," said the widow.

"Now, I shall leave you two to get acquainted, or reacquainted, and you may discuss Emily's quilt." Widow Lankton left the bedchamber, pausing with a smile as she passed the silhouette of her husband.

"Do you think it holds promise?" Emily asked.

Honour rested her hand upon the folds of the white fabric. "Promise?"

"Yes. My husband obtained this fine piece partially quilted. When I told Aunt Eunice about it she offered to have you complete it for my bridal quilt."

A burning sensation shot through Honour's veins. Her chest tightened and she felt as though she could barely breathe.

"Honour? I can return later if you are not up for my visit," Emily said.

"Please stay." Honour found her resolve. "How did your husband come by it?"

"I do not know exactly. Something about the Customs House. Good fortune, really."

'Twas not for Honour. Her mind was paralyzed with shock. Her own whole-cloth bridal quilt at last in her arms, unfinished, like her grieving. Yet belonging to her no longer.

"It will make a fine bridal quilt," Honour said. "A finer one I have never seen."

Emily's face was devoid of the joy Honour imagined a new bride would have, but they both knew her secret—Emily's marriage was devoid of love. Her heart belonged to another. "Aunt Eunice is trying to encourage me to make the best of my situation."

"How difficult for you, Emily. Joshua explained everything, as you know." The hollow look in Emily's pretty eyes almost made Honour think she would have given her the quilt, if only it would cheer Emily. This thought took Honour aback. Honour might never have the love she wanted. Joshua had rejected her and denied the most fervent request she had ever spoken to another. Honour looked down at the quilt again. She drew back a fold revealing a partially quilted serpentine heart. Mayhap this quilt had another purpose, to restore joy to a broken heart. Yet it would not be her own.

Joshua left the office of Mein & Fleeming in great haste. He tramped across the street to The White Horse Tavern as a gust of wind whisked around him. He looked about, not seeing his father's coach. The lad he'd paid to watch it sat on the stoop of the entrance. Joshua went to the boy and pulled the lad to his feet. "Did someone move my carriage? Tell me where it is."

"Sir, you already took it." The boy's face grew pale, his eyes wide with fear. "My dear life, a man drove it away. I thought he was you!" The boy spun around, pounding his fists against his temples as raindrops fell from the sky.

Joshua moaned. Andrew! He grabbed the poor boy by his shoulders. "Stop, lad. It is no fault of your own."

The boy looked up, his mouth hanging open. "It isn't? It was a mistake, I tell you. I am sorry, I am."

"I fear my brother was playing a trick on me." Joshua rolled the newspaper and tucked it inside his frock coat.

"Your brother, you say? He came out from the tavern and I thought it was you . . . though I never saw you go in. There is a side door," the lad said.

"Do not fear. My brother has fooled me on more than one occasion." Joshua brushed the drops of rain from his face.

"You'll not call the sheriff? Or the British officers?" asked the boy, as his coat grew darker from the rain.

"Nay. But I may get the gallows after I wring my brother's neck." Joshua grinned at the boy, hoping he didn't scare the lad into thinking it was Joshua's real intent. "Take care, lad. Get out of the rain now."

"Thank you, sir." The boy ran to his stoop in the shelter of the tavern doorway.

Joshua arrived at the sign of the scissors, after his long walk back to Sutton's Clothiers through intermittent wind and rain-fall. The torrent was brief, and the sun fought its way through the darkened clouds. Joshua hoped he could talk sense into Andrew before Father figured out what was going on, yet he had no way of knowing where his brother might have gone. Joshua slid his hand back over his wet hair, pulling it from its queue, and shook the excess water from his hand.

Andrew came around the corner, nearly plowing into Joshua. "Brother! A good day for a walk, I hear."

"A walk, indeed! In a hurricane, no less!" Joshua grabbed Andrew by the arm and escorted him around the rear of the building.

"Easy, brother! It wasn't as bad as all that. It was only a rainstorm."

Joshua glared at Andrew as he brushed his sodden shoulders.

"'Twas only a joke." Andrew smirked.

Joshua reciprocated the smirk. "The joke is on you. I have learned your secret."

Andrew placed his hand over his heart. "You know my secret. My broken heart."

"'Tis Father's heart will be broken if he discovers what you have done—what you are about to do, this Saturday." Joshua pulled the newspaper from his coat.

Andrew looked around, and hushed Joshua through clench teeth. "Not so loud. How do you know about that?"

Joshua hiked his chin. "I had business at *The Boston Chronicle*. John Mein was more than happy to share the news of your vendue with me when he learned I was a Sutton."

Andrew heaved a deep breath, and the smell of rum hung in the damp air. "I regretted it after I placed the advertisement. I went back, but Mein said he wouldn't retract it."

Joshua smacked the rolled-up newspaper in the palm of his hand. "So what now? You are still planning to hold a public vendue. Those cloths you are planning to auction are the textiles damaged when the warehouse flooded. I thought you gave them out to the poor, but instead you have hidden them and intend to sell them for profit."

Andrew paced around, dragging his fingers through his hair, squeezing the top of it. He halted and pounded the back of his wrist against his forehead, before looking at Joshua with his eyes filled with panic. "Joshua, you cannot tell Father."

"You cannot tell Father what?"

The brothers spun around. Father stood, arms crossing his chest, awaiting an answer.

Joshua looked at Andrew, and released a shallow breath through his nostrils, his mouth clamped tight.

"Father," Andrew spoke up, "it appears I got myself into some mischief today."

"Why does that not surprise me?" Father's stern gaze volleyed from Andrew to Joshua.

"My brother, the trickster, drove the carriage home from my errand today. The only problem was he hadn't gone there with me, and left me to walk home." Joshua cast a fake blow to Andrew's shoulder.

"In the rain?" Father surveyed Joshua's soggy attire. "I would laugh, sons, but I fail to find it humorous." Father shook his head. "Though I do hope it means you have resolved your differences."

"Yes, sir." Andrew lowered his gaze, glancing at Joshua.

"You are no longer boys, so I cannot punish you. But, Andrew, I can keep you from using my coach for the next month. And Joshua, you'd better get out of those wet clothes before you catch your death."

"Yes, sir," Andrew said again.

Joshua nodded and lowered his head, pitching a stealthy glower Andrew's way.

Father glanced around Joshua's back. "What have you there? A newspaper?"

Joshua brought his arm around and held the rolled-up paper by his side. "Yes, it is."

"If you are done with it, I would like to read the news." Father held out his hand.

Joshua reluctantly handed the newspaper to his father. "Mein is at it again."

18

Honour read from Psalm 91 in the small Bible. *He shall cover thee with His feathers, and under His wings shalt thou trust: His truth shall be thy shield and buckler.* The verse reminded her of her dream, so real the vivid memory of it stayed with her. She read the words again, and a truth unfolded. Honour had so longed for the return of her quilt top she'd neglected to see what she had right in front of her. Already in her possession was the indigo bed quilt her mother had made, like the love of her parents that would never leave her. More so, the love and watchcare of her Heavenly Father. The white-work quilt represented all her longings, past and present. She must entrust them to His care. Further, His truth must guide her to receive His protection.

Honour placed the Bible down on the bedside table. She picked up the piece of paper which she had marked with a pencil, the tiny dots indicating part of the design that she would use as a stencil for the bridal quilt. She retrieved a large needle from her workbag, which she now kept by the bedstead. She began the process of poking a small hole through each of the markings. She had copied the partially complete designs she and her mother quilted into the fabric. They had transferred the markings onto the linen by patting ground cinnamon through the holes of their stencil. Yet now those markings were so faded that Honour could no longer make them out.

When Honour finished she took another piece of paper from the table. Though this paper was blank, a clear shape appeared in her mind's eye. She sketched her design with a rounded feather sequence. She repeated the process of marking and piercing the holes through the stencil, all the while thinking of Joshua. Although he had disappointed her, her heart still ached for his love. She would relinquish it, if she must, along with her other hopes and dreams.

From her bed, Honour held the paper up to the window light to make sure she had not missed puncturing any of the tiny dots. Light filtered through the holes, illuminating the shape of a heart which she would incorporate into the design of the quilt. Aye, a new pattern had emerged—for the quilt, and also for her life.

Honour set the paper down and bowed her head, drawing her folded hands to her face. *Lord, my heart belongs to you.*

An angelic voice called to her. "Honour!"

She looked up as Tempe and Mrs. Wadsworth entered the bedchamber. Honour clasped her hands under her chin with a joyous smile. "Tempe!"

Temperance, in a pretty yellow petticoat and flowered print short gown, hurried toward Honour. She leaned over her older sister, giving her a gentle embrace.

"Do be careful, Temperance, as your sister is not yet healed," Mrs. Wadsworth said.

Honour smiled at Mrs. Wadsworth. "This is the best medicine I could ever receive. Thank you for bringing her."

"We would have come yesterday, but for the terrible wind and rain." Tempe handed Honour a nosegay of white blooms. "Abby, Sarah, and I picked this for you, but now it is wilted."

"How beautiful, and it smells lovely." Honour breathed in the scent of the star-shaped waxy blooms. "Tuberose."

"Aye, and it looks like a bridal bouquet." Tempe issued Honour a sassy grin.

"I am no bride, sister," Honour said. "Though I am beginning to believe I am wed to this bedstead. But Widow Lankton's housekeeper promises me if I stay put, my recovery shall be hastened."

"You will be someday," Tempe said.

Honour eyes widened. "Recovered? I hope so."

"I meant a *bride* is what you shall be some day." Tempe twirled around. "And Joshua Sutton shall be your husband."

"Temperance. You must get those romantic notions out of your head." Honour narrowed her eyes. "I've no reason to think in that direction."

"Come, Temperance, sit over here," Mrs. Wadsworth instructed.

Tempe faced Mrs. Wadsworth. "May I first show Honour what I brought?"

"Yes, you may." Mrs. Wadsworth held out a square of embroidered fabric.

Tempe accepted it from Mrs. Wadsworth's hands and laid it in Honour's lap.

"What have we here?"

"My sampler! Mrs. Wadsworth had it returned to me."

Honour smiled at Mrs. Wadsworth. "Thank you for doing that." She inspected the sampler. "Tempe, you have done lovely work on this. Your stitchwork is very fine."

"Like your sister's," Mrs. Wadsworth added.

Honour acknowledged the compliment with a humble nod.

"My new tutor said I may complete it at school." Tempe pointed to the verse she had begun to embroider. "It is going to say, 'Love one another.'"

"Do you know what Jesus said about that, Tempe?" Honour asked.

Tempe tilted her chin.

"It is the greatest commandment of all. He said to love the Lord your God with all of your heart." Honour held up the heart-shaped pattern. "Go place this against the window."

Tempe took the pattern and placed it against the glass. She held it there, and looked back with a bright smile upon her face. "The heart is lit up like an illumination."

Honour smiled at her sister. "Aye, like God's love in our hearts."

The maidservant tapped on the door, smiling over at Tempe before she spoke. "Mrs. Hall has sent me for the girl. Some little cakes have finished baking. She thought Tempe might like to help prepare a tray of sweets for all to enjoy."

Tempe skipped toward Honour, handing the stencil back to her. "May I, please?"

Honour gave an approving nod. "Certainly, and do make haste! Though slowly on the stairs."

Tempe left the room with the maidservant. Mrs. Wadsworth inclined Honour with a slight tilt of her head. "Mrs. Hollister said she would have gladly returned the sampler had you returned her fabric. You had intended to do so, hadn't you?"

Did Mrs. Wadsworth doubt her? The mere thought of it pricked Honour's heart. "Most certainly, though I've had little opportunity."

"I know, dear, but you might have asked someone to return it on your behalf. You mustn't let pride get in your way when your character is at stake."

"I thought I could still do the quilting for Mrs. Hollister—although Joshua paid her—if only to restore her trust in me. Mayhap it would put the rumors concerning my dishonesty away. You know I would never keep something that did not belong to me. In fact, I have something which belongs to me, yet cannot keep."

"Whatever do you mean?" Mrs. Wadsworth asked.

Honour pointed to the folded linen quilt lying on the chest. "The quilt. 'Tis mine."

Mrs. Wadsworth went over to it, and smoothed her hand over the white cloth. She looked at Honour, question in her eyes. "Honour, is this your bridal quilt? How did you get it back? You must be so relieved. Did you get your other belongings?"

"Nay, this is all." Honour stiffened. "Emily Leach's husband obtained it from the Customs House. This is the piece that Widow Lankton employed me to quilt."

"You are certain?" Mrs. Wadsworth looked over at her astonished.

"I am. Look, the pomegranates and fronds I have described to you."

"You could be mistaken."

"The pattern has been etched in my mind. I could have drawn it on paper and shown you before the quilt was ever unfolded." Honour's brow furrowed. "There is a small M in the corner, beneath the pomegranate. Mum was fond of beginning her quilts with our family initial. She said the last stitch would be on my married initial one day, as it was to be my bridal quilt."

Mrs. Wadsworth located the M. "Oh, Honour."

Honour sighed.

"We must tell Widow Lankton. I am sure she will understand."

"I brought it to the Lord," Honour said. "The quilt is no longer mine."

⚬⚬⚬

Joshua shielded his eyes as he peered into Boston Harbor, littered with King George's ships. A boat of redcoats, British soldiers coming to shore from Castle William where many of the troops were garrisoned, rowed inland upon the choppy water this September morn. Their royal stench wafted over the ocean breeze like the low tide. Anxious seagulls shrieked as they flocked overhead, descending near a fishing sloop unloading its morning catch. Gray's Wharf, like the many other wharves encompassing the old town, bustled with activity.

Andrew leaned against his wagon, filled with textiles of various kinds: Marseilles cassimere, linens, brocades—all imports he intended to sell. 'Discounted' the advertisement had said, but lo, it would be no bargain to the Suttons if the Board of Customs or Body of Merchants became alerted to this morning's event. Hopefully, it would be over before any harm could befall them.

Joshua walked over to the wagon, and perused the cloths. Watermarks and mildew stained the rolls of fabrics, though there were enough undamaged portions that could be cut off and salvaged for use by thrifty folk. Father had instructed Andrew to dispose of the damaged textiles many weeks back, dispensing them to the poor, some who had no spinning wheel or loom of their own. With imports decreased by nearly half since the Non-Importation Agreement, textiles had become a precious commodity and many suffered for it. But in Andrew's reckless state of mind he'd ventured to sell the cloth discounted, knowing the poor would flock to the vendue like hungry gulls.

"I convinced myself the sale would do the poor a service, and give them the dignity of not having to accept charity." Andrew stared into the wagon. "I figured it would not hurt to put some coin in my pocket since Father expected no recompense for the damaged goods. It would merely compensate me for my time."

Joshua narrowed his eyes. "You've no need for coin in your pocket, Father pays you well. But the needy must choose whether to feed or clothe their children."

Andrew gripped the side of the wagon, and hung his head. He kicked a wheel, jarring the wagon. The horse harnessed to the conveyance sidestepped and threw his head up in protest. Andrew looked up at the horse. "Easy, boy!"

Joshua continued. "Nor did you count the cost. Let us hope our plan works, so if Father should hear about this escapade, at least we will have thwarted trouble."

The horse stirred some more. "Easy there," Andrew called. "He's not the most docile beast we have in the stable."

Joshua went to the restless animal, and stroked its shoulder uttering calm words.

Though it was not yet time for the auction to commence, a small crowd assembled. People of all classes, shown by their attire, meandered about, peering at the wagon trying to view the textiles piled within.

Tall, pointed red helmets caught Joshua's attention as a pair of British officers escorted one of the king's revenue commissioners toward them, followed by another man, and Sheriff Porter. Joshua elbowed Andrew and their eyes locked in alarm.

As the crew approached, Joshua recognized the customs officer. "Good day, Mr. Clowing." The British officers stood expressionless behind the portly man in his powdered wig.

Clowing held out Andrew's advertisement. It says here you intend to sell imported textiles at public vendue this morning.

Andrew stepped forward. "That is my intent."

"I have come with a writ to search your goods," Clowing said. "Have you bills of lading and receipts?"

Andrew handed him the papers, providing the evidence revenues on the merchandise had been paid. Joshua looked on, his heart thumping hard inside his chest. Joshua had gathered all the papers from Father's office before they had left, doubtful Andrew had planned to do so. Although Andrew was a fine tailor in his own right, his naivety in business affairs was evident by this scheme.

Clowing's assistant rummaged through the textiles, checking the fabric against the invoices. The crowd grew agitated during the search.

Joshua planted his hand on the wagon. "I assure you, all taxes have been paid on these goods. They have been in our warehouse since last year—before the Non-Taxation Agreement."

Sheriff Porter looked from Andrew to Joshua. "What causes you to sell them now?"

A voice shot out from the crowd like a cannon. "I'd like to know the same thing."

Joshua groaned under his breath. William Molineux. British-born merchant and Patriot, staunch organizer and agitator of the merchants against the king's revenues. "Are you not the sons of Jairus Sutton the clothier?" Joshua's jaw grew taut, he'd let Andrew own up to it.

"We are," Andrew said. "Our warehouse was flooded after the big hailstorm. We are here to disburse the damaged cloth to those in need."

"You mean, to sell the damaged goods," Molineux said.

Andrew's jaw pulsed. "This merchandise has been warehoused since the boycott, and is not a new import. 'Tis not breaking the agreement to get rid of it now."

Onlookers murmured, the numbers of those gathered there increased. All they needed now was a riot. Redcoats stood in the rear keeping watch.

"I doubt the Committee of Merchants would agree." Molineux loomed over Andrew.

"The agreement your father signed forbade the selling of British imports until the revenues are repealed, at least until the new year."

Father appeared, pushing his way through crowd. "I agreed to not sell my textiles imported from England. As far as I can tell nothing has been sold here today." Father glared at Andrew. "Am I correct?"

Sheriff Porter interjected. "The law states that you must comply with the intent of your advertisement on imports or you will be prosecuted at the Court of Admiralty."

Someone shouted from the crowd. "We came to purchase cloth!"

"Let's get on with it, I have work to do," another called out.

The assistant commissioner handed Clowing his report, glowering from Andrew to Joshua. "I know not what game you are playing." He shoved the paperwork into Father's hand.

"I assure you, there is nothing untoward here." Father eyed Andrew and Joshua.

Clowing turned to the sheriff with his statement. "All Sutton's Clothiers' invoices and bills of lading indicate no breech of commerce. They are dated 9 July 1768, before the Non-Taxation Agreement."

Molineux narrowed his eyes. "Yet they are British imports to be auctioned, are they not?"

Joshua released an exasperated breath. "Allow me to explain—"

"Who is responsible for this vendue?" Sheriff Porter asked.

Another loud voice, belonging to John Mein, publisher of *The Boston Chronicle*, came forth and pointed. "'Tis that one, Andrew Sutton."

Red-faced, Father turned to face the newspaperman. "There is no sale today."

The crowd grew louder, and the British soldiers moved in.

"Yet it was the intent. Ye son, Andrew, paid me to print the advertisement and I've his signature to prove it."

Father's lips tightened as he stared at Andrew.

Andrew lowered his head, shifting nervously from foot to foot on the wooden quay.

"Andrew Sutton," the sheriff said. "If you refuse to hold this sale, you will see the jail."

The horse grew uneasy as the crowd came closer, the din of voices growing louder. "'Tis the king's enemies! They've done this to stir up the Patriot cause!" a man yelled.

"Upon my word," Andrew said.

"We've done no such thing here," Father barked.

"We came in peace," insisted Joshua.

"Silence, or I shall arrest you all for breach of peace," Sheriff Porter yelled.

"And sedition," Clowing added. The British officers with the revenue official stepped forward, their muskets tight in their grasps.

John Mein wormed his way in front of Father while Molineux, Clowing, and the others looked on. "Ye ought to know, Mr. Sutton, your other son, had intent to soil your good name as well. He came to my office yesterday inquiring about claiming British goods kept at the Customs House for which he would have paid the duties, had they been available. Apparently both of your sons are non-compliant to your Patriotic cause."

A hush broke through the clamor of the assembly.

"The trunks seized from the French frigate?" Clowing asked.

Mein angled his head. "The very lot of it."

Father turned to Joshua, the hurt in his eyes almost more than Joshua could bear. "Is that true, Joshua?"

Joshua exhaled. "Yes, sir."

Father lifted his palms, confusion in his eyes. "What gave you need of that?"

"'Twas a favor for a friend," Joshua said.

"What friend?"

How it grieved Joshua to speak her name. "'Twas Honour Metcalf."

"You are certain?" Mrs. Wadsworth asked Honour, coming to her side. "You are relinquishing the quilt?"

"That, and much more." Honour placed her hand upon Mrs. Wadsworth's sleeve. "I beg you, please do not break this confidence."

The kind woman patted Honour's hand. "If you wish, dear. It is not my secret to tell."

Honour turned toward the wall, wiping the lone tear that trickled down her face.

Mrs. Wadsworth returned to her seat by the hearth. "I have brought you a few of your belongings. Some of your garments and personal items. I was able to remove most of the blood stain from your gown with hot vinegar. Though you will have to wear an apron to cover it."

"Thank you," Honour said.

"We will send the rest of your possessions when you are fully recovered and give you some time to settle into your new employment with Widow Lankton. Temperance shall join you when you are ready. She misses you, but the beautiful indigo bed quilt brings her comfort. She says her prayers and then traces the pattern with her finger until she falls asleep." The corner of Mrs. Wadsworth's eyes crinkled.

"You stay with her until she falls asleep?" Honour asked.

"I sat with her the first few nights after she returned from Deborah's. When she returned it impacted her how unwell you were and she became a little downcast. She is fine now."

"I hope caring for her has not been a burden to you," Honour asked.

"Not at all. After her school each day, Temperance comes home and does her chores. In the evening, she practices her tambour work and we read for a while." Mrs. Wadsworth smiled. "I am rather fond of keeping her."

"It pleases me know she is in such good hands. I sincerely thank you."

"You may thank me by getting well," Mrs. Wadsworth said.

Tempe returned carrying a tray of refreshments and set it down on the tea table. The maidservant set out a pitcher and glasses. "Lavender lemonade," the girl said.

"Thank you," Mrs. Wadsworth said. "I'll see to the serving."

The maid nodded and dashed away.

Tempe set a plate of little cakes and lemonade on the bedside table for Honour.

"This is very kind of you, sister."

Tempe's face filled with pride and she took a seat at the tea table with Mrs. Wadsworth.

"Mrs. Wadsworth told me you started school, Tempe. How do you find your tutor?"

"I like him, though he puts up with little nonsense."

"I would suspect so, as did my tutors."

Tempe angled her head. "Your tutors?"

"Yes. I had several. Education was extremely important to Mum and Poppa."

Tempe rubbed her lips together, glancing down at the floor.

"It is all right to talk about them, Tempe. It may even help," Honour said.

Tempe looked up in earnest. "Wesley and Thomas, too?"

"Of course, pumpkin." Honour said. "They will forever be a part of our lives and we shall see them again in heaven."

"I hope God is taking good care of them." Tempe looked from Honour to Mrs. Wadsworth.

Mrs. Wadsworth squeezed Tempe's hand. "I have no doubt that He is." Mrs. Wadsworth traced her finger along her neckline as she did when she thought about her husband. "I also know God is taking care of Captain Wadsworth, just as He does each of us."

"Then why does Honour keep getting hurt?" Tempe asked.

"Oh, people get hurt, and sadly some die. Though what we often fail to notice is how good the Lord is to see us through such times," Mrs. Wadsworth said.

Tempe went to Mrs. Wadsworth's side and hugged her. "May I call you Grandmother?"

Mrs. Wadsworth's pressed her hand against her chest and blinked back tears. "Of course, you may, child."

Honour's heart filled with warmth as she held back her own tears. Then she noticed the black ribbon on Tempe's ruffled cap, the same black crepe that adorned her own. Mrs. Wadsworth had spared it for them when they had first come to stay with her, as they had no mourning attire. Through the months the black ribbons became almost invisible, a perpetual memorial woven into their lives.

"Come here, Tempe." The child came to her bedside and Honour removed the cap from her own head. She untied the ribbon of black crepe, representing her loss and grief.

Tempe's lips parted in awe of what was transpiring before her. Honour unfastened the black ribbon on her sister's white cap. It broke Honour's heart Tempe had to bear such a grief at her young age. Honour wound the ribbons together and held them between her clasped hands. "Place your hands on mine, sweet sister."

Tears streamed down Tempe's cheeks. "What are we going to do?"

Honour's eyes filled with moisture. "Our time of mourning is done. Mum and Poppa, Thomas and Wesley shall remain in our hearts forever. We shall henceforth wear pleasant colors of remembrance to honor them all the more."

"Do you mean like violet? 'Twas Mum's favorite color," Tempe said.

Honour smiled softly. "Aye. Violet, and orange for Wesley, and blue for Thomas."

"And green for Poppa," Tempe said. "He liked green."

"'Tis the color of your eyes, is why." Honour planted a kiss upon Tempe's nose.

Mrs. Wadsworth looked on, dabbing her nose with a handkerchief.

"I may have some ribbon in my workbag. Would you hand it to me, please, 'tis right there." Honour asked Tempe, pointing to the bag on the shelf of the bedside table.

Tempe handed her the bag and Honour found a length of yellow ribbon, while tucking the black ribbons discreetly inside. Honour wrapped the yellow ribbon around Tempe's cap and tied it in a bow. "There. Yellow to match your petticoat."

The light in Tempe's eyes brightened. "And yellow for the sun."

"Indeed. We shall have sunnier days ahead." Honour hoped her words would prove true. But without Joshua in her life, she might have to settle for cloudy days instead.

19

Father took Joshua by the arm and ushered him to the side, questioning him in a low voice. "Honour Metcalf! What, pray tell, possessed you to do her bidding at the expense of your family's name?"

Joshua's body grew rigid as he met his father's glare. "I went to inquire on her behalf, as she is unable to do so herself. To see if they were indeed her belongings."

"If they were?" Father asked. "Would you have claimed them? Paid the duties?"

Joshua face grew tense, hesitating. "Yes," he nodded, "I would have."

His father's mouth drew into a grim line, and an eyebrow darted upward.

Joshua tossed his palms out to his side. "The items were from the stolen cargo she immigrated with. The items were not to be sold, only redeemed for the owner."

"You are certain she is the owner?" his father asked.

Did Father doubt her? Joshua looked at him, incredulous. "That is what she told me. She recognized the description of them in *The Chronicle*—especially her white-work linen."

"Who would *not* want to claim such a cloth as their own when most have resorted to homespun?" Father asked.

"I believe she is sincere." Joshua looked at his father, pleading. "Father, you know her."

Father looked down, and tapped a buckled shoe against the wooden planks of the wharf. "Not long enough," he muttered, angling his head back at Joshua.

Joshua ignored the complaint. "As much as we despise paying the king his taxes, surely there is no wrong in paying revenues on personal property?"

Father heaved a great sigh. "The only wrong here is subjecting our family to the scrutiny of the untoward." His father glared at that mushroom judge, John Mein.

The crowd that assembled around them continued to grow restless.

"Get on with it, ye!" a woman in a ragged gown bawled. "I've children to sew for."

"I've a quilt to make, I do," an old dame called out, a basket perched on her hip.

A quilt.

The dame continued. "'Tisn't that Honour Metcalf you spoke of, Margaret Wadsworth's quilter from England? She almost stole from the milliner and a schoolmistress."

"Quiet, woman, or you'll get the scold's bridle." Sheriff Porter snarled at her.

"'Tis half past the hour. The auction was to commence at eight o'clock," a man hollered, hoisting up his cane.

John Mein chortled, as he came around and placed a hand on Father's shoulder. "I dare ye. I'll grant Sutton's Clothiers top rank on my list of non-compliers come Monday."

Father cringed, and began to raise his arm. "You unscrupulous—"

197

Joshua discreetly drew his father's elbow down, fearing if spoke he would have popped like a lead ball shooting from a musket. Andrew stood at Father's opposite side.

"You call yourselves Sons of Liberty!" yet another heckler called out.

A fellow merchant in a fancy suit came forward, standing by Molineux. "What about that fancy carriage you own, Jairus Sutton? Did that come from England? Have you paid your carriage taxes?"

Clowing crossed his arms over his chest, awaiting the reply.

"This is not the inquisition, man," Molineux said to the merchant. "Yet, what say you, Sutton, so we may put that matter to rest?"

Joshua stayed his hand on Father's arm. "My father made his purchase from a chaisemaker in Cambridge . . . Massachusetts. *Before* the Townshend Acts were in effect. Further, his taxes are always paid in a timely fashion. Sheriff?"

"I've never had trouble with Sutton on that account," the sheriff said. "As for Miss Metcalf. She has been accused, aye, yet she has never been found stealing."

"Yet she sent you to pay duties on her things," the woman sniveled at Joshua. "How do you know they were her own?"

"Get her out of here," the Sheriff directed one of the redcoats.

Joshua stepped forward, addressing Clowing, Sheriff Porter, Molineux, Mein, and the horde of others.

"These are difficult times, we need not make them worse. We planned to hold a special auction of the textiles here today—to the lowest bidder, *without* charge." Joshua glanced at Andrew, who nodded. "We'd not yet been given a chance to explain. This vendue was halted before it was begun."

Clowing narrowed his eyes.

Molineux grinned. The brilliant master of Boston's spinning schools, and representative of the Body of Merchants, appeared satisfied for the intended help to the poor and plan to avert the greedy pockets of the commissioners.

"Ye cannot do that!" Mein snapped.

Father inclined his head. "Sheriff?"

"There is nothing illegal in it. In fact, it is a clever way to distribute goods in a peaceful and charitable manner," Sheriff Porter said.

"As members of the Body of Merchants and the Sons of Liberty, Sutton's Clothiers devised a splendid plan for the betterment of the community," Molineux said. "Let there be no more interference with it."

The people hearing this grumbled. Had the plan been carefully explained, they would have understood the benefit Joshua had devised. But with tensions high, and this pronouncement coming after their long wait, the 'clever' plan incited them to anger.

A wad of seaweed flew through the air and slapped Joshua in the neck.

A second attack targeted Andrew, sending his cocked hat flying to the ground.

A dead fish smacked the horse in the rump and there he went. Horse and wagon bolted down the wharf through the clamor of people, as they scattered. Andrew chased after it with Joshua trailing behind. The horse turned as some redcoats formed a barrier. At least they were good for some purpose.

Joshua went around, arms extended to each side. "Whoa, now. Easy there."

Andrew slowly approached on the other side, reaching out toward the harness.

A musket resounded into the air with a *boom*! The frightened horse reared back, knocking Andrew onto the quay. Andrew jumped up as horse and wagon jolted around catching the wagon on a wooden post. A wheel slipped over the pier.

Joshua leapt forward, trying to put his weight on the rear of the wagon with the help of some other men, while Andrew grabbed the horse's reins. British soldiers and Bostonians worked together, fencing the horse in so that it would not try to escape again.

While men held on to the wagon, Joshua made his way around the horse. He and Andrew unharnessed the timid creature and walked him away, handing the animal off to their father.

The brothers went back to the wagon and helped the men pull the end dangling over the edge, but it was caught in a tangle of heavy ropes. Someone shook it hard, trying to loosen it, but the heavy textiles broke through the wooden side into the harbor below.

Joshua and Andrew groaned as they looked over the pier. The precious contents sunk into the dredge of briny water, seaweed, clamshells, and muck. A bolt of material sank down into the mire—the machine-quilted French Marseilles. Mother would be horrified, as surely she would be when she learned of this morning's debacle.

Honour stood at the bedchamber window gazing into the backyard of Widow Lankton's estate—pristine gardens with late summer blooms, fruit trees with leaves beginning to show their near autumn shades, and weeping willows whose green fronds were now turning yellow. Everything had changed. This, her home now, and soon to be Tempe's. Widow Lankton, her employer, and Mrs. Wadsworth, her employer no longer.

Moreover, the love she thought Joshua held for her, which had taken root in her heart, was not enough to take root in his.

Honour felt the linen weave of the curtain between her fingers and noticed a small loosened stitch. Mayhap Joshua's affection for her was not unchanging, nor unending, but just beginning to bloom. Had she asked too much of a man she hadn't begun to court? Yet, their bond already felt more significant than a courtship. He oftentimes anticipated her needs and came to her aid, though she knew not how to help him. She'd denied him the opportunity to explain what prevented him from doing her favor. Was it his family? A political reason? Unlike the heart stencil, held up to the light to illuminate its pattern, her heart felt darkened, dull—and until she understood what had transpired between them, it would remain so.

Widow Lankton entered the room with the clacking of her brocade mules against the wooden floor. "Honour, dear. I am surprised to find you out of bed."

"Mrs. Hall informed me I could rise for a short spell. As long as I was no longer dizzy, it would improve my strength." Honour stepped toward the older woman. "Have I thanked you for all you have done for me?"

"I believe you have, dear," Widow Lankton said. "You are entirely welcome."

Honour's face brightened. "Please come into the next room."

Widow Lankton followed Honour through the doorway into the adjoining bedchamber and cast a curious look at Honour. "I smell cinnamon."

"Indeed you do." Honour smiled, extending her hand toward the white quilt which was carefully draped on the bedstead.

"What lovely patterns. Did you do that yourself?" Widow Lankton's brow lifted.

"I instructed Mrs. Hall how to place them so I did not have to bend." Honour pointed to the designs transferred onto the cloth. "Cinnamon is patted through the small holes of the stencils I made to mark the pattern."

"So that is why Mrs. Hall brought cinnamon upstairs," the widow said. "I thought mayhap it was another remedy for you. Another interesting use of the spice."

Honour picked up one of the stencils from a small table by the window. Though not as lavish has her own bedchamber, this tidy room, painted a cheerful yellow, would be perfect for Temperance, once she joined her. Honour handed Widow Lankton the stencil.

"I noticed these on your bedside table. You were napping and I did not know what to make of them. I thought perhaps you'd found a project to help pass the time."

"I did. It made me feel useful. My hands have been idle too long."

"You did not work on them yesterday, did you?" Widow Lankton held up her finger. "I do not abide working on the Sabbath."

"Nor do I. I spent my time in prayer and reading the Scriptures while you were at meeting and supping with Reverend and Mistress Cooper. I had a special visit with my sister and Mrs. Wadsworth the day previous and realized I've much to be thankful for, as well as a future to commit to God's care."

Widow Lankton looked at her with compassion. "I am glad to hear it, dear. Healing is a timely process. I am aware your body is not all that is in need of mending."

"You are?" Honour sealed her lips together. *How does she know my heart is suffering because of Joshua? Had she heard me weeping after he departed the other day?*

"When my beloved husband died, the emptiness and grief seemed more than I could bear at times. You, too, have suffered a terrible loss no one should ever have to endure."

Honour nodded sadly, the lump in her throat preventing her from speaking.

The widow continued. "I found comfort and strength in God's Word. And though I miss Mr. Lankton dearly, I find that my life is purposeful and never lacking the love of others."

Honour gave a faint smile at the elderly woman's empathetic words. "Thank you."

"God sets the lonely in families," Widow Lankton said. "It says so in His Word. You are part of my family now and I know you shall always have one with Margaret Wadsworth."

"Mmm. She has been a great friend to me and Tempe, and more." Honour stared down at the quilt and the light-colored cinnamon markings, soon to be quilted.

Widow Lankton also looked down at the quilt. "A good amount of the quilting has already been done. It makes me wonder to whom it once belonged. I see great care was taken. It must have been stitched with love."

A surge of emotion overcame Honour. She squeezed her eyes tight as she fought back racking sobs. Honour could no longer withhold her tears and buried her face in her hands, her grief pouring forth. Though Honour no longer wore her banner of mourning—the black ribbon upon her cap—she was discovering that grief dispensed in waves, like the ebb and flow of the tide. Someday, it might recede entirely, as the painful manner of her family's demise faded into the unknown. But the memory of her family would forever leave a loving impression upon her heart, like the silhouette of remembrance Widow Lankton kept upon the chest of drawers. When Honour looked at the small portrait it was flat, unmeaning, yet when the widow looked at it, how meaningful it must be to her. Honour had no portraits of her family, save the images she held in her mind's eye. But the whole-cloth quilt before her was their legacy of love. As painful as it was to part with it, the love was meant to share. Mayhap this was part of letting go.

"There now, Honour. 'Tis all right to cry. It is why the good Lord made our tears." The kind woman pulled Honour into an embrace. "Come, let us get you back to bed before Mrs. Hall scolds the both of us."

⸎

Joshua ripped the handbill off the door of Sutton's Clothiers just as mother opened it. He knew what warning it held.

Mother gasped at Joshua as he tripped over the threshold. "What in heavens?"

"Excuse me, Mother, but I must find Father at once. Have you seen him?"

"Of course, he is in his office going through some invoices," she said. "Joshua, what is it? Are matters worse?"

Joshua went to the office, Mother's heels tapping as she hurried behind him. How upset she'd been when Father explained what happened at Gray's Wharf. While doing her bookwork, she'd discovered the missing invoices. He should have been more careful. So when she questioned the sorry trio when they returned from their morning encounter against the forces of Boston, she'd nearly collapsed. Her own family, enemies against her precious cause. Yet the cause belonged to them all, they'd assured her, but now the episode was turned on its end.

Joshua slapped the handbill down on Father's desk, the afternoon sun searing a beam of light onto the paper. Joshua looked over his father's shoulder and read the threat again.

SUTTON'S CLOTHIERS

Sign of the Scissors,
Hanover Street, Boston

It is desired that the Sons and Daughters
of LIBERTY would not buy any one thing
of them, for in doing so will bring much
Disgrace upon themselves and their
Prosperity, forever and ever, AMEN.

"We have suffered dearly for our compliance with the boycott. Now it is for naught!" Father moaned. "These handbills will be distributed all over the city."

Mother picked up the notice and read. "It is we who are disgraced!" She plopped onto a chair, and wept.

"'Tis worse." Father handed Joshua *The Boston Chronicle.*

Joshua read the print aloud, as Mother would beg to see it anyway. Maybe his voice would soften the blow.

A list of those who audaciously continue to
counter the united sentiments of the Body
of Merchants throughout North America by
importing and selling British goods according
to the AGREEMENT:

Jairus Sutton, SUTTON'S CLOTHIERS
William Jackson, BRAZEN HEAD
Theophilus Lillie, LILLIE'S DRY GOODS
James McMasters, McMASTERS & COMPANY

He twisted the newspaper in his fists. "This is slander!"

"You know John Mein has a penchant for telling the truth as he sees it." A grim scowl crossed Father's face.

Joshua sneezed and turned away and wiped his nose with his handkerchief. "Excuse me."

Mother pinched he eyebrows. "Dear, I hope you are not coming down with a cold."

"'Tis nothing." Joshua looked from his mother to his father and cleared his throat. "Does Andrew know about this?"

"Yes, he was with me when I bought a copy of the paper. He is beside himself with regret." Father wiped the perspiration from his brow.

Joshua's jaw tightened. "Let us hope he does not attempt another reckless endeavor."

"He went to see Reverend Cooper for some spiritual guidance. Though I do not know how he can get us out of this disaster." Father shook his head. "Mayhap some goodwill comes out of it, for his sake if not for our own."

Mother got up. "I am retiring to the parlor. You shall find me on my chaise, should you need me. I shall pray. There is nothing more to be done. Should the Lord see fit to untangle our plight, I shall praise him."

Untangle our plight. Like the wagon wheel caught on the rope at the pier, Joshua would not allow the whole load of goods to go crashing into the mire. There must be a way to repair this damage. He would solicit the Lord's help for direction, and work with Him in tandem. He'd not go off on his own, as Andrew seemed so fond of doing. *Lord, help me to forgive my brother again. And please help me to know Thy way.*

Father rose and retrieved the crumpled newspaper from the waste barrel where Joshua had tossed it. "There is more." His father pointed to an article John Mein printed, reporting on Saturday's affair. It was bad enough how word got around. The murmurs at Sunday meeting were almost his parents' undoing. Thankfully, Reverend Cooper preached a sermon about making hasty judgments.

Joshua tossed back his head. "Hasn't Mein eked enough out of this inquisition?"

"The man is greedy. His lust of power is not like many others. But I fail to see how it benefits him in any way, save selling his newspapers and infuriating the masses." Father exhaled. "Hear me, he shall pay for his words one day."

"I have no doubt he shall. He is an evil man." Joshua rubbed his scratchy throat.

"Son, did you see what he wrote concerning you and Honour?" Father asked.

Joshua scanned the print in haste.

> The publisher reports his own encounter with Joshua Sutton whom, Friday last, inquired of *The Chronicle* regarding imported British textiles and goods held at the *Customs House*, for which he was prepared to pay duties.
>
> He confessed to the public that said items were on behalf of Miss Honour Metcalf, quilter at Mrs. Wadsworth's Mantua Shoppe; some accusing the maid of thievery.

"As a tailor you are apt at making a right assessment of a suit of clothing within the span of a passing chariot, but as for your estimation of Miss Metcalf I cannot say the same," Father said. "Trouble befalls the young woman at every turn."

Joshua looked at his father dumfounded. "I thought you were fond of her! You know these accusations are untrue." Joshua paced like a caged panther.

"I am, son," Father frowned. "But we must put feelings aside, especially as yours blind you so. With her character in question, we cannot afford to have you associate with her, no less court her."

20

Joshua sat upon a window-side table in the workroom, stitching the seams of his father's new suit. At least Father would be well dressed when his business went under, due to the expanded pattern. How like the ever-increasing resolve his father bore, his example of how to face these trying times.

To add to it, Joshua had been abed for several days, at Mother's insistence, with a spell of cold and fever. Andrew's trick, which had left him wet and cold, had caught up with him, Mother said. Although he tended to believe Mr. Benjamin Franklin, who disagreed with this theory of illness, Joshua was satisfied to attribute his misery to his brother.

All the while, he'd worried about what he could do to help resolve the tribulation his family had fallen prey to at the hands of that vulture, John Mein. He'd like to blame the man for everything from his family troubles to his discord with Honour, in the same way he'd blamed his brother. But blame served no one, least of all himself. It was meaningless. Meaningless—like his life seemed without Honour. *Oh, God, I beseech Thee to help me to take my eyes off others so I may see Thy way. Please restore my relationship with Honour. Be with her now as her loving Father and help her through trials of her own.*

From his perch, Joshua looked out at Boston Harbor, into the distance where sky and sea appeared seamless. The words Reverend Cooper had proclaimed from his pulpit on Sunday, following Joshua's illness, returned to him. "Do not judge hastily." But how could Joshua not judge the rash words John Mein printed after the vendue? Mein's evil tactics were apparent, and he'd wasted no time publishing them in Monday's edition of *The Boston Chronicle*. But words more poignant came to mind, those shared by Reverend Cooper read from the book of Proverbs. Unlike the Puritan churches in Boston, which distained any resemblance of Anglican worship, the manifest of the Brattle Street Meeting House allowed the reading of the Holy Scriptures at each turning of the hourglass. "Seest thou a man that is hasty in his words? There is more hope of a *fool* than of him."

Joshua slipped the tape measure through his thumb and forefinger. A tape carefully measured and marked for use as his guide, so he could make a correct measure. "Judge not, that ye be not judged," Reverend Cooper had also read from the gospel of Matthew. "For with what judgment ye judge, ye shall be judged: and with what measure ye mete, it shall be measured to you again." Judging Mein according to the man's own corrupt manner would not serve the Suttons at all and would only make Joshua as great a fool as Mein. God's Word must be his measuring rod—the standard of truth was the only way to refute the damage.

Joshua lowered his head and closed his eyes. *Please show me how to fight this battle, Lord, according to your statutes.*

The battle is mine.

As if a ghost appeared in his mind, Joshua saw the face of Reverend Cooper through the crowd at Gray's Wharf. With his distinct features, white bob-wig, and black parson's garments, the esteemed and learned Reverend Doctor Samuel Cooper was unmistakable. Joshua had only regarded him briefly and hoped that the Reverend kept the Suttons in prayer during their time of inquisition.

The screeches of seagulls beckoned Joshua's attention from the window. He looked down into the street where he could make out the form of Reverend Cooper, in his usual black frock. The reverend often walked this way, but today rested on a bench befriending the scavengers with crumbs of stale bread. What had Reverend Cooper said the day he walked with Joshua to the Lankton house? "Do not grow weary in doing good, for in time—"

Joshua would not give up. At once, he jumped off the table, securing his woven cap over his head. He kicked off his work slippers, wiggled his way into his buckled shoes, and donned his coat. Call him a fool, but he had some seagulls to feed.

Honour pulled her silk thread through the fabric. Each tiny stitch continued to reveal more of the design of the beautiful whole-cloth quilt. The lamb's wool batting, so carefully carded by Temperance during their voyage from England, and tacked to the linen quilt top with a linsey-woolsey bleached as white as the linen. Honour sighed relief that it remained intact, despite the quilt's own precarious journey. But the manner in which Honour found this quilt in her lap once again remained a curiosity to her. Was it God's way of sending her a message? A message to trust Him for the direction of her life? Each stitch was but naught, yet strung together, part of a unique pattern. Her stitches were purposeful, sometimes pleasant and other times tedious, yet, one stitch at a time she pressed on. She liked this work, though her fingers grew weary after laboring long hours, it was a joy to be employed at a satisfying endeavor.

Bittersweet though it was, each precise stitch wrought healing somehow.

A fortnight had passed, even more, since she'd last seen Joshua. He had chosen to stay away. Would she ever see him again so she might tell him she never should have imposed on his good graces? It tore at her she'd offended him so, a man whom she so ardently admired. Mayhap it was better this way, and her rent heart might have chance to mend. Yet, she prayed for him still.

Widow Lankton entered the parlor, her maidservant following, carrying a tray. "I am so pleased to see you so well recovered, Honour. The pink in your face is becoming. Though I fear you shall wear your fingers to the bone with your stitching from morning until night."

"'Tis pleasing work," Honour said.

Widow Lankton took her seat on the velvet settee and smoothed her brocade gown. "I must insist you take a respite. We shall enjoy some 'Indian Tea' this afternoon with some currant scones."

Honour rose, laying her quilting down on the chaise and joined Widow Lankton. "Thank you," Honour said, accepting her tea from the gracious lady.

"The tea is made from redroot grown in the Province of Maine. It tastes like Bohea, don't you agree?" Widow Lankton asked.

Honour took a sip of the hot beverage. "'Tis delicious. Who needs teas from England when plenty can be found on American shores?"

"My sentiments precisely," the widow said. "I am pleased to know you share them."

The maidservant entered and handed the Widow Lankton a newspaper. "*The Boston Gazette*, Mistress."

"Thank you, dear." She said, and the girl scurried away. "Let us see what tidings abound in this edition." Widow Lankton viewed the front page through her bejeweled magnifying lens, making note of the entries. "There is a frontiersman named Daniel Boone, who began an expedition across the wilds of Kentucky. What danger he must be encountering."

"I am astonished one could be so brave," Honour remarked.

"There is not just one form of bravery, my dear," Widow Lankton said. "You exhibit great courage when you face your trials."

Honour nodded and a surge of warmth washed over her.

The widow continued reading. "It says here, French pirates were captured off the coast of Massachusetts and will be tried for the attack on a British ship last year. The Admiralty is summoning witnesses for the prosecution."

Honour's heart propelled at the rate of a spinning wheel in motion. "What will become of them?"

Widow Lankton looked up. "Hanged, I suppose."

Honour gasped. "Does it report the name of the ship?" She bit her lower lip as she awaited the answer.

Widow Lankton scanned the article. "The *Luna*, it says . . . dear me, is that the ship . . . ?"

Honour released a deep breath. "No. It is not the ship my family was on." Honour turned away and shook off a bitter chill.

Widow Lankton placed her hand upon Honour's arm. "It shall all come to pass, here or in eternity."

The widow sipped her tea and resumed her perusal of *The Gazette*. "Hear this. An alphabetical list of the names of the 350 Sons of Liberty who dined at the Liberty Tree in Dorchester in August. The roll is impressive. Samuel Adams; John Adams, Esquire; John Hancock, Esquire; William Molineux; Honorable James Otis."

"May I?" At Widow Lankton's nod, Honour looked on at the list, under the S's. Jairus Sutton, Joshua Sutton. True Patriots. Perhaps Andrew was not listed as he was not yet a freeman, or could it be there was division within their own household?

"The Suttons are listed." Widow Lankton pointed at their names. She slanted her head toward Honour. "We've not seen Joshua in some time. Would you like to invite him to the quilting party?"

"Quilting party?"

"Didn't I tell you? I thought when you were done stitching the motifs we could invite some ladies to assist with the border and complete the quilt."

Honour smiled. "What a lovely idea."

"'Tis a custom to bring the ladies to quilt in the day and the men in the evening to celebrate," Widow Lankton explained. "Of course, your Joshua shall be welcome."

"My Joshua?" Honour sighed. "I am not so certain he is my Joshua."

"Do not lose heart, my dear. There must be some worthy reason he has not called on you recently." Widow Lankton gazed absently at the newspaper. "It is imprudent to speculate. It only leads to worry."

The sound of someone arriving through the front door hearkened their attention. "Your niece and her husband have arrived," Mrs. Hall announced.

"Do send them in," the dowager instructed, promptly greeting her niece as she entered the room. "Welcome, Emily. Where is your husband?"

Emily lay her reticule on the secretaire. "Good afternoon, Aunt Eunice. He shall be along momentarily." She smiled at Honour. "How nice to find you looking well again. We've come to see how the quilt is coming along."

"It is . . .," Honour began, when an imposing figure emerged in the doorway. The bewigged man, clothed in a pretentious suit, fastened his gaze on Honour, overlong. In spite of his foreboding presence, he cast a debonair grin.

Widow Lankton lifted her chin. "Miss Honour Metcalf, please meet Emily's husband, Mr. Edmund Leach."

Honour stiffened, then proffered a conciliatory nod. "Mr. Leach."

He approached the settee and graciously bowed and kissed Widow Lankton on the cheek. He turned to Honour and took her hand in greeting. "The pleasure is mine."

She cringed.

Widow Lankton led them to the whole-cloth linen quilt, making much ado of it when showing it to the couple. "Honour's handiwork is unmatched. I am glad to have hired her for the task. Her work is exquisite."

Mr. Leach looked on, casting scathing, furtive glances Honour's way. "My wife's quilt is progressing well. What good fortune I had in acquiring it. Don't you agree, Miss Metcalf?"

Despite Honour's hard work, Mr. Leach gloated on his find. He put his arm around his wife's waist, "You are pleased, dear?"

"I am," Emily said, "A more beautiful quilt could not be found." Though the quilt met with Emily's approval, Honour knew the sorrow hidden beneath Emily's pleasant countenance.

"Then, Emily, you will be pleased to participate in the quilting bee I am hosting on Saturday for its completion," Widow Lankton said. "The men will join us in the evening for a feast and dancing. You will attend, Edmund?"

Leach looked down at his wife, receiving an obligatory nod, and returning his regard to Widow Lankton. "We shall be delighted. 'Tis our wedding quilt, after all." He cocked his head toward Honour and issued an obscure smirk.

Honour could bear it no longer. "If you will excuse me. I am in need of some fresh air. I am going to take a turn about the garden so you may continue your visit privately."

Mr. Leach cleared his throat. "I shall escort you, Miss Metcalf." His gaze scanning over her. "I would not be a gentleman if I allowed you to sojourn alone, in your weakened condition."

"I am recovered, sir. It is not necessary."

"I insist. It will give my wife and her aunt a chance to visit. You would not deny them, I am sure." Mr. Leach extended his arm. "Shall we?"

The stress of it overwrought her every nerve, yet she had no choice but to acquiesce. Mr. Leach followed Honour out the door. They walked in silence—while Honour's heart beat so loudly she was sure he could hear it—until they passed into the backyard, behind the brick wall laden with ivy. When they turned the corner, he boldly pressured her against the wall.

Mr. Leach's gaze pierced through her like a coiled snake ready to bite. "You seem distressed, Miss Metcalf. Perhaps I can ease your discomfort," he said, taming his forked tongue.

Honour breathed in deeply. "Mr. Leach, you are *married*."

Fondling the coil of her hair, he said, "Yes, and you have met my lovely wife, Emily."

"No, sir. You are married. *Twice*."

Honour slid a step away, but he halted her by pushing his knee against the outer portion of her gown, pinning her to the wall. She'd heard of men like that, with their schemes to come to America and marry, only to steal their "wives" dowries, spoil them, and return to England, never to be heard from again. More so, she knew him as the son of her father's business associate who had helped her after arriving in Boston. It sickened her.

Leach scoffed. "Aye, I remember you. Though you were younger when you attended my wedding in England with your family." He feigned pity. "Sorry thing about them."

Honour swallowed back the whimper rising in her throat.

"You have become quite a prize," he sneered, angling closer to her. "A pirate's prize. Hmmph. They could have taken you . . . and your pretty little sister." He sniffed her hair and hissed in her ear, "They were only to take your father's gold, his investment was substantial."

Honour's eyes burned with shock, and a wave of nausea passed over her at his revelation.

"Ah, but you cannot trust the French. They took it upon themselves to make a show of it. Simply Byzantine, don't you agree?" A crooked smirk formed above his narrow chin.

Honour spun her head aside. Her breathing grew heavy, but at last her voice rose from the depth of her hurt and anger and she faced him. "You are bold to show yourself to me. Are you not afraid I will reveal your secret?"

His hand slithered its way up the side of her neck and grabbed the hair at the nape. He glared into her eyes. "Ah, you haven't the heart. Besides, I prefer to face my enemies." He had not pulled her hair from its coif, however, a sign of his experience in not exposing his ill deeds.

Honour glowered at him, clenching her teeth. "Let me—"

He cuffed his palm over her mouth. "You will not speak a word of this, Miss Metcalf. I have been watching you for some time, after I learned how my father cleaned up my, shall we say, little scrape." He lifted a knife from his pocket and pricked beneath her chin within a hair's breadth. 'Twould be a pity for your sister to lose her only living relative. I suspect you might feel the same. You'd miss your little 'pumpkin', would you not?"

How did he know the term of endearment she used for Temperance? She felt as though she would wretch. Leach pressed her closer to the wall, until she could move no more. He pulled the knife down, pointing it toward her abdomen, over her now-healed wound. "Do not try me."

21

Honour paced the floor of her bedchamber, recalling her unbearable encounter with Edmund Leach. When she'd encountered him in Widow Lankton's parlor, Honour could barely school her breaths to maintain their normal rhythm. She had needed no introduction to the man, for at once she had recognized him and knew what he was about—or so she had thought. His clandestine glowers at her were disturbing enough, but his bold declaration to her about his involvement with her family's demise shocked her to the core. He was responsible for killing her family and taking everything they owned. What would she do about his threats to Temperance and her? She held no doubt that the menacing beast would follow through on them if she were not careful. The unnerving exchange still made her shudder.

Honour clamped her lips together, her temples pulsing. *Heavenly Father, please protect us from this evil and grant me wisdom.*

Trust me, daughter.

Honour rubbed her arm as a chill tickled her flesh. *Trust Him, I shall.*

She turned her head toward the doorway at the clomping of footsteps coming up the stairs announced company.

"Honour!" Temperance bounded into the room and wrapped her arms around Honour's waist. Tempe stepped back. "Did I hurt you?"

"Of course not. You could never hurt me." Honour embraced her sister, as she hadn't done in so long. She could scarcely let her go.

Tempe looked up at Honour, a pretty orange ribbon adorning her cap. "I am here to move in with you. Mrs. Wadsw— Grandmother—said 'tis time."

Honour smiled, wiping the moisture from her face she had not been able to contain.

Tempe pouted. "You are crying."

"I am sore happy to see you!" Honour looked up as Mrs. Wadsworth entered the room, followed by Widow Lankton. Mrs. Hall opened the door to Tempe's new bedchamber from the adjoining side where she and the maidservant had brought up baskets and satchels filled with their belongings.

The group of ladies, Tempe included, crossed the room, but Mrs. Wadsworth stayed Honour by her arm. "What is it, my dear? Are you unwell?"

"I am all right now that Tempe is here. Truly."

"Though I must ask, is something upsetting you? A certain tension is born on your face."

"I shall miss Temperance dearly." Mrs. Wadsworth hesitated, tracing her finger at her neck. "And . . . well, I have misplaced the pearls that my husband gave me. Rather, I fear someone may have stolen them."

Widow Lankton gasped. "Stolen? Your pearls?"

"I am afraid so. I believe they may have been missing for some time now."

"Have you asked Maisey if she's seen them? You know she will help you look for them."

Mrs. Wadsworth's brow wrinkled. "We already have. We've searched high and low."

Tempe tugged on Honour's sleeve. "I helped Grandmother, too. They have disappeared."

"Perhaps they shall yet turn up," Honour said, attempting to offer some hope.

Widow Lankton turned around. "Have you reported it to Sheriff Porter?"

"I have. It pained me to do so." Mrs. Wadsworth shook her head. "You know they shall put the thief in jail. Or send him to the pillory with a *T* branded upon his hand."

Tempe sucked in an audible breath.

Honour looked down at her hands and cringed. Looking up she met Mrs. Wadsworth's grave expression.

"Let us get this room put together, shall we?" Mrs. Hall fluffed a feather pillow and inserted it into a fresh embroidered pillowslip. The maidservant had already begun putting away Tempe's garments.

Widow Lankton's footman appeared at the hall doorway carrying the indigo quilt that Tempe had been using in her room at Mrs. Wadsworth's. "You may place it on the bedstead," Mrs. Hall instructed him, and after he did, he departed.

"Tempe, your quilt. Now you shall feel right at home." Honour smiled.

Tempe tipped her head. "*My* quilt?"

"Aye. It belongs to you now, pumpkin." Honour crossed her arms across her middle, caressing them absently. Might Edmund Leach really follow through with his awful threats?

Mrs. Hall and the maidservant placed the quilt carefully upon the bed.

Widow Lankton placed her hand upon her chin, looking at the quilt. "It is charming. What a pretty color. Some of the motifs remind me of Emily's quilt. Yes, the pomegranate, and some of the feathered patterns. They must be common patterns used in England. 'Tis lovely."

"Aye." Honour pressed down on her lower lip.

Mrs. Wadsworth reached for the hem of the quilt, tugging it into place. "There—"

A pearl dropped onto the floor planks with a plop, rolling straight to the tip of Honour's damask mules. Another fell, and then another. Tempe scurried to gather them.

Mrs. Wadsworth grabbed at the hem, kneeling down at the end of the bedstead. "The hem has come loose and here lie my pearls! How could this be?" Hurt and horror filled her eyes.

"Honour! What have you done?"

⁂

Joshua waited in the guest parlor, the wainscoting closing in on him. It had been several weeks now since he'd seen Honour. He hardly knew where he'd begin. He had not heard from Honour, nor had she from him, as he'd been detained with other matters. He presumed she was angry with him still. Would she receive his company now?

Widow Lankton's housekeeper addressed him. "Miss Metcalf and her sister are outdoors, enjoying the Indian summer. It may be her last chance."

Joshua eyed her curiously. "Whatever do you mean?"

"She will have to explain it to you herself. Widow Lankton has granted permission for you to seek her."

Joshua exited the grand house and found his way to the backyard, much as he had that day he sought her when she was so upset. Yet today he dared not rush. What if she rejected him, as he had rejected her—rather, her request, which caused the breach between them?

"Joshua!" Tempe ran to him, unreserved, throwing his arms around him. He twirled her around and placing her down, kissed her atop her bonnet.

Joshua looked up as Honour strolled toward him. How demure she looked in her *robe à la anglaise*. The pink lustring gown, with ivory quilted petticoat, made her look every bit an English lady. He had not thought it possible for her to look more beautiful than the day he had swept her out of the street during the hailstorm.

"Honour." He nearly croaked out her name.

She nodded demurely. "Joshua."

Tempe took hold of Joshua's hand.

"Your manners, Tempe," Honour said.

"I have missed him, Honour. Haven't you?"

Honour parted her lips, then closed them. "It is not becoming for a young lady to be so forward."

Joshua took Temperance's small hand in his and bowed. He placed a diminutive kiss upon the back of her hand. "Milady."

Tempe giggled and stepped back.

"Something is different about you, Tempe." Joshua cocked his head, narrowing his eyes. "Ah, yes. I see you have removed your mourning ribbons and exchanged them for something brighter. Green becomes you."

"'Twas my father's favorite color," Tempe angled her head toward Honour. "Honour said 'twas time to cease our mourning, but not our memories."

"'Tis good to know." Joshua offered Honour a tender glance.

"How is Anne?" Honour asked.

"She is well, thank you. Past the worst of it," Joshua said.

"I am glad to hear it. I have been keeping her in prayer," Honour said.

"You look well. Are you much improved?" he asked.

"Aye," Honour said.

"Tempe, would you mind if Honour and I had a few moments of private conversation?"

"I shall be your chaperone. 'Tis only fitting." Tempe shielded her eyes from the sun. "I shall play by the fountain and you may have a seat on the stone bench."

"Very well. If your sister agrees." Joshua rested his hand upon his hip. Meeting Honour's eyes, he earnestly sought her reply.

Temperance skipped off, humming as she went, although Honour had yet to grant her permission.

"The girl has no manners." Honour shook her head with exaggerated dismay. "I suppose I have failed her."

"You have done nothing of the sort. She is a wonderful child, as—" Joshua hesitantly held out his elbow. "Come, let us find the bench."

Joshua and Honour crossed the lawn in silence. He allowed her to sit first, remaining undecided as to whether he should sit by her or remain standing.

"I shall not bite, Joshua Sutton."

Joshua lifted his eyebrows. "We are sure?"

"Very."

A hint of the scent of lavender and cinnamon emanated from her, and he dared breathe it in. Breathe her in.

She clasped her hands together in her lap.

He straightened, facing her. "Honour. I must apologize for my absence."

"You needn't," she said.

"I must. I have been indisposed for these last weeks, with an urgent family matter, and then my illness."

She looked at him with concern. "Family matter? Illness?"

"I am well now. 'Twas only a cold and fever." He grinned. "My mother, you know how she fusses."

Honour smiled. "Aye, she is a good caregiver."

Joshua nodded.

"And your family?" she asked.

"They are well, but we have come upon some trouble. I have been consumed with the matter, and thus my reason for not coming to see you sooner. I had hoped you did not conclude it had anything to do with . . . your request." He was rambling. Did what he said make any sense to her? "I want you to know that I did inquire at *The Chronicle* concerning your belongings. But some other party had already claimed them."

Honour glanced down at her lap and said softly, "It matters not." She looked up at him from beneath her dark lashes. "I am only glad it did not cost you anything."

"Nay, Honour, it cost me a great deal."

Alarmed at his statement, Honour faced Joshua, her eyes pleading. "Joshua, you must tell me. What happened?"

"Besides my brother and I nearly being jailed?" Joshua's brilliant blue eyes tried to emit humor.

"'Tis no time for jesting." She could not bear the possibility of him spending time in jail. Yet, she knew not what her own destiny would bring on that accord.

"I am not," Joshua said. "Albeit, we managed to get away with some mere lashings from John Mein, picketed by some miscreant lads, and served a hefty fine."

Honour flattened her palm against her chest. "On my account?"

"Not at all. 'Twas Andrew's doing mostly, and my own involvement to aid him. You see, he tried to hold a vendue without Father's knowledge and it ended . . . well, let me say a wagon of our damaged textiles were disposed into the harbor at low tide." Joshua cast a sidelong glance at her, casting a dimpled grin.

Honour covered her mouth, holding back a small laugh. Oh, how she had missed him.

"Looking back at it, it does lend humor to the situation." Joshua chuckled. "You should have seen the British soldiers rallying around with Boston citizens, trying to corral our loose horse and wagon." His eyes widened and he released a hearty laugh.

Honour could restrain herself no more as he regaled his tale of woe. Her own mirth at this telling could scarcely be contained until the merry tears filling her eyes betrayed her. But then she turned away, weeping.

Joshua's hand reach around her, and he rested his chin upon her shoulder. "Honour," he whispered. "Look at me."

She hesitated, but something deep inside told her she would find safe harbor with him. She turned her head back, and their eyes met. He stroked her chin, gently, lovingly, as he entreated her to listen. "I know all about it, Honour. You will not go to jail."

She turned, her mouth opened trying to form words, though none could be found. She licked her lower lip, and he soon found it with the featherlight touch of his fingertip. He withdrew his finger, brought it to his own mouth, and kissed the moisture from it. "Take heart, Honour. All is well."

All is well.

"I learned of your situation this morning when Mrs. Wadsworth was visiting with my mother. They felt it best that I know."

Joshua enveloped her hands in his. "Mrs. Wadsworth does not believe that you are the one who took her pearls. She trusts you. She knows you are a woman of honor."

"She, she told you this?"

"Yes, upon my word. Not only mine, but others." Joshua retrieved a news clipping that he had tucked within the breast pocket of his frock coat and handed it to her. "Here, please read this. The first part concerns the notice I penned to reflect an accurate account of the vendue that created such a trial for my family's business. There was an accusation made against you there. You will find yourself fully vindicated for that and the incident of the pearls. Please, read it."

The Boston Gazette, 26 September 1769

Letter to the PUBLICK

Sutton's Clothiers hereby begs pardon for the cancellation, due to an unforeseen situation, of a special vendue to be held Saturday, 9 September 1769 at Gray's Wharf. Further, we humbly submit these indisputable true accounts as recorded by the Reverend Doctor Samuel Cooper, he being witness to the events on said occasion:

"We planned to hold a special auction of the textiles here today—to the lowest bidder without charge."—*Joshua Sutton, Sutton's Clothiers*

"There is nothing illegal in it. In fact it is a clever way to distribute goods in a peaceful and charitable manner."—*Sheriff Porter, City of Boston*

"All Sutton's Clothiers invoices and bills of lading indicate no breech of commerce. They are dated 9 July 1768, before the Non-Taxation Agreement."—*Edmund   Clowing,   Customs Commissioner, City of Boston*

"As members of the Body of Merchants and the Sons of Liberty, Sutton's Clothiers devised a splendid plan for the betterment of the community."— *William Molineux, Body of Merchants*

In regard to Miss Honour Metcalf, quilter —

"As for Miss Metcalf. She has been accused, aye, yet she has never been found stealing."— *Sheriff Porter, City of Boston*, who further adds the report testified to him by Widow Eunice Lankton, Mrs. Emily Leach, and Mrs. Margaret Wadsworth, that Honour Metcalf, quilter, "is of the utmost character and honest in every way."

Joshua Sutton, Sutton's Clothiers

Sign of the Scissors, Boston

Honour rose from the bench, smiling at Joshua. "I can hardly believe what I see. You did this for me?"

He stood, taking her hands in his as he faced her. "I did. For us."

Honour glanced down, shyly, feeling her face warm. She took a step away and spun around with joy. "I am so relieved our reputations have been restored. It means so much to have Mrs. Wadsworth trust me. That you also trust me."

"Do you trust me, Honour? Please tell me you do."

With everything she had inside her, she trusted this worthy man. "Aye, Joshua, I do."

He slanted his jaw, giving her a coy grin. "Enough to grant me permission to court you? In fact, I've proof you already did."

"Upon my honor, I did not."

Joshua took a small slip of paper from his waistcoat and handed it to her. "I found this inside the needle case you gave to me on my birthday."

"Did you?" Honour opened the paper, eyeing it curiously and read the little rhyme.

Inside this fish, an answer find.
Have your wish, love is blind.

"You think *I* wrote this?" Honour looked at him chagrined.

Joshua narrowed his eyes. "Didn't you?"

"I positively did not." Honour clamped down on her lip, the heat returning to her face. "It is entirely possible I could have written you such verse. But it did not come from my pen."

"Then who wrote it?"

Honour tapped her finger against her chin. "I have a suspicion a certain strawberry-blonde imp I know may have done the deed." The pair turned, surveying the yard where Temperance was tossing flower petals into the fountain.

"I had hoped to gain an answer from you that day as to whether you would allow me to court you, and when I read 'Have your wish', I believed it to mean you were giving your approval." Joshua lifted his shoulders and the corner of his mouth curved.

"I confess, Joshua, I had no intent to court you then. I thought I had seen you with Emily, and was quite distressed over it." Honour winced.

"It said '*love is blind*' so after I'd talked to Emily, I believed it true . . . that you loved me, as I love you. I have been keeping this near my heart for all of this time."

"Have you?" Honour smiled up at him. "Even when I felt you did not love me at all, you loved me still? Even when you refused my request, and then again when you honored my request?"

"Even then. Even now."

Honour released a slow breath, summoning renewed courage from within. "That be true, Joshua, I have a matter I must trust you with now—it involves a quilting party and the husband of one Emily Leach."

22

Honour surveyed the beautiful white linen whole-cloth quilt, pulled taut within a wooden frame put together for the quilting party. Joshua and Andrew had come in the afternoon to set it up in Widow Lankton's ladies' parlor, the servants having already pushed the furniture against the walls. The eight-foot square filled the center of the space as it rested on a large table, the corners supported by ladder-back chairs.

Lovely ladies in their pretty gowns gathered around it, adding delicate stitches to join the layers of the quilt and complete its border. Joining Honour were Widow Lankton, Emily, Mrs. Wadsworth, Maisey, Mrs. Cooper—the reverend's wife, Mrs. Sutton, Deborah, Anne, and the three girls—Sarah, Abigail, and Temperance.

Tempe was so excited about the party and the opportunity to lend her own stitches to the project she nearly bubbled over like a boiling kettle of water on the hearth. She had not recognized the bed quilt as the one that Mum and Honour had worked on aboard ship. Mayhap because it had remained carefully folded in their laps much of the time as they worked on it. When Widow Lankton had commented on how Tempe's indigo quilt had similar qualities to Emily's quilt, Honour had thought her secret exposed. The reason she suggested, of the motifs being common in England, had apparently appeased the group of women—and Tempe—until the pearls dropping from its hem had distracted them all. Perhaps it was a risk for Honour to have her precocious sister there for the quilting, yet the risk of not having Tempe safely by her side may be greater.

The feathered serpentine pattern embellishing the border framed the center motifs splendidly. Having quilted from dawn, it was nearly time to break for the midday meal.

As she looked up from her stitching, Widow Lankton smiled around the circle of women whose hands remained busy at their task. "We have made great progress on the border this morning. Many hands make light work. Thank you all, again, for coming to help complete Emily's bridal quilt."

Emily smiled demurely. "I appreciate all of your help. 'Tis humbling."

"Every bride deserves a quilt," said Deborah.

Mrs. Cooper smiled. "I do agree. The reverend and I still have our bridal quilt upon our own bedstead." She lowered her gaze, blushing.

"Perhaps someday I shall have a bridal quilt of my own. 'Tis what I hope." Maisey collected her sewing items as she spoke.

Maisey's future was yet to be determined. Honour only hoped their plan would work.

Mrs. Sutton made her way around the quilt, admiring the handiwork of the ladies. She paused behind Anne, resting her hands upon her shoulders. "We shall have to gather again to make your new babe a quilted coverlet."

Honour smiled at Anne. What joy to look forward to the birth of a new child.

"That sounds wonderful," Anne said.

"Mayhap Sarah, Abby, and I can make it," Temperance chimed in. "It shall be so small surely we could do it." Sarah and Abby beamed at the prospect.

"That is quite ambitious of you, Temperance," Mrs. Wadsworth said. "Though you must realize a small quilt is no small task. It takes many years of practice. Isn't that so, Honour?"

"'Tis true, though you have a natural ability and are doing superb work. Mum would be proud of your skill." Honour kissed Tempe on the forehead, who sat at her side, yet it occurred to her she should have refrained from stirring her sister's memories this day. The Lord had told her to trust Him, and this day required exactly that. Honour tapped her shoe on the floor. She was trusting God for the outcome of the day, but she anxiously awaited Joshua's arrival later on, when the true event would get underway.

Mrs. Hall entered and announced the midday meal. "I have prepared a luncheon for you in the keeping room. 'Tis a light repast with Liberty tea, as you will be feasting heartily later."

Mrs. Wadsworth signaled Honour to remain for a moment. "Honour, dear. I must apologize once again for suspecting you of stealing my pearls." She placed her hand over the strand of pearls at her neck.

"There is no need," Honour said. "It was a logical assumption."

Mrs. Wadsworth's mouth drew into a grim line, her brow creasing beneath her white pleated cap. "Mayhap. Yet it did not last long, I assure you. It was evident by the stitch work that you did not weave the string of pearls into the hem of that quilt. Your stitches are too fine." Mrs. Wadsworth lowered her voice, leaning closer. "'Twas also evident the pearls were meant to be discovered. No person with intent to steal would be so careless. The true malefactor meant to incriminate you."

Honour and Mrs. Wadsworth shared concerned glances, for they both knew the identity of the culprit. "Let us have some refreshment," Honour said. "The others wait."

In the afternoon, the ladies resumed their quilting. Honour marveled at the progress being made as the quilt neared its completion. The needlework would help keep her thoughts occupied until the men arrived. She smiled, thinking of Joshua and how much he meant to her—how much she loved him.

"Penny for your thought?" Widow Lankton asked, her eyes crinkling.

The girls giggled. Tempe covered her mouth, her eyes wide. The girls giggled again.

"Temperance Metcalf. Do not be impolite," Honour said beneath her breath.

"Oh, dear, I am low on thread," Deborah said.

Widow Lankton turned to her maidservant, who remained in waiting to assist the quilters. "Bring that spool over to Deborah please, would you?"

"I haven't mentioned what fine linen this quilt is made of," Mrs. Sutton said. "An English weave. It is rare to find such a textile in these times."

"Here in the colonies we have come to rely on homespun, especially with Mr. Molineux's spinning schools," Mrs. Cooper said.

Deborah and Anne glanced at Mrs. Sutton.

"Has it been hard on your husband's business?" Mrs. Cooper asked Mrs. Sutton.

"'Tis short-term punishment for long-term gain," Mrs. Sutton said, pulling her silk thread through the fabric.

Mrs. Wadsworth glanced around the table. "Do any of you recall the spinning bee of 1753 on Boston Common?"

"I do believe my ears are still humming from the sound of all those spinning wheels," Widow Lankton said.

"How many were there?" Maisey asked.

"Three hundred spinsters all dressed in homespun," Mrs. Wadsworth said. "A loom was set up on a stage for demonstration."

"What was the occasion?" Honour asked as she knotted her thread.

"The Society for Promoting Industry among the Poor was celebrating their fourth anniversary. The women demonstrated their skill and the art of using the spinning wheels. Women from every social class joined together for the event, and music played all day."

Mrs. Cooper snipped the end of her thread. "The great crowd of spectators later attended a special sermon for the occasion, and a contribution was taken up for the society."

"It was a grand spinning bee," Mrs. Sutton said, addressing Abigail and Sarah. "Your mothers attended that day, sitting behind their own wheels. They were not much older than you."

"Will you teach us how to spin, Grandmother?" Abby asked.

"Perhaps I might. My wheel is presently in storage, but I cannot think of a better time to again put it to use."

"I dare say, we have shown great industry here today with our own quilting endeavor," Mrs. Wadsworth said, beholding the completed quilt. "Honour, you have created a lovely quilt and it has been a joy for each one of us to contribute to it."

"It is kind of you to say. I owe the skill to my mother, the talent to the Lord, and my gratitude to you all for your assistance." Honour appreciated this quilt now more than ever, from the beautiful material she had taken for granted, to the loving hands helping complete it. It did not escape her notice how quiet and forlorn Emily had been. Honour hoped her heart would soon mend, though she feared it first must fully break. Honour prayed that Emily would find comfort in God's love, as she herself had found.

Mrs. Sutton folded her hands in her lap. "What a delightful day this has been."

"The Lord hath provided," Widow Lankton said.

"The Lord is pleased to see His children joyful. He wishes also that we delight in Him," Mrs. Cooper said, "just as Psalm thirty-seven proclaims, in verses three through seven." As she recited the passage, the others joined in.

> Trust in the Lord, and do good; so shalt thou dwell in the land, and verily thou shalt be fed. Delight thyself also in the Lord: and he shall give thee the desires of thine heart. Commit thy way unto the Lord; trust also in him; and he shall bring it to pass. And he shall bring forth thy righteousness as the light, and thy judgment as the noonday. Rest in the Lord, and wait patiently for him: fret not thyself because of him who prospereth in his way, because of the man who bringeth wicked devices to pass.

The longcase clock in the corner chimed four o'clock. Honour sucked in a tiny breath, glancing toward the door. The hour of reckoning had come.

"Ladies, ladies, we have come to celebrate your handiwork," Joshua's father announced as the horde of men gathered at the parlor doorway. Jarius, Anne and Deborah's husbands, and Joshua had traveled to the Lankton mansion in their carriage. Reverend Cooper had followed in his Boston chaise. Edmund Leach apparently had not yet arrived.

"Do come in, gentlemen," Widow Lankton instructed.

"We shall be glad to, but first we would like you to greet our special guest." Father turned to the side, extending his arm toward the entrance. "Captain." The men parted, and Mrs. Wadsworth's husband stepped forward.

Mrs. Wadsworth's hands flew into the air, as she rushed toward her husband. Captain and Mrs. Wadsworth embraced, and he peeked up. "Excuse me while I give my wife a proper greeting." He planted a kiss on her mouth, unabashedly. He looked up and chuckled. "I won't get fined for that, I hope."

"I care not," Mrs. Wadsworth cupped her hands around his white beard.

"Sorry, Margaret, I hadn't the chance yet to see to my ablutions. I was eager to see you." Captain Wadsworth addressed Father. "Jairus told me I could find you here."

Honour looked on at the joyous scene, her eyes misting. As she glanced around at the other ladies, she did not think one of them had a dry eye.

After the men filtered into the room, Mrs. Hall stood in the doorway.

"Yes, Mrs. Hall," Widow Lankton said.

"The feast shall be ready in the dining room, momentarily, and the musicians shall arrive within the hour," Mrs. Hall said.

Joshua huddled the girls together. "The three of you shall follow Mrs. Hall. The adults shall join you shortly. She has a special meal prepared for you in the kitchen. I hear that Mrs. Wadsworth brought her fashion babies for you to play with later."

Mrs. Hall acknowledged the girls and ushered them from the room.

Widow Lankton faced the gentlemen, clasping her hands with enthusiasm. "We shall retire to the dining room in a moment. But first, gentlemen, be sure to admire the exquisite bridal quilt you see before you. The ladies have worked diligently on it this day to complete the work Honour had previously quilted."

"It is a fine quilt," Father said as Mrs. Sutton joined him. "Exquisite, indeed."

Honour donned a demure smile. "Thank you, sir."

"Many of the patterns were designed by Honour herself," Mrs. Sutton said.

Joshua gazed at Honour, so proud of her accomplishment. So taken in by her loveliness and courage. He ambled up to Honour where she stood by the quilt frame. He looked down at the large white quilt laden with raised feathered motifs of pomegranates and serpentine swirls. "You have done an extraordinary work here, Honour."

She glanced up at him, her dark brown eyes radiant, trusting, despite what soon would transpire. He pointed to the central design at the top, a feathered heart, and he sensed the mutual devotion passing between them.

Widow Lankton clapped lightly to garner everyone's attention. "Let us adjourn to—"

Edmund Leach stumbled over the threshold, into the room. "Ah, I hope I am not tardy for this grand affair."

Joshua squeezed Honour's hand gently before moving toward the incorrigible lout.

Emily walked toward her intoxicated husband, who leaned against the door frame. "Edmund, please. What is the meaning of this?"

Sheriff Porter stomped into the room. "That is what I would like to know."

Joshua glanced at the opposite door, where Andrew discreetly waited in the dark hallway.

"You are under arrest, Edmund Leach," the sheriff said.

Leach leaned closer the Sheriff and growled. "On what charges? Can a man not partake of a little spirits at a private party?" Leach pulled Emily over to him. "I am here to share a celebration with my bride."

Joshua heaved a deep breath. "This is no bride of yours. Your wife resides in England."

Honour came beside Emily and drew her away from Edmund, the poor woman quivering.

Leach glared at Joshua. "Upon my word!"

"Your word is no good here," Jarius shouted.

Leach pointed at Honour. "There is your criminal! She stole Mrs. Wadsworth's pearl necklace."

Sheriff Porter shoved Leach's arm down.

Mrs. Wadsworth came forward, the captain at her side. "She stole nothing. The stitching in the quilt was not Honour's."

"Her then!" Leach pointed at Maisey, who huddled against the wall.

Mrs. Wadsworth waggled her finger. "No one stole anything, Mr. Leach. There is no law against sewing pearls into a quilt. Furthermore, I brought the quilt into this home myself. One cannot steal from one's self."

Captain Wadsworth scowled at Leach. "You blackmailed Maisey by threatening to burn down my wife's mantua shop." He turned back to Maisey, his weathered face softening. "Isn't that true, girl?"

"It is." Maisey narrowed her eyes. "Your threats are no good here, Edmund Leach."

Sheriff Porter pushed him against the wall. "Edmund Leach, you are hereby charged with bigamy, piracy, and murder."

Leach snarled at Honour, "They should have killed you and your spoiled sister!" At once, he lunged for her. "You—"

Honour screeched.

Joshua leaped in front of her, and grabbed Leach by his ruffled cravat.

"Restrain that filth!" Sheriff Porter pulled out his pistol.

Joshua's brothers-in-law jumped at him, but Leach ran past the guests like a wild animal toward the door at the end of the room.

Andrew bounded forward, plowing into Leach, as chairs and sewing baskets toppled to the floor.

The sheriff pulled his trigger. The report of his gun echoed through the room, amidst the cries of the women.

Andrew and Leach fell to the floor with a thud. Leach lay crumpled on top of Andrew, blood seeping from his back.

Joshua sprang forth, pulling Leach's body off his brother. *No!*

"Andrew," Father cried out from behind Joshua.

Joshua kneeled over his brother, trying to rouse him. At last, Andrew opened his eyes.

"Are you all right, brother?"

Andrew rubbed his temples, shaking as he sat up.

Joshua stood and tugged Andrew to his feet. Father pulled him into his embrace and Mother rushed toward them.

Sheriff Porter stood over Leach. The pitiful soul groaned and released his last breath.

Joshua looked back and saw Emily's head buried against Honour's shoulder. Honour glanced up and met Joshua's gaze across the parlor—just beyond the pristine quilt, untouched in the center of the room.

"The marriage would have been nullified, under the circumstances," Reverend Cooper said, his wife standing near, "but it matters not, because now he is deceased."

Honour observed the reverend explaining the situation to Widow Lankton, thankful the elderly woman had blessedly fainted and been ushered from the chaos by the reverend and his wife. Deborah had taken Anne to safety, given her delicate condition. Moreover, Honour was relieved when she'd learned Mrs. Hall had instructed the maidservant to take the children to a neighbor's house. The girls knew little of what happened, save the unsavory outburst of a drunken man.

Joshua took Honour by the hand. "'Tis a fine way to begin a courtship."

"I believe you were merely attempting to impress me, saving me from harm as you did. I do thank you." Honour sighed. "Oh, Joshua, what a dreadful evening this has been."

"I know, love. I never anticipated it would turn out as it did," Joshua said. "Yet, we followed Sheriff Porter's plan for confronting Leach. The trap was set, but it was not for us to know the outcome."

"Where is Emily?" Honour asked. "Have you seen her?"

"She is with Andrew and Mother in the other room. I believe Maisey has gone to fetch the girls. My sisters and their husbands will be on their way soon. Mrs. Wadsworth and the captain are waiting for Maisey to return."

"Your father?"

"I believe he is in the kitchen pestering Mrs. Hall for something to eat." Joshua grinned.

Andrew, Emily, and Mrs. Sutton returned to the parlor.

Widow Lankton approached the group. "Joshua, Andrew, would you mind setting the quilt frame against the wall so my servants may reassemble this room? Though, I do not know what will become of it after this debacle." The widow glanced at her niece. "Sorry, dear. We shall get through this, fear not. I am only glad your parents were not here to witness this.

They shall be shocked to learn what has transpired upon their return from their trip."

Emily glanced away, apparently lost in thought.

Andrew and Joshua each took an end of the quilt frame and carefully leaned it against the far wall of the long room. The small group gathered around, admiring the coverlet.

"Even after all of this, something beautiful remains," Mrs. Cooper said.

Reverend Cooper nodded. "So are the ways of the Lord."

Temperance came skipping into the room, unawares. She halted in front of the quilt, and stared, tilting her head from one side to the other. "Honour, your quilt!"

"You are mistaken, Tempe. This belongs to Mrs. L—it belongs to Emily," Honour said.

Tempe looked up at her with such certainty on her face it nearly broke Honour's heart.

"The designs are like the indigo quilt Mother made. I know it is yours. I couldn't tell when it was lying down," Tempe said.

"Tempe, the quilt is not mine."

"It could be, should you accept it." Emily gave Honour a gentle nod. "I would like you to have it, Honour. It truly belongs to you with all the time and effort—and love—you have invested in it."

Widow Lankton smiled approvingly at her niece, and turned to Honour. "Take it, dear."

Honour rubbed her arms, a feeling of warmth encompassing her like the familiar cloth of a quilted counterpane. "Thank you, I shall." Her eyes filled with tears of many emotions, but she brushed them back, willing only the joyful ones to remain.

"Temperance, why don't you go home with Abigail tonight? We can bring you there on our way home," Mrs. Sutton said. "Would you like that?"

"Oh, yes." Tempe turned to Honour. "May, I?"

Honour smiled. "You certainly may, pumpkin."

"Shall we release the quilt from its prison?" Andrew asked with a grin.

"It would be very nice of you," Honour said.

Andrew and Joshua removed the frame, and folded the quilt with care.

"You may set it in the best parlor, for the time being," Widow Lankton said. "Joshua, you won't mind taking it in there for Honour, will you? Honour, please show him where to place it."

Honour blushed as she left the room, fully aware the dowager offered them a few moments of privacy.

Once inside the best parlor, Honour sat on the rolled-arm velvet sofa.

Joshua held the quilt over his arms. "Where should I place this?"

Honour patted the top of her quilted petticoat. 'Twas her favorite of blue calamanco. "I would like to hold it for a little while."

"I thought that you might." Joshua sat beside her and draped the quilt across their laps.

Honour traced the heart shape which, perchance, was on the top. She scarcely could believe the quilt had been safely returned to her, though the course it had taken to find its true home was as astounding as her own journey.

Joshua brushed a loose tendril from her face. "'Tis yours, isn't it? The quilt you had lost."

Honour glanced up at him. "Aye, the very one my mother and I began on our journey to America."

"You amaze me, Honour Metcalf. You knew all along, yet you relinquished it for the joy of another." Joshua gazed into her eyes, full of admiration.

"Emily needed it more than I," Honour said. "Yet giving it up proved to provide a blessing for me. I shall forever wonder at the mysteries of the Lord."

He moved closer, the warmth of his body radiating from him. "And I shall forever wonder at the mystery of you, my love."

Honour dared touched his face, trailing her finger along his jaw. "I have other secrets for you to discover."

"I intend to rectify that at your earliest convenience." The corners of his mouth curved.

"Allow me then, to confess my love to you," she whispered. "For you have filled every crevice of my heart."

At last, he kissed her, lovingly, longingly . . . until a little giggle came from the doorway. Tempe inched her way into the room. Mrs. Sutton called after her, soon appearing at the door.

"Do come in, ladies," Joshua said, stroking back his hair.

Honour looked at him, astonished.

"I was about to offer something to Honour and you have arrived precisely in time." Joshua grinned mischievously, and pulled something from his waistcoat pocket. He held it up, pretending to inspect it. "Look what I found at Mr. Greenleaf's mercantile, Mother. Imagine that. Someone with the initials *H E M*, hem. It must belong to a quilter."

Honour recognized it at once, and grasped it from his fingers. "My thimble!" She rubbed her finger over the engraved initials. Her initials.

Tempe giggled.

Mrs. Sutton tsked. "You never know what that son of mine will do next."

Joshua retrieved another item from his pocket. He held the shiny item, again feigning to inspect it. "I am not sure. I think I prefer this one. I bought this silver thimble from Paul Revere and had him engrave it." He held the thimble within Honour's view, though not allowing her to have it. "Tell me, what do you think of those initials, my love?"

Honour beheld the intricately fashioned thimble, with the three letters *H E S* engraved upon the front. Her heart soared. *Honour Elizabeth Sutton!*

"Mayhap you would like to exchange the one you have for this one?" Joshua grinned, his dimples creating deep contours by his handsome mouth. "What say you, Miss Metcalf? Will you exchange and *M* for an *S*?"

Honour handed him her thimble. "I feared you would never ask."

Joshua placed the new thimble in her hand, enclosing her hands in his. Honour glanced down, their clasped hands resting atop the heart-shaped pattern on her bridal quilt.

Epilogue

September, 1812

Honour Sutton gathered the white whole-cloth quilt from the chest at the end of her bed and pulled it close to her breast. Squeezing her eyes, she breathed in its faint fragrance with the barest hint of lavender, cinnamon, and the scent of years. Oh, the wealth of memories, seemingly woven into the very fabric of the white linen whole-cloth quilt.

She closed the lid of the chest, and lay the quilt down upon her bed. A canopy of rich fabric draped over the tester bed with the print of vines and floral motifs in crimson, gold, and indigo on a background of ivory. The white quilt had graced her marriage bed for many years, though after some time she had decided to tuck it away to preserve it, using it to mark special occasions such as the month of her wedding anniversary, October.

Honour longed to see it on her bed once more, before she relinquished it to the care of another, much the same as she did those many years ago. The joy had returned to her tenfold, and now the time had come to share it again. Honour unfolded the quilt over another quilted counterpane upon her bed, its fabric matching the draped canopy. She searched each corner of the quilt, locating the first and last stitches—the small *M* placed there by her mother at its beginning, and the *S* Honour stitched at its completion after Joshua asked for her hand in marriage. As she smoothed her hand over the white cloth, another hand covered hers, that of a younger woman. The pale satin hand gently took hold of Honour's own hand, with its silky sheen and wrinkles.

"This quilt must have quite a story, Grandmum," the sweet voice said.

Honour traced her finger around the feathered heart pattern. "Aye. It contains plentiful memories, with many yet to behold. Though the cloth has faded, the memories are as fresh now as ever." She glanced up at her granddaughter and smiled.

Her eldest granddaughter kissed her on the cheek, Honour in turn patting the spot, feeling the lines of time beneath her palm. Honour grasped the edge of the quilt, pulling it into place over the feathered mattress.

"Let me assist you with that." Her granddaughter went to the opposite side of the bed and helped lay the quilt in its proper place. They both ambled to the foot of the bed, admiring the beautiful quilted counterpane.

"The patterns are beautiful. Did you design them yourself?" her granddaughter asked.

"I did—with the help of my mother on our journey to America. My mother taught me the skill, which we enjoyed in the leisurely days of my girlhood in England. We passed the time on our voyage working on my bridal quilt for my dower chest."

"I am blessed to have learned how to quilt from both you and my mother." Her granddaughter lifted her shoulders and smiled. "Perhaps I shall pass the skill along to my own daughter someday."

Honour beheld the young woman before her. Her dark auburn tresses so resembled her own in her days of youth, though Honour's were now silver. She noted her granddaughter's high-waisted lawn gown, lace fichu, and flat satin slippers. "'Tis a lovely dress, my dear. How the fashions have changed through the years. Indeed, much has changed, as much will. Yet, so many things remain the same."

"Thank you," the young lady said, fingering the fine embroidery of the buttercream-colored fabric. "The cloth came from Grandfather's store. Great aunt Temperance created the dress for me in the spring. She is a fine seamstress."

"She is, at that. She was taught by the best mantua-maker in Boston, Margaret Wadsworth, the wife of a sea captain. She owned Mrs. Wadsworth's Mantua Shoppe where I worked when Temperance and I first came to Boston." Honour smiled with a fond sigh of remembrance. "She was so dear to us and treated us as her own daughters, having no children of her own. She was like a second grandmother to your mother in her early childhood. Your mother loved visiting her shop as a child, with all of Mrs. Wadsworth's lovely gowns, fripperies, and fashion dolls."

"You were a mantua-maker? I did not know that."

"Nay, I was a quilter then. The skill my mother had taught me, and talent bestowed on me by my Heavenly Father, proved to be a saving grace when I arrived in Boston with nary a shilling to my name, and a young sister to provide for."

"Mother has told me about the tragic circumstances leaving you and Aunt Temperance orphaned. It must have been devastating."

"'Twas a troublesome time." Honour's mouth grew taut, and she brushed her finger across her lips as her thoughts drifted back over the sands of time. Her eyes became moist pools, even after all of these years.

"I fear I could not have endured it. You have great strength."

Honour blinked back her forming tears, a habit she'd grown accustomed to, having grown more stoic in her maturing years. "'Twas the Lord's strength that bolstered us. We trusted Him to see us through it and learned to walk with Him, not in perilous times alone, but to walk each day in His truth."

Her granddaughter sidled up to Honour and hugged her arm.

"Sweet, Honour. My namesake."

Her granddaughter smiled. "My sister, Margaret, is she named for Mrs. Wadsworth?"

"She is. And your sister, Olive, for your grandfather's mother," Honour said. "And your own mother, I named after my Mum, Susannah."

"Let's sit by the window." The two Honours rested upon a pair of upholstered winged-back chairs.

The elder Honour released a soft laugh. "Time passes so fast. Here we are and another war has begun. Your mother was about thirteen when the last war ended. We called her our little daughter of liberty, because she helped me mend soldier's uniforms and care for her younger siblings whilst I was busy with those tasks."

"They are calling this Second War of American Independence," Honour's granddaughter said. "Grandfather Joshua fought in the first war, did he not?"

"He did, along with your great uncle Andrew. How proud their mother was to see them in their uniforms, though it was worrisome to see them go. Aunt Anne's and Sarah's husbands also enlisted."

"Thankfully they all returned."

"Indeed." Honour looked heavenward, and sighed. "Yet when Joshua and Andrew returned, they provided another service to our country at home, by sewing uniforms for officers and soldiers alike. Great-grandfather Sutton received a com-

248

mission from the Continental Army, by George Washington. Though he worked long hours, I was glad to see him at the end of the day to encourage him with his work. And to have him kiss our children good night, your mother among them!"

Young Honour smiled.

"Folks tend to forget about the faithful service many performed at home for the cause of liberty. Everyone did his or her part in those days, and many works of service to our country remain unspoken of today."

"Like your mending uniforms?"

Joshua appeared at the door, his white hair pulled back neatly in its tie. "Yes," he interjected. "Has your grandmother told you it was her plan to invite soldiers to bring their worn and torn uniforms to Sutton's Clothiers? She'd take them up to the house to mend them, without charging for her services."

"Grandfather, would Sutton's be willing to participate in the cause again?"

Joshua tilted his jaw in interest. Honour looked on with pride.

"Perhaps we could collect quilts and blankets for the soldiers. People could drop them off and should they need mending, my sisters and I could patch them with spare cloth from your workrooms."

Honour raised her eyebrows as she met Joshua's gaze. His bright eyes sparkled at his granddaughter's idea. "What do you say, dear?"

"I say she has a heart much like her grandmother." The crevices at the corner of Joshua's mouth deepened and he smiled. "We shall do it."

"It will not interfere with your business, Grandfather?"

Joshua rubbed his chin. "Nay. The only thing interfering in my business is Jefferson's trade embargoes these past years. It has been disseminating the economy, though we are holding our own. There is always a need for textile. Despite the Enemy Trade Act and this new war, the British are not keeping as tight a blockade on the Northern states so we are able to receive goods from the West Indies."

"Thanks be to God," Honour said.

Joshua adjusted his waistcoat. "Enough of politics. I hear my lovely granddaughter shall be wed at the Lankton mansion. Your Uncle Andrew and Aunt Emily are looking forward to having you at their home."

"I've spent many of my girlhood days playing there with my cousins. It is the perfect setting for my wedding."

"How is Aunt Temperance coming along with your wedding gown, dear?" Honour asked.

She could scarcely believe her granddaughter's childhood days were bygone, and now she was a young lady about to be wed. Had her own face glowed similarly all those years ago?

"It is nearly done, Grandmum, and so lovely. I cannot believe I shall soon be a bride." Their granddaughter's eyes misted.

Joshua gave his granddaughter a gentle squeeze on the shoulder and walked across the room to the bedstead. "What have we here?" He turned toward Honour, his eyes wide. "'Tis not our anniversary, is it?"

Honour swatted her handkerchief into the air.

Joshua looked from his wife to his granddaughter. "I might forget our anniversary, but I shall never forget our wedding day. We, too, were wed at the Lankton estate . . . in October." Joshua leaned over Honour's shoulder and kissed her on the cheek, while their granddaughter looked on demurely.

"We shall share the same wedding month," young Honour said.

Honour glanced over to the bed. "Then it is especially fitting, granddaughter, that we gift you with our bridal quilt."

"Grandmum! Grandfather! Truly?"

"'Tis an honor to bequeath it to our eldest granddaughter." Honour rested her hand upon her shoulder.

"And your namesake." Joshua squeezed Honour's hand. "You must honor the Lord in all things, Granddaughter, especially in matters of love."

Honour entreated their granddaughter, "And be sure to let the quilt remind you that the best pattern for romance is stitched with faith, honesty, and trust."

Discussion Questions

1. What did the indigo quilt represent to Honour and Tempe? Do you have a belonging that holds special sentiments? Do you own a quilt that is meaningful to you?

2. Many of Honour's possessions were stolen from her including her wealth, family's valuables, and her bridal quilt. She also lost her workbag and thimble. Have you ever lost something significant or sentimental to you? Is it all right to grieve for lost material possessions?

3. Joshua and Honour were each falsely accused. How did they deal with their situations? Did they react or respond? What is the difference? What is the best way to deal with falsehoods about you or someone you care about?

4. What did the bridal quilt represent to Honour? How did its significance change for her throughout the story (while it was lost, when she tried to get it back, when it was returned, when she gave it up, when it was given back to her, when she gave it away)?

5. How did Honour come to the point where she relinquished her longings? Was it right for her to do so? Did it make her a martyr or did it free her? Have you ever had to relinquish longings of your own?

6. Honour endured a tremendous amount of hardship with her health, finances, relationships, and grieving. Have you ever experienced times like that? How did you manage? How did your relationship with God change during those times? Was it difficult to continue trusting Him? How did He show himself faithful during those times?

7. Like each quilt, every love story is unique. There are however certain elements required to create each

one: cloth, thread, pattern, tools. What elements did Honour and Joshua build their romance upon? What other elements make for a healthy relationship? A happy romance?

8. When reading a novel you have the experience of seeing both the hero's and heroine's points of view. Sometimes we assume that others know what we are thinking when we have not yet disclosed it. How would your relationships change if you better communicated your point of view? If you took the time to understand another's perspective?

9. Were you happy to see that Emily and Andrew ended up together? They each encountered a great deal of hardship preventing them from being together. How could it have been avoided? What mistakes did they make along the way? What did they do right?

10. The colonists of Boston experienced difficult times that affected their values, the economy, etc. How were those times similar to those we have today? How did they face their challenges? What encouragement from their resourcefulness and resolve can inspire you to face your own challenges?

11. God's Word provided a compass of truth to guide Honour, Tempe, and Joshua. In what practical ways did they follow His guidance? In what ways does God guide you?

12. Psalm 37:3-7 sums up the theme of *Pattern for Romance*. What does it mean to delight in the Lord? Though Honour desired her bridal quilt, what was her true desire? Will you trust the Lord to reveal the true desires of your heart? The more we trust Him, the more His desires become our desires. What do you desire of God? What does God desire of you?

Want to learn more about author
Carla Olson Gade and check out other great
fiction by Abingdon Press?

Sign up for our fiction newsletter at
www.AbingdonPress.com
to read interviews with your favorite authors, find tips
for starting a reading group, and stay posted on
what's new on the horizon. It's a place to connect
with other fiction readers or post a
comment about this book.

Be sure to visit Carla online!

http://www.carlagade.com

We hope you enjoyed *Pattern for Romance* and that you will continue to read the Quilts of Love series of books from Abingdon Press. Here's an excerpt from the next book in the series, Sandra D. Bricker's *Raw Edges*.

1

Gray glanced at the dashboard clock before he pulled the key from the ignition and pressed the button to lower the garage door.

"Ten twenty-six," he said aloud, punctuating the time with a weary sigh.

Sadie would likely be fast asleep by now, probably floating over angry strains of resentment toward her careless father who had missed their Friday pizza night together for the first time in years. He tried to justify it with the fact he had a good reason, but he knew it was one Sadie's nine-year-old mind couldn't understand.

He closed the door behind him and walked softly through the kitchen into the family room where Essie Lambright sat reading.

"Oh, good evening, Grayson," she said in her barely-there trace of Florida twang.

Essie smoothed her silver hair and removed her reading glasses, placing a ribbon to mark where she left off before closing the book on her lap.

"Hi, Miss Essie. How were things tonight?" he asked. "I didn't notice any torches or pitchforks when I came in. Am I safe?"

"I'm sorry to say you are not," she replied. "I think you're going to have to earn your forgiveness, and she's a pretty tough customer."

"She certainly can be," Gray said with a chuckle. "Can I give you a lift home?"

"No," she chided. "It's a beautiful Tampa night. I can walk the two blocks and enjoy the breeze off the bay."

Gray hadn't even noticed the weather on his drive home. He'd been lost in the maze of his thoughts and, looking back on it now, he couldn't remember a thing about the commute.

"There's chili in the slow cooker," she told him on her way toward the kitchen, "and fresh cornbread wrapped in foil on the counter."

"She didn't go with pizza?" he asked, surprised.

"Apparently, it's not Friday pizza night if you're not here. So we decided to enter into the realm of the unknown with turkey chili."

Gray grinned. "Well, thank you."

"Oh," she said, placing a finger to the side of her face and stopping in her tracks. "She is considering the merits of going vegan, by the way. But she's still on the fence."

"Vegan," he repeated. "Where does she come up with these things?"

"It seems Steffi Leary is going that direction, and they share a table in the lunchroom."

Gray shook his head and followed Essie through the kitchen toward the back door. "Thanks again."

He flipped on the light and watched after her as the older woman followed the sidewalk around the curve of the house.

When she disappeared from sight, he turned it off and bolted the lock on the door.

The spicy scent of the chili caused a rumble to erupt deep within his stomach, and Gray pulled a bowl from behind the glass cabinet door, scraping the silverware drawer open and plucking a large spoon from inside before gliding it shut again. Just about the time he sat down on one of the stools at the island and took his first bite, the familiar rub of sock-against-ceramic-tile drew his attention to the doorway.

"What are you doing awake?" he asked, and Sadie *groan-sighed*, as Jenna used to call it.

"It's her anniversary, you know," she sort of spat out at him. "And you missed it."

Gray's heart pounded hard before flopping over and sinking. He'd convinced himself that she wouldn't remember.

"I'm sorry."

Sadie scuffed toward the refrigerator and removed a small carton of sour cream and a plastic container of grated cheddar cheese. She slid it across the marble counter toward him and climbed up on the closest stool.

"Miss Essie says her chili cries for these. I tried it, and I think she's right."

The corner of his mouth twitched as he allowed her to sprinkle cheese into his bowl, followed by a dollop of sour cream. As he took a delightful bite, Sadie unwrapped the cornbread and grabbed a hunk for herself before pushing the foil mound toward him.

"We had warm honey butter," she said over a full mouth. "You woulda had some, too, if you'd come home at a decent hour."

Gray arched one eyebrow and gazed at his daughter.

Nine, going on twenty-nine, he thought.

"Today is one year since Mommy left," she announced. "Did you even remember?"

Gray took another bite of chili before he replied, "I remembered."

"Then why didn't you come home?" she asked, narrowing her eyes at him. "You didn't want to be with me and remember her?"

He pushed the spoon into the chili and left it draped over the side of the bowl as he leaned against the stool's wooden back. He couldn't imagine a response sufficient for that particular question, so he sighed and answered, "I'm sorry, Sadie."

"Especially because it's Friday, Daddy. We always spend Fridays together."

"I know."

"Well then? What do you have to say for yourself?"

Gray couldn't help it, and he blurted out one puff of a laugh. "Miss Essie is right about you. You're one tough customer."

"When it's called for," she said, and Gray's heart constricted. Jenna used to use exactly those words and tone when he'd irritated her. "I think you owe me an apology—"

"Which I have already delivered," he pointed out.

"Right. And a present."

"A present!" he repeated with a chuckle.

"Yes. It's Mommy's anniversary of when she got to be with Gramma and leave behind her pain. And we always give presents on anniversaries and birthdays and stuff, right? I think we should really have a cake too, but Miss Essie made cornbread that's really more like cake than bread anyway, so that's okay, I think."

Gray smiled as she took another big bite of the cornbread. When she tried to talk right through it, he raised his hand and shook his head. "Uh-uh. Chew and swallow first."

After a few dramatized chews and a noisy gulp, she pulled a folded piece of cardboard from the pocket of her red pajama bottoms with a giant tan puppy screened across one leg. After first ironing it out against the counter, she pushed the large postcard toward him and said, "Here's what I want for my present."

Several things crossed Gray's mind in those couple of seconds.

I want a Great Dane.

I'd like a trip to Africa to see the giraffes, please.

Can we get a swimming pool? Steffi Leary has one.

But what he saw on that card was the most remote and unexpected thing he ever might have imagined his nine-year-old daughter asking of him.

Ovacome Support Group Meeting. Tuesday night. St. Joseph's Hospital in Tampa.

"Where did you get this?" he inquired, trying to remain casual as he set it down on the counter and turned his attention back to the chili before him.

"It came in the mail today, and I think we should go."

"We?"

"Yes. I called them, and—"

"You did what? You called them? Sadie!"

"—they said I could come, as long as you come with me. So can we go?"

"No," he replied without looking up from the ceramic bowl.

"Why not? That's what I want as my present."

"Is it your birthday again?" he asked her seriously. "Because I'm pretty sure we just celebrated that last month. And it's too warm for Christmas. Those are the times when I'm even marginally okay with you assuming you're owed something."

He knew how ridiculous it sounded. He only owed his daughter something special twice a year? Jenna might have rolled over in her grave at the sound of it. He owed her something each and every day of the year, and twice on holidays!

When Sadie didn't reply, he looked back at her again and waited. Before he could apologize for such an outlandish statement, she smiled at him.

"The thing is, Daddy," she said softly, "I know you didn't mean that. And I know you didn't mean to miss our Friday pizza night either, because you can't help it, I think. You miss Mommy so much you can hardly stand it. And I guess I might make you think about her, too, don't I? Is that why you didn't want to eat pizza and read to me out of her journal, like always?"

Gray groaned. Closing his eyes for a moment, he rubbed his throbbing temples. With a sigh, he smacked his leg twice. "Come here."

She hopped down and rounded the island before lifting her arms and letting him pick her up and plant her on his leg. He wrapped both arms around her tightly, pulling her into him.

"I'm sorry, Sadie," he whispered. "I'm so sorry."

After a full minute of silence, she pushed out a gravelly reply. "It's okay, Daddy. Don't worry. We'll nabigate it together, that's what you said, right? So we will. We'll nabigate it."

Gray blinked back the tears standing in his eyes. "Navigate. And how old are you again?"

Sadie's giggles sounded like music. "I'm nine now, Daddy. You know that!"

"Annabelle, line two for you."

"This is Annabelle Curtis."

"Hi. It's Carole Martinez."

"Ah, Carole. How are you?" Annabelle flopped down on the yellow leather sofa at the far side of her crowded office and pushed a section of blondish curls behind one ear as she held the phone up to the other. "Are you calling about tonight?"

"Yes, just checking to make sure you're coming."

"I wouldn't miss it. My friend Paula gave me her employee discount at Honeybaked Ham. I've got box dinners for fifteen," she said. "I think that will be enough, don't you?"

"Plenty. I don't really expect more than ten or twelve of us. Tonight will mostly be a planning session for the quilt project. I'll see you at around six-thirty then?"

"See you then."

Annabelle smiled as she disconnected the call. Carole and the Ovacome support group had become a fixture in her life since The Dark Days—a term she used to describe the five months and six days between the initial diagnosis at the young age of thirty-four and the day that her oncologist broke out the long-awaited "cancer-free" stamp of approval. Annabelle had thought ovarian cancer was an older woman's disease; but then, as her brother had reminded her, she'd always been one to step out ahead of the pack.

"If everyone else is getting it at age fifty, leave it to my big sis to rush in there at thirty-four," Nathan had said when he flew in from Oregon just in time to see her before they rolled her in for surgery.

A complete hysterectomy.

The words were daunting back then. And not much less so now that she'd come through the chemo and the radiation and the seed implant surgery—radioactive seeds implanted for several days in hopes of a more up-close-and-personal treatment.

The hysterectomy had stolen so much more than her uterus and ovaries! The surgery had also taken all of her latent maternal dreams, mashing them up in a blender already chock full of pain, fear, anger, and regret. Adding insult to her incisions, fiancé Peter had been the perky rubber spatula that wiped out any final remnant of hope about children when he'd peeled out of her driveway after a short fifteen-minute discussion about their future. Annabelle chuckled bitterly at the irony. Peter had made his *escape* in his brand new pretty, green Ford Escape.

"I just can't do cancer," he'd told her from the other side of the kitchen table, two mugs of untouched lukewarm coffee between them. "I saw what it did to my aunt and her family, and I'm just not prepared for it, Belle." She hated it when he called her that. "Look, I've read the statistics. You're almost guaranteed to get it back again."

"Thanks for the pep talk," she'd interjected.

"I'm sorry, but it's true. Only half of the women who get it make it through another five years before it comes back with a vengeance. And I just can't see doing it again."

"That's funny. I sort of thought I was the one who *did* the cancer, Peter."

The sad truth: He'd been little more than a bystander in the tragedy that had consumed her life. And now, there he sat with his too-white teeth and his perfect wavy hair, telling her she was going to get it again? Never mind the fact she hadn't even completed her full course of treatment yet. Never mind the wounds from the hysterectomy hadn't even healed completely. Never mind—

"And the thing is, Belle, I really do want kids. You know I saw that as part of the picture for my life."

Annabelle had always envisioned having children in *her* life picture, too. But between the hysterectomy and the quick glance she caught of Peter streaking from her life in his ironic choice of vehicle, the idea dove directly into the blender with the rest of her emotions and hopes. She could almost hear it now, grinding again, so many years later.

Looking around her cramped office, Annabelle grinned. She wondered what Peter would think if he saw her now. She'd quit her lucrative—yet unfulfilling—job managing public relations for an upscale Central Florida restaurant chain to become an underpaid, overworked—but extremely enthusiastic—employee of her beloved Florida Aquarium. Her lawyer ex-fiancé would likely have left her anyhow once she'd morphed her volunteer hours into a full-time job where she sometimes wore no makeup at all, donned mostly jeans and tennis shoes, and often went home smelling just a little bit like one of the aquarium's promenading penguins.

"I have box lunches in three brown bags in the fridge with my name on them," she told young Jeremy as she passed him, one arm clamped around a small bundle of folded clothes, and the other struggling to force the strap of her large leather tote up to her shoulder. "Would you mind schlepping them out to my car for me?"

"Sure thing."

Annabelle piled the clothes on the floor of her Volkswagen, leaving the passenger door open for Jeremy while she rounded the small yellow car and climbed behind the wheel. Jeremy jogged toward her and slid the bags to the passenger seat.

"What is all this?" he asked her, leaning down into the car. "Support group meeting tonight?"

"Yep. We're combining our regular meeting with the memory quilt project," she explained with a nod toward the floor. "I'm donating the blouse I was wearing the day I was diagnosed, and the ducky jammies I practically lived in until the incision healed."

Jeremy chuckled. "You don't strike me as the quilting type, Annabelle."

263

"What I don't know about quilting could fill the shark tank," she teased. "But they needed someone to work on it with Carole, and I was the lucky one."

She couldn't bring herself to add the reason they needed someone new this year. Carole and Sharon Chaulk always handled the project together, but that third and final return of Sharon's cancer had just been too much for her. At the too-young age of fifty-seven, Sharon had lost her battle. Annabelle's stomach did a little flop as Jeremy slammed shut the door and waved.

"See you tomorrow."

Annabelle took Channelside Drive over to Kennedy, and headed down to Martin Luther King Boulevard. While she waited at the stoplight, she noticed Kim Snyder as she turned in front of her and sped through the entrance to St. Joseph's Hospital. The green arrow pointed the way, and Annabelle followed Kim and parked right next to her.

"Excellent!" she sang, tossing her door open. "I was wondering how I would manage to carry all of this inside."

"Glad to help," Kim returned, and she rounded the VW bug and tugged on the passenger door.

The two of them shared the load and hiked to the double glass doors and inside toward their regular meeting space. By the time they had the room set up and the boxed meals set out on the table adjacent to the door, there were ten women gathered in small groups.

"Annabelle has brought us ham and turkey sandwiches from Honeybaked," Kim announced. "And there are bottles of water in the ice bucket next to the coffee. Help yourselves and let's get started."

Annabelle had just found a chair next to Carole Martinez and twisted open the top on a bottle of water when the door burst open.

"Are we too late? I told you, Daddy. We're late."

Standing in the doorway, a wild-haired little girl clutched the hand of her father, her eyes open wide and dancing with excitement.

"Don't be silly," Kim said as she approached them. "We're just getting started. Come on in."

Annabelle watched as Kim exchanged greetings and a few words with the pair and led them toward the food table. The little girl made an immediate beeline to the coffee, pouring a cup and handing it to the tall, lean man behind her.

"We have some new visitors with us tonight," Kim proclaimed. "This is Gray McDonough, and his daughter, Sadie. Some of you might remember Gray's wife, Jenna."

Carole leaned over toward Annabelle. "Jenna McDonough's family. I talked to the little girl last week. I didn't think for one minute she'd be able to get her dad here."

"Who's Jenna McDonough?" she asked, but Carole missed the question as she stood up and headed toward them.

Little Sadie looked quite grown-up as she shook Carole's hand and nodded. "Daddy," she said, rolling her arm to call him over. "This is the lady I told you about."

"Carole Martinez. So glad you could make it."

Annabelle guessed Gray McDonough to be in his late thirties, maybe forty. His salt-and-pepper hair was trimmed short on the sides, longer on the top, and his striking blue eyes seemed tired and sad, making her wonder about the ovarian cancer connection. Was Jenna his sister or mother? Another glance at Sadie made Annabelle's heart flutter. *His wife.*

Sadie took her father's hand and followed Carole's lead. They took the two folding chairs on the other side of her.

"That's Kris," Carole told them, pointing to the smiling woman next to them. "And on this side is Annabelle Curtis. She's the one heading up our memory quilt project."

"Hi," Sadie grinned at her. "I think it's neat about the blanket."

"Thank you," she returned. "Maybe you can help us cut some squares, huh?"

"Really?" she asked, and she turned toward her father. "Can I?"

"We'll see," he said softly, before nodding at Annabelle. "Hi."

His eyes darted away before she had the chance to return the greeting.

A year or less, she thought, calculating the time since his loss. He still had that uncomfortable, tentative look in his eyes. *Definitely no more than a year.*

"Daddy, eat your sandwich," Sadie prodded in a slightly-too-loud whisper. "It's really good."

His daughter had obviously taken on a bit of a caregiver role with him. It was adorable and sad at the same time. Annabelle's eyes caught Sadie's as she took a bite of her sandwich that was just a little too large for her small mouth. The girl's bluish eyes glinted, and she giggled out loud as she struggled to chew it.

"Use your napkin," Gray muttered in her direction.

She wiped mustard from the corner of her mouth, smearing it on her chin. When Gray took the napkin from his daughter's hand and tended to the mess himself, Sadie looked directly at Annabelle, shrugged slightly, and grinned.

Dogs & People Don't Have to Be Scary

Sweet, silly Sadie,

This one's very important. Don't be afraid to try new things and meet new people.

When I was your age, it seemed like I was afraid of everything, from roller coasters to dogs, and all the stuff in between. But when I met Aunt Bebe's dog Trent, I realized that even the biggest, sloppiest dog can be a sweet puppy if you treat him right and talk nicely to him. This will be the case with people you meet, too.

Always talk nicely, and follow The Golden Rule about doing unto others as you want them to do unto you. You'll make a lot of friends that way, and I think you'll find some lovely surprises along the path, too.

Love you to the moon and back,
Mommy

Matthew 7:12 (CEB): *Therefore, you should treat people in the same way that you want people to treat you; this is the Law and the Prophets.*

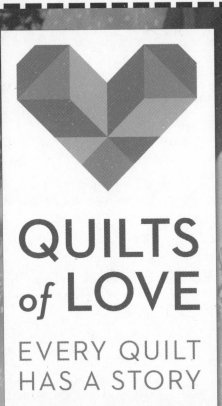

QUILTS of LOVE

EVERY QUILT HAS A STORY

There is a strong connection between storytelling and quilts. Like a favorite recollection, quilts are passed from one generation to the next as precious heirlooms. They bring communities together.

The Quilts of Love series focuses on women who have woven romance, adventure, and even a little intrigue into their own family histories. Featuring contemporary and historical romances as well as occasional light mystery, this series will draw you into uplifting, heartwarming, exciting stories of characters you won't soon forget.

Visit **QuiltsofLoveBooks.com** for more information.

For more information and for more fiction titles, please visit AbingdonPress.com/fiction.

Abingdon Press fiction
a novel approach to faith

BKM122220005 PACP01223825-01

What They're Saying About...

The Glory of Green, by Judy Christie
"Once again, Christie draws her readers into the town, the life, the humor, and the drama in Green. *The Glory of Green* is a wonderful narrative of small-town America, pulling together in tragedy. A great read!"
—Ane Mulligan, editor of *Novel Journey*

Always the Baker, Never the Bride, by Sandra Bricker
"[It] had just the right touch of humor, and I loved the characters. Emma Rae is a character who will stay with me. Highly recommended!"
—Colleen Coble, author of *The Lightkeeper's Daughter* and the *Rock Harbor* series

Diagnosis Death, by Richard Mabry
"Realistic medical flavor graces a story rich with characters I loved and with enough twists and turns to keep the sleuth in me off-center. Keep 'em coming!"—**Dr. Harry Krauss, author of *Salty Like Blood* and *The Six-Liter Club***

Sweet Baklava, by Debby Mayne
"A sweet romance, a feel-good ending, and a surprise cache of yummy Greek recipes at the book's end? I'm sold!"—**Trish Perry, author of *Unforgettable* and *Tea for Two***

The Dead Saint, by Marilyn Brown Oden
"An intriguing story of international espionage with just the right amount of inspirational seasoning."—*Fresh Fiction*

Shrouded in Silence, by Robert L. Wise
"It's a story fraught with death, danger, and deception—of never knowing whom to trust, and with a twist of an ending I didn't see coming. Great read!"—**Sharon Sala, author of *The Searcher's Trilogy: Blood Stains, Blood Ties,* and *Blood Trails*.**

Delivered with Love, by Sherry Kyle
"Sherry Kyle has created an engaging story of forgiveness, sweet romance, and faith reawakened—and I looked forward to every page. A fun and charming debut!"—**Julie Carobini, author of *A Shore Thing* and *Fade to Blue*.**

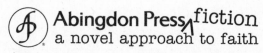

Abingdon Press∧fiction
a novel approach to faith

AbingdonPress.com | 800.251.3320